Into the Fire

The Texan Quartet #4

Claire Boston

D1797815

BANTILLY
PUBLISHING

First published by Momentum in 2016
This edition published by Bantilly Publishing in 2017

Into the Fire: The Texan Quartet 4

EPUB format: 978-1-925696-06-6
Mobi format: 978-1-925696-07-3
Print: 978-1-925696-08-0

Cover design by XOU Creative
Edited by Kate O'Donnell
Proofread by Jason Nahrung

About the Author

Claire Boston is a contemporary romance author who enjoys exploring real life issues on her way to the happily-ever-after. She writes heart-warming stories, with resilient heroines and heroes you'll love. In 2014 she was nominated for an Australian Romance Readers Award for Favourite New Romance Author.

When Claire's not writing she can be found creating her own handmade journals, swinging on a sidecar, or in the garden attempting to grow something other than weeds.

Claire lives in Western Australia with her husband, who loves even her most annoying quirks, and her grubby, but adorable Australian bulldog.

You can connect with Claire through Facebook (https://www.facebook.com/clairebostonauthor) and Twitter (https://www.twitter.com/clairebauthor), or join her reader group (http://www.claireboston.com/reader-group/).

Also by Claire Boston

DEDICATION

This book is dedicated to those who want to change the world for the better.

Chapter 1

The bar was one of those hip places where the design was minimal and the prices were maximal. The tables were small to encourage intimate groups and conversations. Piper Atkinson scanned the faces in the dim lighting, hoping to catch sight of her friend, George. Stagehands were checking the microphone and equipment up front. George would be somewhere nearby, perhaps giving his client Adahy some last-minute words of encouragement.

Piper hadn't heard the singer yet, but Adahy had played at her friend Elle's café and she'd said he was fabulous. A fusion of modern music with Native American beats.

Close to the stage there was an empty table with a reserved sign on it. It was probably reserved for George.

She ordered a drink and something to eat, and stood at the bar, waiting.

"Is your daddy a baker? Because you've got a nice set of buns!" a deep male voice behind her said.

Piper rolled her eyes and debated whether to ignore the pickup line or tell the guy off, when someone grabbed her butt. She whirled and slapped at the hand. "What the hell are you doing?"

The man who'd both groped her and tried the cheesy pickup line was tall and built like a linebacker. His muscles bulged out of his too-small shirt and the glaze in his eyes told her he'd been in the bar a while.

"Just checking out how fresh they are."

"Take a hike," she said.

Before he could respond, there was a *tap-tap* on the microphone. They both turned to the stage where one of the staff stood. He cleared his throat. "Let me introduce you to tonight's entertainment. He's a born and bred Texan – Adahy Woods."

A young man in his mid twenties walked onto the stage. He had short, dark hair and was wearing jeans and a T-shirt.

"He's a damn Indian," the linebacker said. "Didn't think they'd let that sort in a place like this."

Luckily his comments were drowned out by the applause. Disgusted, Piper grabbed her drink and moved away.

There were now two people seated at the reserved table and one of them was George. She wandered over, and George looked up and smiled. The other man didn't notice her.

"Hi, George, mind if I join you?" Piper asked.

"Sure, we've got an extra seat." George indicated one of the chairs and she put her drink on the table and pulled it out.

As she sat, the other man tore his attention away from the stage to look at her.

His gaze was intense. Chocolate brown eyes, glaring in annoyance at the interruption, chiseled features and loose, wavy, shoulder-length brown hair. Piper's whole body flushed warmly, and there was a delicious shiver down her spine.

"Tai Woods, this is Piper Atkinson, she's a friend and a reporter for the *Houston Age*." George turned to Piper. "Taima is Adahy's brother."

The name sparked something in Piper's memory. She'd just read it at work. "The chef of the Wooden Spoon."

Tai looked surprised but nodded once before turning his attention back to his brother.

Piper's editor had assigned her to do a set of profiles on people of Houston. Taima Woods was the one person on her list of interviewees she actually wanted to interview, but the reclusive chef famously didn't talk to the media. This was a great opportunity to break the ice.

"He sounds great," Piper said to George, and nodded

toward Adahy.

"He does. We're going to release a single next month."

The waitress delivered Piper's order of nachos to the table.

"Help yourself," she invited the others.

Tai frowned at her. He was obviously there for the music and not the company.

Pity even his dirty look made Piper shiver. What was wrong with her? She'd dated plenty of men, but none had given her this kind of frisson, especially not a man who was completely uninterested in her.

Still, if she was going to be interviewing him, she didn't want to get him offside. She shut up, ate her nachos and listened to Adahy sing.

He was amazing. His tone was warm and the way he mixed Native American drums and pipes with modern pop/rock music gave it an edge, a difference that was refreshing.

Piper found herself tapping her foot to the music and when he finished his set, she added her voice to the shouts of approval coming from the crowd.

George got to his feet. "I'll be back in a minute." He headed to meet Adahy.

The applause died down and was replaced by voices.

"Oh my God. He's so hot. I can't wait to hear more of his songs," said a woman who was sitting at the table next to theirs.

"Sounds like he was a success," Piper commented.

Tai grunted non-committedly.

"You must be proud of him," she tried.

"Ada's achievements are his own." Tai scanned the crowd.

Wow. This guy really didn't do small talk.

Interviewing him was going to be a whole lot of fun.

She wondered whether the paper had contacted him about the special feature yet. The woman she'd phoned this evening had been expecting the call. She guessed Tai wouldn't be.

As she was about to broach the subject, he pushed back his chair and left, walking toward Adahy and George, who were standing next to the stage.

No. Social skills really weren't his forte.

Tai said something to his brother, gave him a hug and then wove his way through the crowd and out of the bar.

Piper sat there, unsure whether to be amused or offended by the man's lack of manners. She decided on amused and made a mental note to ask her editor, Geraldine, why Tai was on the interview list.

George brought Adahy over to the table and introduced them.

"That was a fantastic set," Piper told him. "Let me know when you next play and I'll tell our music reporter."

"Great idea," George told her and grinned. "I'm getting drinks, do you want one?"

"Yes, please." She wasn't in any rush to get home and tomorrow was miraculously free, with no interviews booked or events she had to attend.

Adahy took the seat next to her and sighed in satisfaction. "That was fun."

Fun.

When had Piper last thought her work was fun? She couldn't remember associating that descriptor with her job at all. Even the usual positive fallbacks *interesting*, *fulfilling* and *educational* couldn't be used to describe the last few months in her new position. "You looked like you were enjoying yourself," she said.

He nodded. "You work for a paper?"

"The *Houston Age*," she told him. "I was hoping to talk to your brother about a series we've got coming up, but he left before I could."

Adahy laughed. "Good luck with that. Tai's not one for talk."

"I noticed," Piper said.

He laughed again.

George returned with the drinks and handed them out. "What brings you out tonight, Piper? No one to interrogate?"

"Not tonight. I felt like going out and Elle said you'd be here." She'd tried all of her friends – Libby, Imogen and Elle – but none of them had been available. Elle had suggested Piper meet her fiancé, George, at the bar.

"We haven't seen you much lately," George said.

Piper felt a twinge of guilt. "I'm sorry I wasn't there to help clean up after the break-in at Elle's café." Elle's ex had trashed the place in a fit of jealousy.

"We had plenty of hands," George said. "Besides, the piece your reporter buddy did when Elle reopened the café got so many people interested that she's constantly busy. She's pretty happy."

"I'm glad." Piper had called in a favor and asked the social pages reporter to attend Elle's bookshop café reopening. The guy had been so impressed by the setup he'd done more than a little paragraph – he had requested his editor make it the spotlight of the week.

George turned to Adahy to discuss the performance. Piper found it fascinating to listen to people talking about subjects she knew little about. Here it was all about the music – pitch and tone, notes and keys – as well as the performance itself.

Some of George's suggestions were good and made Piper review the set in a whole other light. It wasn't just about singing and playing: it was about entertainment. She'd like to interview George about his work, but she'd never be allowed to because the music reporter guarded her turf.

Still, she'd chat to George about it some day when they were both free.

Piper stifled a yawn and checked the time. If she wanted to do anything constructive tomorrow – and she had to do more research on those profiles – she should go to bed. She got to her feet, said goodbye and headed home.

On the way out she caught herself looking for Tai, wondering if he had indeed gone or was waiting for her to leave.

Annoyed he was on her mind when he'd not paid her the slightest bit of regard, she reminded herself it was a purely professional curiosity. She had to interview him.

She ignored the fact her body didn't usually respond like that to people she interviewed.

It was nothing to worry about.

***

Tai sat on his motorbike in his driveway and breathed in and out.

He hated reporters.

He never gave them the time of day, knowing the kind of article they would write about him. Knowing they would make some misinformed error about his culture, about his people.

But he shouldn't have let Piper scare him off.

He wished George hadn't invited her to join them in the first place.

Then she'd sat down and flashed him a friendly smile that reached her light hazel eyes, and shifted her head so her short honey-blond hair flicked back. It had hit him right in the chest.

She should come with a flashing red light that screamed *Danger, Danger* above her head.

Reporters couldn't be trusted.

Female reporters were the worst, because they made you think they were your friends before *bam*, they wrote some ridiculous piece about you that made no sense whatsoever. Unless you were a non-native person with no idea what life as a Native American was like.

The worst thing about Piper was that she'd been genuinely enthusiastic about Adahy's performance. She'd whooped and clapped, and he was sure she'd really liked it.

It was hard for him to dislike someone who had such good taste.

So he'd left rather than get sucked into whatever trap she was preparing for him and instead he'd spent the whole ride home fixating on her words, her hair, her curves, and her friendly, open smile.

Mountain lions looked friendly enough until they attacked.

Now he was home and still he was tense. He refused to carry the tension inside with him. Inside was his sanctuary.

So he breathed in deeply and out again before taking off his helmet and getting off his bike. He walked around his front garden, grounding himself with the touch of the tree bark, the smell of the honeysuckle, the song of the crickets.

Gradually he found his center and entered his house.

The light was on in the kitchen and heading that way he found his cousin drinking a glass of water.

"You're up late," he said.

"Your bike woke me," Rayen replied, running a hand through her long, dark hair. "When you didn't come in straight away, I was worried. What's bothering you?"

It didn't matter that she was sleepy, she knew him well

enough to know when something was wrong. Still, he didn't want to talk about it.

"Nothing." He went to the sink and poured his own glass of water.

"Didn't Adahy's performance go well?" she persisted.

"He was great," Tai told her, the pride he'd pretended not to feel with Piper welling up inside him. His little brother was going places. "George is talking about releasing a single soon."

"That's fantastic," Rayen said. "You trust George, right?"

He nodded. When Adahy had first found representation, Tai had grilled George to make sure he was on the level and that he wasn't going to cheat Adahy. George had passed muster – he continued to impress Tai with his integrity and drive.

"So what's wrong?"

"There was a reporter there."

"Ah." Rayen nodded. "What did he say?"

"*She* didn't say much. I ignored her."

Rayen rolled her eyes. "Tai, you can't judge everyone based on one experience. You'll get a reputation of being rude."

"I don't care what people think of me." He'd learned not to.

"You're lucky your reclusive behavior adds to your mystique," she said. "Sometimes I think people come to your restaurant just to catch a glimpse of you."

He grunted but didn't disagree. His restaurant was five star and popular for its food alone, but he'd lost count of the number of times his maître d' had come into the kitchen telling him a guest had requested an audience.

As if he was some kind of trained monkey.

No, he wasn't interested in the rich people who came to his restaurant. He just wanted to cook and help his people.

"I'm going to bed. I'll see you in the morning." Rayen gave him a hug and left the room.

Tai stood at the kitchen window with his glass of water, looking out over the dark yard. The thought of Piper made his chest tight again.

He'd make sure he didn't see her again.

He didn't need that.

Chapter 2

Piper spent Saturday researching her ten Houston profiles, as well as prepping for more articles she would write during the week.

She'd been so excited when Geraldine had given her the assignment; here finally was a chance to show her investigative skills, which had lain dormant since she started at the *Age*, but then came the rules. The subjects were non-negotiable, and the questions should focus on what they'd done for the city, not on any issues – in other words employ a massive positive bias.

They were all prominent people: some politicians, a couple of CEOs, a socialite known for her charity events, a few sports people and Taima. She'd recognized immediately the political leaning of all of them – except for Tai – and knew the timing of the profiles was related to the upcoming election.

It grated on her. Newspapers had a responsibility to report the facts, not have a bias.

Tired of finding negative and therefore unmentionable facts about her subjects, she switched to search for the chef.

There was surprisingly little about Tai online, considering his restaurant was one of the most expensive and desirable places in Houston. She couldn't find any photos of him, and the articles about the restaurant focused on the food, only briefly making mention of the reclusive chef.

How could anyone keep such a low profile in this digital age?

It only intrigued her further.

She dug a little deeper, looking for smaller journals or blogs that might have something, and found an article from a travel journal mentioning the Wooden Spoon. As she read, she frowned. Whoever had written the piece had had an agenda.

It was supposedly a piece on eateries in Houston, but it focused on the fact Tai was of the Queche tribe. The reporter or the editor had chosen the stereotypical image of an Indian in a headdress to accompany the story and expressed amazement that someone from that culture knew what a wooden spoon was, let alone could cook a decent meal.

It was condescending, full of statistics that didn't ring true, and barely addressed the subject it was meant to be about.

It was horrendous.

Reporters like that gave all journalists a bad name.

She saved a link to the piece in case she wanted to refer to it later and typed in a new search query.

The statistics in the article about the Native American cultures had seemed wrong – it talked about massive handouts, alcoholism, obesity, and painted Native Americans as deservedly third-class citizens. Piper knew very little about the culture, but she was fairly certain the "facts" were incorrect.

She began to read.

***

The strain on Piper's eyes was the first indication she'd been at the computer too long. She glanced away from the screen and blinked, surprised to find it was dark. It was eight o'clock and her stomach rumbled, reminding her she hadn't eaten since lunch.

She got to her feet, stretched, and headed for the kitchen. As she opened the pantry door there was a tinkle of bells and Moggy, her ginger cat, ran in from wherever she'd been sleeping.

"Poor thing. I'm surprised you didn't tell me it was past your dinner time," Piper said, giving her a stroke and dishing some cat food into Moggy's bowl.

Moggy meowed and started eating.

Piper opened her fridge. Not a lot of options. It was past time she went grocery shopping. There were a couple of eggs and some ham and cheese which were still good – enough to make an omelet.

As she cooked, her mind processed what she'd discovered during her afternoon of research. She'd known there were Native American reservations in the US. From what she'd read, the living conditions were vastly different depending on where they were and what source of income they had. Some had extremely poor living conditions, and there were housing shortages and sanitary issues. How was it even possible in the United States today? Why weren't people doing something about it?

She'd always spoken up for the poor and disadvantaged on her blog. It was the one place where she could have her say, express her opinions on the things that mattered to her, and raise issues. It gave her freedom of speech that working on the paper didn't. She had a large following, which told her there were others out there who felt the same way she did.

She had to do a story on the reservations, or write a few blog posts – she had to find out more about the tribes of Texas and what life was like on the reservations in the state. Even Geraldine would have to support a piece like that.

As she ate, she drafted up her article pitch and reread it. It was confident, clear and concise. Plus it was a good idea.

Checking the time, she realized if she was going to get to the start of the fun run she had to cover in the morning, she should head to bed. She'd spent her day off working and would be straight back to it Sunday morning.

She needed to get a life.

***

Tai was happy to head into the restaurant on Saturday morning. There he didn't have time to brood, not even about the blond who'd ruined his sleep the night before. He just couldn't get Piper out of his mind.

But he was determined to.

Some of his staff were already there, prepping what would be needed for the day.

"Morning, Tai," his sous chef, Kath, called. "What are you doing here so early?"

"Thought I'd try a dish," he said. He'd been playing around with the idea for a new entrée for a couple of weeks. He'd stopped at the local markets to get the ingredients he needed on the way to the restaurant.

"Can't wait to taste it," she said and continued her work.

Tai was grateful Kath had chosen to come with him when he'd opened the Wooden Spoon. They'd both been working at another five-star restaurant across town but hadn't been happy with the head chef. Kath was the best organizer he knew and his restaurant ran so smoothly largely because of her work. He never forgot to thank her for it.

Today he immersed himself in what he was preparing, a new twist on a crab recipe he'd discovered after chatting with a Powhatan tribe member who'd visited the reservation.

He experimented with spices, sauces and accompaniments until he was happy with the flavor, texture and color.

"You almost done there?" Kath asked. "I'm dying to taste it."

Tai blinked then grinned. "Let me plate it up."

He made up three plates with the different options and gave Kath a fork.

"You're planning on serving this as an entrée?" she asked.

"Yeah."

She called one of the line chefs, Jared, over and handed him a fork as well. Tai waited until they had tried each dish. He had his preference but he liked to involve his team, find out if there were any issues with the dish such as difficulty to prepare or similar flavors to an already existing menu item.

"That one," Kath said, pointing to the plate in the middle.

Jared nodded. "It has the right balance and is really fresh."

Tai grinned. It was the one he preferred as well.

"If you write up the ingredients we need, I should be able to add it to the specials board next week." Kath retrieved a notebook from a nearby shelf.

Tai rattled off the ingredients and quantities, then turned to Jared. "You got time after lunch to go through the method?"

Jared was his seafood chef and would be in charge of the preparation of the dish.

"Yes, chef."

Tai glanced around his kitchen, which was busy now with people preparing lunch for the early-comers. This was his place, his business, and he'd built it himself, knowing exactly what he wanted it to represent. Sure, he still had a loan to pay off, but that was just part of doing business.

His food was described as a fusion of Texas barbeque, Mexican tang and Native American flavors. There was nothing else like it in Houston, which was one reason it had become so popular so quickly.

His menu was slowly leaning more toward the Native American flavors. He wanted to move away from the barbeque and Mexican food, and focus on the food of his people – the dishes that were in danger of being lost due to western influences.

Tai wouldn't let it happen. He wrote down all of the traditional recipes he was taught, and had lists of foods his tribe used to eat before Europeans arrived. He planned to do a cookbook one day.

He was also considering branching out, opening another restaurant in Austin or San Antonio. The Wooden Spoon was running well and he wanted to discover if his success could be replicated in another city and whether he could spread his traditional culture further.

But that would also drag him out of the kitchen. Cooking was his passion and the administrative side of the business already took up too much of his time. Perhaps it was time he hired someone to deal with those day-to-day tasks he hated.

"Need an appetizer for table five," someone yelled.

Tai grinned as the call brought him back to the kitchen.

It was time to get to work.

***

On Sunday Piper woke at a ridiculous hour to get to the triathlon start line before it began. She'd been allocated the event because the sports reporters were covering the more important sporting events taking place in Houston that day. She'd been told to focus on the charity it was raising money for rather than the race itself.

She took her camera and got a number of good, early-morning shots of people milling around with their race numbers on, some doing stretches, some checking their phones, a number of people looking bored or nervous.

Piper caught up with the event organizer after the race began and listened to his monologue about the cancer research program that would benefit from the proceeds of the day. It was a cause most people were prepared to get behind – and one Piper supported herself.

After speaking with him, she interviewed a couple of volunteers, asking why they chose to volunteer for this particular cause and what they thought of the turnout.

Finally she drove to the finish line to interview the first people across the line. They were the ones who didn't necessarily care about the charity, but were competing because it was what they loved to do. They were racing against their own times and their fellow competitors. Piper spotted one of the athletes she was meant to be interviewing as part of the People of Houston series.

She grabbed a bottle of water from the supply for competitors, and wandered over to the seven-foot-tall African-American basketball player who was bent over, catching his breath.

"Not your usual sport," she commented when he glanced up at her.

He took the bottle she offered and took a long swig. "Thought it would improve my stamina," Russell said.

Piper grinned at him. She supported his team, the Houston Rockets, and knew he was an excellent player, but couldn't last four quarters. "You've done well: top ten percent I'd say." Then because she didn't want to mislead him, she added, "I'm Piper Atkinson, reporter with the *Houston Age*. Can I ask you a few questions?"

Russell straightened, still breathing heavily. "Sure."

She asked him about the race and his training regime. He dropped the names of his sponsors and talked up his dedication to his team. Someone had done a good job training him to be media ready.

"I'm doing a series of in-depth profiles of the people of Houston for the *Age*," she told him at the end. "I'd love to interview you for it."

"Sounds great. Call my agent and he'll set you up with a

time." Russell wiped his sweaty palms on his shorts and then shook her hand.

"Thanks for your time."

"Pleasure's all mine," he said and winked.

Piper smiled at him, used to the reaction. She'd interviewed many people who'd thought she was a ditsy blond and she wasn't above using it to her advantage. Often people confided things to her that they wouldn't have if they'd been more on their guard. Of course she only used the information if it was relevant to the story, but she had on occasion received some very angry complaints when the article came out.

She didn't mind. She was doing her job and she was always very clear from the start that she was a reporter, and that anything they said could end up in the newspaper. If they felt comfortable with her, then she was doing her job well.

Happy she'd got what she needed for her article, she headed to Elle's bookshop café, Eat, Drink, Read, for some brunch. She hadn't bothered with breakfast and was now desperate for something to fill the hole in her belly.

She carried her laptop into the café and noticed a single wingback chair free in the book area, so she hurried over to grab it.

Elle waved at her and called, "The usual?"

"Yes, please."

Piper fired up her laptop and plugged in her digital pen to upload the voice recordings and notes she'd taken that morning.

"Did you enjoy Adahy's session on Friday?" Elle asked as she delivered Piper's cappuccino and pecan pie.

"Yeah, it was fantastic. I can't wait for the single to be released."

"He's so nice as well. George is always saying how down to earth he is and how easy he is to work with."

"Pity his brother didn't pick up some of those traits," Piper said.

Elle laughed. "I've met Tai. He's a bit scary, all intense and quiet. He and George get along well though."

"George gets along well with everyone," Piper said. Perhaps he could be a gateway to Tai. "Weren't you cutting back your hours?" she asked. Elle had been working almost constantly since she opened the café a few months earlier, but with its success, she'd been able to hire more people and cut back on her own hours.

"I am, but Mary-Beth called in sick today. George has taken Toby over to visit Kate so I was free to come in." Toby was Elle's five-year-old son.

"You must be so pleased with how it's all going."

Elle beamed at her. "I am. I never dreamed it would be this successful, especially after I left Dean with next to nothing." She glanced around. "I'd better get back to it. I'll call you when I get a spare table."

"Thanks."

Piper ran the conversion software on her computer to convert her handwriting and voice to text, and took a sip of her coffee. Russell was fourth on her list of interviewees but if she interviewed him sooner it would give her a little bit of breathing space. The ten profiles would be run each week for the next ten weeks.

She debated whether to send some introductory emails to the other interviewees but decided against it. She always had a better success rate calling people than emailing, so it could wait for Monday.

She read over the notes she'd taken and then she started writing.

***

When Piper got to work on Monday morning, after interviewing the first person on her People of Houston project, she headed straight into Geraldine's office.

"I'll have the first profile on your desk by tomorrow evening," she said by way of greeting.

"Good. How's it going?"

"The interview with Shirley went well and I'm arranging a couple more today. I did want to ask about the last person, Taima Woods."

Geraldine looked up. "What about him?"

"What made you choose him?"

"The man's a recluse. If you get an interview with him, it will be the scoop of the year," Geraldine said. "Keith wants it badly."

So there wasn't a political agenda with him – just status. It was slightly strange but she'd work with it. "I've been doing a bit of research and a great follow-on series from Taima's story could be an investigation of Native Americans in the Houston area, or perhaps even Texas."

Geraldine raised an eyebrow. "What's our readership demographic?" she asked.

Piper stifled a sigh. "Middle- to upper-class conservative white Americans."

"Do you think they want to be reading about Indians?"

"They would if they realized the appalling state some of them are living in," she said.

"No. They wouldn't. You know that, Piper. People are only interested in what's in it for them. They don't want to hear about the impoverished or be blamed for stealing land they were born on." She paused. "Besides, there aren't many Native Americans in Houston. Tell me if you have any sensible ideas." Geraldine turned back to her computer screen.

Piper had been dismissed. She bit her lip to stop herself from arguing. She'd already been in trouble once this month after disagreeing about the way her article on a women's shelter had been cut so the meat was gone and all that was left was a fluff piece. It wasn't what she'd expected when she got the job. She thought then that they'd want well-written, fact-filled pieces, real investigative journalism, but that hadn't turned out to be the case. She didn't know why she still bothered doing all her research properly.

She had to stop expecting the best from the *Age*. They were just going to keep disappointing her. No. She'd work on the series in her own time, write the articles she wanted to write and then put them on her own blog.

Heading back to her desk, she made a few phone calls and lined up more interviews, including the one with Russell. Then she flicked through the press releases that had come through, flagging those with enough interest to convert to a story. She spent the next hour writing up the articles she needed, before a phone call came in and she headed off to cover a story about a new baby giraffe at the Houston zoo.

Somehow she'd become a dogsbody journalist, doing stories no one else had time for. As she walked out of the building, she wondered when her dreams of being a hard-hitting investigative journalist had evaporated.

***

It was the end of the day before Piper got a chance to follow up any more of her profile people. Needing a challenge, she rang the Wooden Spoon.

"Hi! This is the Wooden Spoon; you're speaking with Kath." A perky female answered the phone.

Piper crossed her fingers and began her spiel in her friendliest tone. "Hi! This is Piper Atkinson from the *Houston Age*. We're doing a series of profiles about the people of Houston and would love to highlight Taima Woods and the Wooden Spoon." Piper went into detail, explaining the series and who else she was interviewing.

"I'm sorry. Chef Woods doesn't do interviews." Kath's voice was still polite, but more subdued.

"Perhaps he'd make an exception for me. I met him Friday night at his brother's show. We have a mutual friend in George Jones. If I could speak with him that would be great."

"Hold on a minute."

The hold music was surprisingly soothing, a gentle drumming and pipes tune that sounded Native American in origin.

Kath's voice came back on. "I'm sorry, Chef Woods isn't interested." She hung up.

Chapter 3

Piper put down the receiver with a smile. She'd known it wasn't going to be easy. The exhilaration of the challenge thrummed through her veins. It was the most excited she'd been about a story since she started at the *Age*. Which was perhaps a sad indictment of the amount of pleasure her job usually gave her.

What was her next step?

She could go to the restaurant and talk her way in, but it was close to dinnertime and she knew better than to interview anyone in the middle of his busy period.

Perhaps she could call George and see if he would put in a good word for her. No, she didn't want to put him in a difficult position between two friends.

She typed Adahy's name into her search engine and brought up his website and its list of his next performances. If Tai had been at one, perhaps he would go to more.

There was one Wednesday night. She picked up the phone and called the music reporter downstairs. "Patti, have you heard of Adahy Woods?"

"That name has been cropping up a lot but I haven't been to a show."

"He's so good. He's doing a gig Wednesday night. You want to go with me?"

"Is George looking for free press?" she asked.

Piper laughed. "No. I'm trying to get an interview with Adahy's brother, so if I can convince you to come, he might put in a good word for me."

"In that case, I'm always willing to help out a fellow reporter. Who's his brother?"

"He owns the Wooden Spoon."

Patti whistled. "High class. All right, I'll get us tickets and you can owe me one."

Patti was one of the few reporters Piper could rely on. She suspected it was because she was friends with George and Adrian, who also went by the name Kent Downer and was the biggest rock star in the world, but Piper was fine with that.

If Adahy didn't pan out, she'd drop by the restaurant and hope to catch Tai there. If she could get him to listen to her, she was confident she'd get an interview.

Pleased she had a plan, she began work on the first article for the series.

***

"Reporters don't normally get you so worked up," Kath commented as Tai dropped the hot pan on the floor.

He swore. "I don't know what you're talking about." Grabbing a thicker glove, he scooped up the pan and dumped it in the sink then turned to find one of the kitchen hands was already cleaning up the rest of the mess. "Thanks."

The kid smiled at him and hurried away.

"You've been distracted ever since I told you about the call," Kath insisted.

He wished she'd drop it. He wanted to forget about Piper but there was something about her that stuck to his memory like chewing gum to hair.

"The series sounds great. They're interviewing a lot of high-profile people. You should be pleased to be asked."

"So they can have their token Native American?" he asked. So they could show their wonderful diversity of coverage by once a year deigning to put a minority race in a positive spotlight for once.

"Tai, don't be like that. You've made a huge success with the Wooden Spoon. It doesn't matter what race you are: people want to know about the man behind the restaurant."

Kath didn't know what it was like. She'd been a white

middle-class American all her life and he'd never shown her the piece the travel journalist had done when the Wooden Spoon opened.

"I'm not interested. You can do the interview if you want."

Kath sighed. "They don't want me; they want you. At least think about it."

"Sure." He agreed quickly, to get her off his case. He needed to focus on his cooking and get his equilibrium back.

***

Piper attended Adahy's concert with Patti on Wednesday night. She didn't catch any sight of Tai but she had arranged Patti an interview with Adahy, courtesy of George.

They went backstage together and waited for Adahy to get changed. George kept them company, chatting to Patti.

When Adahy came out he charmed the music reporter, and Piper knew the article would be great.

At the end of the interview, Patti said, "Thanks for your time, Adahy. I hope Piper has as much luck with your brother."

Adahy turned to Piper with a frown.

Quickly she said, "I mentioned the series I'm doing last time we met. I rang the Wooden Spoon earlier this week and was told Chef Woods doesn't do interviews. I'm not sure whether the woman who answered the phone actually passed on my message."

"Who was it?"

"Kath."

Adahy nodded. "She would have. I'll talk to Tai and give you a call."

They swapped numbers and Piper left, feeling a whole lot more positive about getting an interview.

***

Tai pulled into his driveway, just behind his brother. He took off his helmet and asked, "How did it go?"

"It was amazing. The biggest crowd so far." Adahy waited for him as he dismounted his bike and walked inside.

"George's friend Piper arranged an interview with the *Houston Age* music reporter," Adahy said. "You met her the other night, didn't you?"

His happiness for his brother fled. Why did her name keep cropping up? "Yes."

"She wants to do some kind of profile of you," Adahy continued. "You should consider it. She seems nice."

"She's a reporter. She's supposed to seem nice," Tai told him, heading for the kitchen.

"Who's supposed to seem nice?" Rayen asked, looking up from the laptop she'd set up on the kitchen table.

Normally Tai didn't mind sharing a house with his brother and cousin but at that moment he'd have preferred to be alone.

"The reporter who wants to interview Tai," Adahy told her.

"Is she cute?"

Tai didn't answer. No way he was stepping into that minefield.

"Yeah, she's pretty hot, wouldn't you say?" Adahy asked him.

He had to say something. "Hadn't noticed."

"You gone blind all of a sudden?" Adahy laughed and then screwed up his face. "Is that what this is about? You're attracted to her?"

Tai was too tired for this. They'd been so busy at the restaurant and he wanted some peace and quiet.

"Leave it. I don't need to do interviews. The restaurant's doing well."

"But you've got things to say," his brother said.

"Nothing they want to hear," Tai told him. "I'm going to bed."

He escaped the kitchen and the grilling.

***

Piper didn't get a chance to put the next part of her Operation Woods plan into action until the following week. Adahy had called to let her know he'd had no luck, but did tell her what time Tai usually turned up at the restaurant.

With that in mind, she cleared a spot in her schedule on Tuesday, explaining to Geraldine her plan, and headed to the Wooden Spoon.

She'd eaten there once, a few months back when Libby was

celebrating a new book deal. The food had been out-of-this-world fantastic, but when she'd asked to speak to Tai to thank him, she'd been refused. Now she stood outside the locked front door, thinking. There had to be a back door, somewhere they received all their deliveries. Heading around the side she discovered one such delivery in progress. A van from a seafood company had its doors open and the driver was unloading crates of produce.

The door to the restaurant opened and a woman stepped out. She was about Piper's height, had black, curly hair and was wearing jeans, runners and a pink T-shirt.

"Howdy, Steve," she called.

The driver passed her a delivery docket. "Kath, how are things?"

"Great." The woman signed the docket and handed it back to him before noticing Piper. She frowned and held the door open so Steve could wheel the crates inside. "Usual spot," she said and then turned to Piper.

Piper smiled at her, approaching slowly so she didn't seem threatening. "Hi, my name's Piper. We spoke on the phone last week," she said, holding out her hand for Kath to shake. "I'm a reporter for the *Houston Age*."

"Persistent, aren't you?" Kath said, but smiled.

"Sometimes it pays," Piper agreed.

"Sometimes." Kath held open the door. "You can come in, but I won't guarantee you a friendly reception."

"Noted." Piper acknowledged the nerves bouncing around her stomach. She hadn't seen Tai since the bar where she'd met him, but she remembered exactly how her skin had sizzled that night.

Piper followed Kath into the kitchen, standing aside to let the deliveryman past and out of the door.

The kitchen was all stainless steel and white. There was a mass of stoves, ovens and cooking implements, but everything was clean and organized and in its place.

"He's in his office," Kath told her and showed her to the small room at the back of the kitchen.

Tai was sitting at his desk, typing something on his computer.

He had his hair braided today and he was wearing a green T-shirt.

Looking at him didn't give Piper the jolt he had when they'd first met.

She breathed a sigh of relief.

"Chef, you've got a visitor," Kath said.

Tai looked up. His eyes met Piper's.

It wasn't a jolt: it was a lightning bolt.

***

Tai clenched his jaw at the interruption. He was in the middle of ordering supplies for the next week. Kath knew better than to disturb him and besides, she knew he didn't take visitors.

His eyes met the hazel ones that had been haunting him and he inhaled sharply before controlling himself. He frowned. "I said no interviews," he said and focused back on his screen, well aware Piper wasn't moving.

"I'll leave you two," Kath said and disappeared.

Friend or not, he'd have words to her after this.

He kept typing, not really paying attention to what he was doing on the screen. He was too aware of the woman hovering at the door.

She stepped forward. "I know you don't want to be interviewed, but if you'd just hear me out, I think you'll agree it's a good opportunity."

"For you or for me?" he asked, eyes still on the screen.

"For both of us," she said. Her voice was warm, light and friendly. The type of voice that might lull you to sleep, or make you believe. A reporter's voice.

"I'm not interested."

She didn't listen. "The series is a collection of ten interviews of prominent people in Houston. The *Age* wants to highlight their achievements and what they are doing for the city." She named a few of the other people involved in the series.

"Tell me, what am I doing for the city?" he asked, curious what kind of information she had, what kind of spin she'd put on the story.

There was a pause. "You're providing employment, fabulous food and making Native American cuisine part of the gourmet experience."

Tai hid his surprise. He didn't make a big thing of his culture's influence – it was enough for him to know what he was doing; he didn't need others to.

Still she didn't seem to know anything else.

"So I'm your token Indian?" he asked. "You need to make sure you get your quota?" He glanced up as anger flitted across her face.

He'd hit a sore point.

Then she sighed, stepped forward and sat down on the seat across from him. Way too close for comfort. He pushed his chair back from the desk.

"I'll be honest with you," she said.

He barked out a laugh. An honest journalist. That was a contradiction in terms.

She ignored his reaction. "I know why my managing editor chose the other nine participants. They all have a leaning toward his political agenda and elections are coming up. But I found nothing like that about you. When I asked my editor, all she said was getting your interview would be a coup because you're such a recluse."

So he was a challenge. They didn't care about his politics, because they didn't even make a blip on their radar.

He scowled. "So what would your piece be about?"

"What do you want it to be about? What do you want to tell me, to tell Houston about?"

It was tempting, but he knew better than to be tempted. That had gone wrong before. "It doesn't matter what I say. You'll twist my words to represent whatever your paper wants to suggest."

Piper sat bolt upright and as good as bristled. "Like that tacky travel writer? The one who wrote that condescending piece about you and this restaurant? I'm not like that. I report the truth."

Tai stared at her. "How do you know about that?" He'd hoped it had been well and truly buried.

"I did my research."

Though he didn't want to, he had to admire her dedication. For her to find that little article, she must have dug deep.

Though he was pretty sure she still hadn't discovered his true passion.

"I'm willing to show you the article before it goes to my editor," Piper said. "I can't promise she won't make any changes, but I will show you what I submit."

"Do I get the opportunity to veto it?" he asked, curious in spite of himself.

She shook her head slowly. "I can't promise you that. If I tell my editor I got the interview, I have to deliver it."

She wasn't making promises she couldn't keep. He admired that. Some would have promised just to get the interview. What would she say if he told her about his tribe, if he explained how he was trying to help them, promote their culture, provide opportunity and employment, and bring back those who had fallen into despair?

Would she think his culture was history and that he needed to move on? That they needed to assimilate with western society?

Or would she understand and want to learn more?

He wasn't sure.

Finally he said, "I'll think about it." He wanted time to do his own research, find out more about Piper Atkinson, read some of the other articles she'd written to see what kind of person and reporter she was.

"It's all I ask," Piper said with a smile. She handed him her business card and her soft fingers brushed his.

He ignored the resulting warmth spreading through him.

"I'll call you next week to see if you've made your decision," she said as she stood.

She left the room and he breathed out a sigh of relief. Something told him she was going to be trouble.

***

"So, did you agree?" Kath's voice came from the doorway.

Tai scowled at her. "I said I'd think about it."

"Come on, Tai. This is a great opportunity for the restaurant and for people to hear about what you've done. You've given so many people a chance to get their lives back on track."

"I don't need people to know." He didn't need acknowledgment.

"But you deserve recognition. You've worked so hard. And you could inspire others to be a part of what you're doing."

Tai looked at his sous chef. Recognition was something that was important to her. She was always striving to be the best. They'd worked their way up the ranks of different restaurants and she had his respect, but about this they had different opinions. He was used to keeping his head down, not attracting attention, and getting the job done.

"I'll think about it," he repeated in a tone that said it was the end of the conversation.

She took the hint. "Seafood has been delivered and I've added the crab dish to the specials menu. Jared knows how to make it, doesn't he?"

"Yes."

"Great. I'm going to do the roster for the next month and then I'll review the customer orders, check if there's any dish not being ordered that we might need to change."

"Sounds good."

Finally she left and he was able to consider Piper's offer. He had other work he should be doing, but he was distracted now. He searched the internet for her name and came up with several social media sites, her personal blog and the *Houston Age* website.

Her social media showed she had a passion for the environment and for the downtrodden. She had quite a good following. In her blog she spoke up about illiteracy, poverty, global warming and recycling. She wrote with passion and an easy-to-read, persuasive style.

On the paper's website she wrote in various sections and none of the articles had much substance to them.

It was completely different from her blog posts. Perhaps she had little control over what she did for the newspaper – which only increased his mistrust. He'd been taken in by journalists before.

He picked up his phone and dialed a number. There was one person who might be able to give him details about Piper Atkinson, one person he'd trust to tell him the truth.

"George, it's Tai," he said when George answered the phone.

"Howdy. What can I do for you?"

"I want your honest opinion about Piper Atkinson. She wants to interview me for some series."

George didn't hesitate. "Piper is about as honest as they come. She is always balanced in her reporting and she fights for what she believes in. I've never known someone so determined and still relatively optimistic, given her job."

"You'd trust her to do an accurate interview?"

"She was the only reporter who defended Adrian when his identity was released to the press by Kate's nanny. Emily was playing the jilted lover and the press just ate it up until Piper interviewed her and showed her to be the liar she was."

Tai leaned back in his chair. That was interesting.

"The only thing I would caution is she doesn't get the final say in her articles. She often complains her editor makes changes to soften her articles. Piper can be a little confrontational at times and doesn't play politics."

She'd said as much to Tai that morning.

"Thanks, man."

"Why don't you come to dinner on Friday? We're having a few friends over and Piper will be there. You can get to know her."

Tai hesitated. Did he want to get to know Piper? She did something to his equilibrium, messed with his calm. He flicked over the roster.

He was free.

Seeing it as a sign, he said, "Sure. You want me to bring anything?"

"Don't tempt me." George laughed. "Or I'll have you cooking the whole thing."

Tai smiled as he hung up. George was one of the most genuine guys he'd ever met, which was surprising considering he was in the music business.

So George trusted Piper.

Was Tai willing to do the same?

***

Piper hadn't stopped all week. She'd skipped breakfast most days and eaten her remaining meals either at her desk or on the drive to her next news story. With the extra work on the profile series, she'd been lucky to finish work before ten o'clock.

The humidity hadn't helped matters. Being outside was like walking through a sauna and it sapped some of her energy.

Finally it was Friday evening and she'd sent off her final article for the day. Summer vacation was winding up, so she'd been working on the usual back-to-school articles, finding new spins to put on them.

She reviewed her emails, flagged those she had to follow up on Monday and then shut down her computer. She was going to leave on time. Elle had invited her over for dinner and she was looking forward to catching up with her friends. She packed up her laptop and, with a wave to a couple of colleagues, headed out the door.

When she got home, she indulged in a long, cool shower and dressed in a green summer dress she'd bought ages earlier but hadn't had a chance to wear. She checked the time, grabbed her satchel and headed to George's place.

When Elle let her in, Piper heard kids' laughter from the garden.

"Everyone's in the living room," Elle told her, giving her a hug.

"I'm not late, am I?" she asked.

"No. We're still waiting on Tai," Elle said.

Piper stopped walking. "Tai Woods?"

"Yeah, he's a friend of George's."

Piper knew that, but she hadn't been expecting him there. She had to make sure she didn't mention the interview. She would be off-duty tonight. If she pressured him she suspected he'd say no just to spite her.

She walked into the open-plan living room and kitchen. Libby and Adrian were sitting on the couch chatting to Imogen and Chris while George stirred something on the stove. Outside Toby was playing on a swing with Adrian's niece, Kate.

She breathed out, allowing herself to relax. George handed her a glass of white wine and she took a seat on one of the sofas as the doorbell rang. Elle left to answer it. Piper smiled.

Elle had recently moved in with George, and Piper was happy for them both. Before George, Elle had been in an abusive relationship and she'd found it difficult to trust again. But once she'd seen George would never hurt her the way her ex had, there'd been no reason not to take the next step of moving in.

Tai walked in, wearing black jeans, a leather motorcycle jacket and black backpack. Piper's eyes were drawn to him. What was it about him that fascinated her? She wasn't usually into the strong, silent type.

He actually smiled when he greeted George, and the smile was large and friendly. Piper's heartbeat increased. She watched their interaction with interest.

Tai took his backpack off and unpacked a large insulated metal container. "This needs to go into the freezer," he said.

"You didn't have to bring anything," George said to him.

"My grandmother always told me never to come empty-handed," Tai said. "I know it's your favorite."

George chuckled. "Maybe we should skip dinner and go straight for dessert."

Piper had never seen Tai so relaxed. It was like he was a different person, someone who was even approachable.

"What has the paper got you working on, Piper?" Libby asked, turning toward Piper.

At her name, Tai turned, saw her and tensed.

So much for approachable.

Piper smiled at him, keeping it friendly, before turning to answer her friend. "Same old stuff mostly, but I am doing a profile series – the People of Houston."

"Like who?" Imogen asked and suddenly everyone was listening.

"I haven't confirmed everyone," Piper said, not wanting to bring Tai's name into the mix. "I've got an interview with Russell Sventer from the Rockets next week, and I've interviewed a few politicians." She named them.

"Russell will be interesting," Chris said. "He's been doing those basketball camps for the underprivileged kids all summer."

She nodded. "The first couple of interviews have been really interesting. I hope they all will be." She didn't look at Tai.

"So has Geraldine given you a break from the local news

while you do this?" Libby asked. She knew how much Piper wanted to get more interesting assignments.

Piper shook her head and laughed. "Nope. It's business as usual; this is extra."

Imogen squinted at her. "You're looking tired. Are you getting enough sleep?"

If anyone in their group of friends was a mother figure, it was Imogen. "I'm fine," she insisted. "What's the latest on the Ryder brand?" Imogen was a fashion designer who was working on her own label of clothing.

"It's all still on paper but I'm getting ready to put it into motion. Chantelle has hired a new production manager and I'll be handing over to him in the next month or so. Then I can concentrate on my own stuff."

Piper was glad. Imogen had worked for her father's haute couture fashion label since leaving high school, but had never had the chance to do her own designs. She'd left the company earlier in the year to work with a friend, but was almost ready to go it alone and make the clothes she really wanted to make.

"Dinner's ready," George called and they made their way into the dining room. The table was set with a white tablecloth, linen napkins and flowers on the table.

"Is this a special occasion?" Piper asked as she took a seat. They were never this formal.

George gestured to Chris, and both Chris and Imogen stood up, holding hands. "I'm pleased to announce Imogen has finally accepted my proposal. We're getting married."

Piper squealed.

She jumped to her feet to hug both Imogen and Chris, exclaiming over Imogen's gorgeous ring. She was so happy for them. Imogen had hesitated to accept Chris's proposal at first, not because she didn't love him, but because she had just embraced her independence after years of trying to please her father and didn't want to rush anything.

It hadn't taken Imogen long to realize Chris wasn't controlling, and that she could have her own life with him.

Stepping away from the couple she noticed Tai was standing back. It must be difficult for him because he didn't know Chris or Imogen.

Walking over, she said, "I've known Imogen since middle school. I'm so happy she's found someone she loves."

He glanced at her. "And someone who loves her back."

It was a strange comment to make. Why would they marry if they both didn't love each other?

When they'd sat down again, Imogen said, "We're going to have a fall wedding at Chateau Fontaine."

"That's not far away," Piper commented. Weddings were hard to organize.

"There won't be too many guests and I'll make all the dresses. I'm sure Mrs. Povey will make us a cake if we get stuck and so really it's just catering and photography."

"I know a good caterer," Tai said. "I'll give you his details."

Imogen beamed at him. "Thank you."

Piper was surprised. She hadn't expected Tai to say anything.

"You should get married in the treehouse," Kate said. "Up at those windows so everyone can see – and then you can slide down the slide together."

Imogen glanced at Chris. "That's a great idea. We'll have to check it out."

Piper laughed. Imogen's treehouse was one of epic proportions and was where Imogen and Chris had first met as teenagers. She liked the idea they would marry there.

Talk covered plans for the wedding, which Imogen had already given a lot of thought to, and then shifted to other topics. Tai was quiet through most of it, but he listened.

When George collected the plates, Tai stood. "I'll get dessert."

What had he brought with him? Piper tapped her foot on the floor, her anticipation high. His restaurant was renowned, not to mention she'd had the best meal of her life there.

Ten minutes later George and Tai came back carrying bowls of dessert.

It was some kind of sorbet covered in a berry compote and topped with strawberries.

When she tasted it, the flavor burst onto her tongue and her eyes rolled back into her head. "Oh my."

"Mom, this is better than pecan pie," Toby said.

Elle grinned at him. "It sure is."

"Pecan pie's Toby's favorite at the moment," George told Tai.

"The highest of compliments then," Tai said and smiled. Piper was glad he wasn't always so serious.

She focused on the dessert, savoring each mouthful. There was so much taste from each bite. She tried to work out what the flavors were, but then gave up and enjoyed.

When she had finally finished scraping her bowl, she looked up straight into Tai's eyes. They were darker than normal and the intensity was back. Piper's body went immediately to burning.

He looked at her lips and she ran her tongue over them, wetting them. Holy hell, the man was hotter than the August sun.

"Piper, have you finished with your bowl?"

Elle's voice broke through Piper's daze. She was waiting next to her with her arm outstretched.

"Yes. Thank you." She passed Elle her bowl and then glanced down at the table, refusing to look at Tai again.

Why did she have to be attracted to someone who clearly wasn't interested in her? She had to get him out of her system. Hopefully she could get the interview and then stay away from him.

That was the safest plan.

***

When Piper mentioned she had to go, Tai was ready. "I'd better make a move as well," he said, getting to his feet and gathering up his backpack.

He'd had fun and he hadn't been expecting to. He'd watched the occasional baseball game at George's place, and he'd met Elle and her boy, but the others were strangers to him.

Except Piper.

She was beginning to interest him more than she should.

Watching her enjoy the dessert he'd made had been an erotic experience, the way she'd sucked every last bit from the spoon. He'd found himself wishing he was the spoon, and when she'd finally looked up, he'd realized the attraction was mutual.

So he could admit now he found her hot.

But it didn't change the fact she was a journalist.

Not that she'd acted like it during the evening. He'd been expecting her to hound him, ask him questions about the restaurant and try to convince him to do the interview. Instead she hadn't mentioned his involvement at all.

Because of that, he was willing to be interviewed, on a couple of conditions.

He grabbed the helmet he'd left by the door and followed Piper, Elle and George out the front.

"Thanks for dinner," he said to George and was surprised when Elle hugged him and kissed his cheek.

"Thank you for dessert," she said.

He shrugged. "You're welcome."

He straddled his motorbike and called out to Piper, "Do you want to call me about the interview tomorrow?"

Her mouth dropped open, and he put his helmet on so she couldn't see him smile.

"Ah, sure. What time will you be at the restaurant?"

"From ten," he said. He started his bike, felt satisfaction from the purr of the engine and gave a salute.

Then he drove away, already looking forward to tomorrow.

Chapter 4

Piper picked up her phone and put it down without dialing several times before she got up the courage to call the Wooden Spoon the next morning. She'd been replaying the moment last night when Tai had oh-so-casually said to call him about the interview. She certainly wasn't confident he would do it. He might want her to call just so he could tell her he wasn't interested. They hadn't talked much the night before, but she'd been utterly conscious of him after the dessert incident. It was doing her head in, second-guessing his response.

Annoyed with herself, she dialed the number.

The person who answered put her on hold and a minute later Tai picked up.

"Thanks for calling, Piper." He actually sounded friendly.

"You wanted me to call about the interview," she said, keeping her tone business-like, professional.

"Yes. I'll do it on two conditions."

Piper knew better than to get excited. "What are they?"

"I get to read and edit the copy you submit to your editor," he began.

"Read, yes. Edit, no," she said. "They need to be my words, but I will rewrite sentences you think may be misleading or ambiguous, within reason."

Tai was silent for a moment and she thought he would refuse. "Agreed."

"And the second condition?"

"You need to spend an evening in my shoes, at the restaurant."

Piper laughed. "Trust me, you don't want me to cook."

"Not cooking, watching the process."

Surprised he was letting her have so much access, she asked, "Can I interview your staff?"

"Only if they agree, and you make it clear to them that what they say is on the record."

"Of course. When would you like me to come?"

"Are you free tonight?"

She had a couple of stories to cover that afternoon, but they weren't big ones. She could do them quickly. "I can be there by five," she said.

"I'll see you then." Tai hung up.

Piper stared at her cell and then grinned, pumping her arms in the air.

This was a huge turnaround. What had made him change his mind?

She had no idea, but she wasn't going to miss the opportunity.

It was likely the only one she'd get.

***

Just before five o'clock, Piper stood outside the Wooden Spoon. She'd debated what to wear and settled for smart-casual. She didn't want to be too dressy if all she was going to do was sit around the kitchen all night, but she wanted to look professional.

The maître d' took her through to the kitchen and into Tai's office. He wasn't there, but the man told her to wait, so she took a seat.

The office had a window in one wall overlooking the kitchen, which was already busy with people dressed in white chef uniforms at different stations doing different things. A number of the staff appeared to be of Native American descent like Tai.

It was very busy and there was only one table of customers.

Then one of the chefs clapped his hands together and called

for attention. Instantly there was silence as all the staff stopped what they were doing and turned to him. Piper got up and moved to the door. The chef who had got everyone's attention had his brown hair tied back in a braid. It had to be Tai.

Tai's voice rang out loud as he spoke some kind of tribal blessing. He then issued a few instructions to which the other chefs said, "Yes, Chef." And they got to work.

Tai turned and his eyes met Piper's. She'd never seen him in his chef's uniform before. The double-breasted jacket fitted him well and he wore it with calm authority. It was definitely a good look for him.

He walked over and smiled. "Glad you could make it."

"Thanks for inviting me." Before she could get distracted by his smile, she asked, "What kind of blessing was that?"

"Straight to the point," he commented. "It's from the Queche tribe. It's a prayer to the ancestors for good luck."

"Do you do it every night?"

"Before lunch and dinner." He waited for her next comment.

"It's obviously been working," Piper said. She wasn't sure what she thought about prayers and good luck. She'd always believed you made your own, but she wasn't about to question his beliefs. The interview wasn't about that. She made a note.

"What do you want me to do tonight?" she asked.

"Observe, ask questions. Kath or I will be able to answer most of what you want to know, and I've told the other staff you may want to talk to them on their dinner break, but that they don't have to if they don't want."

"What are the different stations for?" Piper asked, starting with the basics.

He gestured for her to follow him and he took her around, introducing her to the line chefs, explaining which part of the meal they were each responsible for.

She had never been behind the scenes in a restaurant like this and had often wondered how it ran. She'd never realized her meal was made by several people.

"Order," someone called.

Tai pointed to a large monitor mounted on a wall. A new order had appeared on it. "The wait staff have mobile devices that allow them to take the orders and send them straight through to the kitchen. The device then notifies them when the order is ready to serve. This way they can stay out on the floor where they're needed, making sure the customers are happy.

"We have an average time it takes to get the meal on the table, and the device also flags when this is past. If the table hasn't got the meal yet, the wait staff will check with the kitchen and, if it's going to be more than five minutes, we offer them a complimentary drink."

"Wow, that's service. Does it happen much?"

"Maybe once a week."

He must have the restaurant running like a machine.

"Do you get many people with food allergies?" Piper asked. They would surely throw off the routine.

"A few each night. Usually it's a matter of leaving out a certain ingredient, but occasionally we have to be real careful. They get flagged on the monitor so everyone is aware. Either Kath or I make sure those dishes are correct before they go out."

More orders were coming up on the monitor and the kitchen was coming alive with the clang and sizzle of cooking. Scents of fried garlic and other delectable aromas assaulted her nose.

"How do you stop eating everything you cook?" she asked.

Tai chuckled. It was low and soft, but made her insides vibrate. "When you're cooking it, you lose your appetite a little. Besides we're constantly tasting to make sure it's all correct."

"What's the shift length?"

"Between five and seven hours. Everyone gets a dinner break."

"Do they bring their own sandwiches?" she joked.

"Someone is always allocated as the dinner chef," Tai told her.

"What do you mean?"

"Each of my staff gets a cooked meal every shift. They choose anything from the menu and the dinner chef prepares it."

"How do I get myself a job here?" she asked, not altogether kidding. She could imagine having meals cooked like that every time she went to work.

"You'll get your meal tonight," he told her.

"Oh, no, I didn't mean that." She didn't want him to think she was taking advantage of her situation.

"You're walking in my shoes, so you get a meal." He handed her a menu. "Choose something and write it on the board over there." He pointed to a whiteboard where there was a list with time, name and meal on it. "I need to help out. Take a seat in my office and you can watch everything." He joined the fray before she could argue with him.

Not one to look a gift horse in the mouth, she scanned the menu, her mouth watering as she read the descriptions. There was a large selection of seafood – fish, oysters, clam and crab – as well as deer, rabbit and turkey. The dishes were flavored with chili, persimmon or berries, and other amazing combinations. Finally she wrote her selection on the board and made herself comfortable in Tai's office.

A busboy poked his head around the door. "Can I get you a drink, ma'am?" he asked. He was distinguished from the chefs by his black pants and black apron and he didn't look old enough to be out of high school.

"A bottle of water would be great."

"Sure thing." He disappeared and reappeared a few minutes later with a bottle and a glass.

"I'm Ralph," he said. "Give me a yell if you need anything else." He winked at her and left.

She chuckled. He was definitely a charmer. She settled in to observe the dance of the kitchen.

It really was a sight to behold. Each station was in use: mountains of food appeared, transformed and then disappeared out into the restaurant. Tai floated through the area, relaxed and at ease despite the frenetic pace. He was in his element, helping out where needed, putting the finishing touches on plates and giving his OK for them to be served.

The wait staff collected the orders from the heated area behind the bar. They appeared almost like magic as soon as the order went up and the plates were whisked out to the right person.

At one stage one of the line chefs swore and dropped a pan,

clutching his hand.

Tai moved to him, checked the injury and ordered him to the first-aid station. One of the busboys had already begun to clean up the mess and Kath appeared to take over the cooking at that station.

It *was* like clockwork.

Piper watched in fascination until about seven when the first person got his break. Tai ducked his head into the room. "Break room is next door," he said, pointing. "Jared will be in shortly if you want to speak with him."

Piper got to her feet and stretched before grabbing her satchel and heading to the next room.

It was simply furnished. There was a round wooden table with four chairs around it as well as a navy blue two-seater sofa. In one corner was a small fridge, and as Jared came in he swiped a drink from it and sat down, dropping his chef's hat on the table and taking a long swig from the bottle.

"It must be hot work," Piper commented and introduced herself.

"It is, but you get used to it." He took another sip. "What do you want to know?"

Piper decided to start simply. "How long have you worked at the Wooden Spoon?"

"Since it opened. As soon as I heard Tai was going out on his own, I wanted in."

She was surprised by his confidence. "Had you worked with him before?"

"He was the sous chef at a restaurant where Kath and I worked. Work was always better when he was in charge and the head chef was away."

"Why was that?"

"He cares." Jared lifted his bottle and gestured out to the kitchen. "See when Howell burned himself? Tai made sure he got the proper first aid. Other head chefs would have been annoyed and yelled at him to get back to work. Some would take the spilled food out of his paycheck."

"Really?"

"Yeah."

Tai came into the room carrying a plate of food that

smelled divine. He put it in front of Jared. "Duck with persimmon sauce and micro greens."

"Thanks, Chef."

Tai left and Jared got stuck into the food. "I always love it when it's Tai's turn to be dinner chef."

"Tai cooked that?" Piper asked. So much of what she'd seen of the chef surprised her. She'd expected him to be surly and intense, because that had been her initial experience with him, but with his employees he was friendly and kind.

"Yeah. He's dinner chef at least once a week. You got lucky tonight."

"So do head chefs at other restaurants cook for their staff?"

"Some do. Some don't even provide a break, depending on the shift length. Tai makes meals for everyone from the busboy to Kath."

"Must get expensive." Some of the ingredients on the menu weren't cheap.

"I suppose Tai believes it's worth it. There isn't a single person here who isn't loyal to him. No one wants to leave, even when their apprenticeship is finished. But Tai finds them other places to go, places where they'll be treated right."

"Are there a lot of apprentices?"

"We've always got a couple, and the busboys and wait staff are generally studying either at high school or college. Tai insists they must be getting an education to work for him."

That was strange. Why should he care? Especially when it meant he would have to train new people when the old ones went on to bigger and brighter things.

Jared got to his feet. "Better get back to it. Nice meeting you."

After Jared left there was a stream of people coming through for their break. Some came two at a time, but Tai always served them their meal almost as soon as they sat down. They all sang Tai's praises.

A girl in her early twenties walked in and took a seat. She smiled at Piper and said, "I'm Rayen."

"Your earrings are gorgeous." The woman wore silver earrings with turquoise teardrops hanging from them.

"Thanks! The design is traditional Queche."

It was the opening Piper was looking for. "I noticed there are a lot of Native Americans working here," she said. "Does Tai advertise locally?"

Rayen nodded. "I grew up on the rez like most of the others here. There aren't a lot of jobs available and so Tai trains us and gives us hope."

"Jared mentioned all the wait staff are students as well," Piper said.

"That's right. It's a condition of employment." Rayen smiled. "Many of my people can't afford a higher education. They get blue-collar jobs either waitressing or laboring. Neither pays well and so they're stuck in the cycle like their parents before them.

"Tai gives us jobs, but makes sure we can move on to better things. I'm studying education and will go back to the rez to teach when I'm done. One of the other waitresses is studying medicine, and Ralph has got a scholarship at a school nearby. He stays with his aunt and this job gives him a little bit of pocket money and keeps him out of trouble."

"Is Tai from the reservation?" How did he know all these people?

"You'll need to ask him," Rayen said and got to her feet. "I'd better get back to work. My break's over."

Piper added some notes. Tai had asked her what she thought he was doing for the city and she'd given him an answer, but there appeared to be a whole lot more to it than she'd been able to find.

Most people liked to crow about their achievements and their philanthropy, wanting people to congratulate them for their work.

Tai wasn't most people.

He came into the room carrying two plates of food. "Thought you'd be ready for dinner now," he said, putting her order in front of her.

"Thank you." It smelled delicious, but her brain was too busy thinking to eat. When Tai sat next to her she asked, "Is it your break?"

He nodded. "Everyone else has eaten."

"So you have the last one?"

"The dinner chef has the last one," Tai corrected her.

"I'm told not all restaurants have dinner chefs," Piper said as she took a bite of her meal.

"No, they don't. I believe if I'm going to ask my staff to work demanding hours, the least I can do is provide them with a decent meal."

"One of your apprentices finishes at the end of the month," Piper said, checking her notes for a name.

"I'd like to keep her on, but I don't have the space," Tai said.

"But she said you'd found her a place nearby." The meal was delicious but she was too focused on her questions to really savor it.

He nodded. "The industry is quite close. I asked around and found out who was hiring."

It was very generous of him. He could have left her to fend for herself. As it was, she was starting in another five-star establishment as soon as her apprenticeship ended.

He continued to eat as if unconcerned about the questions. This restaurant was his domain; perhaps that was why he was so relaxed.

"Your wait staff are all studying," Piper said. "Isn't there a risk they'll all find new jobs and you'll be left with no one?"

Tai chuckled. "No. Their courses finish at different times. Sometimes my staff find part-time jobs in their chosen fields before they finish their study but I'm always happy for them. It makes sense for them to move on to a job which will further their career. There are always people looking for work."

"People from the reservation?" Piper asked.

His gaze sharpened on her, but he didn't tense. "That's right."

Piper hesitated and then said, "Can I go off topic for a minute?"

He nodded.

"While I was researching you for the interview, I read some statistics about the reservations and the quality of life there. Their wealth varies according to where they are and what their income is. Do you know much about life on the reservations?"

"I grew up on one. What do you want to know?"

His admission surprised her.

She'd considered herself a well-informed individual. For some reason she'd assumed people who chose to live on the reservations did so because they wanted to live a traditional life. It hadn't occurred to her they might leave.

Which was silly really.

"Which one?"

"The Queche reservation. It's not far from Houston."

Piper hadn't realized that. She wanted to know more but she focused on her original topic. "The statistics I read don't make sense. They talk about the lack of housing, the percentage of people living under the poverty line and the lack of education. Then there's the suicide rate which is number eight in the top causes of death for Native Americans." She threw her hands in the air. "If things are that bad, why aren't we doing anything about it? Why is there no focus or reporting, highlighting the situation?"

"Why would the government care when they've been screwing us over for centuries?" he asked, keeping his tone mild.

She paused. She could see his point of view. "It's not right. People should not be living in third-world conditions in the United States of America."

"What would you do about it?"

She sighed. "I'm ignorant. I don't know enough about it. There mustn't be an easy solution, otherwise someone would have done it by now."

"Do you think people who live on the rez are unhappy?" he asked.

The question made her stop. "I can't imagine being happy living in poverty," she said.

"If you investigated and found issues, would you do an article on it?"

"I know you'll probably think I have a white savior complex, but my parents taught me to stand up against injustice. I'd like to do a whole series, but I'd need to convince my editor." Which would be hard. "But in order to pitch the idea I need to know more."

"And you believe I might be able to help?"

Piper leaned back in her chair, her cheeks flushed. "If you're already doing so much on your own, you might want to bring the issues to the public's attention."

"Do you really believe they will care? We're drunks, gamblers, bums and drug addicts."

"We need to break down those stereotypes, don't you think?"

"Yes, I do," Tai answered.

Piper let out a breath.

"Have you plans tomorrow?" he asked.

It was her one day off that week. "Nothing I can't adjust."

"I'll show you what you want to know," he said. "But everything you write will be vetted by me."

Piper hesitated. "For this series of articles."

Tai inclined his head.

"All right."

He grabbed a pen and wrote his cell phone number on her notebook. Then he said, "Write down your address."

She did as he asked. "Where are we going?"

"To see how rez Indians live," he told her. "I'll pick you up at seven. Wear sensible clothes."

He gathered their empty plates and left the room.

Piper sat where she was, not quite sure what she'd agreed to, not quite sure how she'd gone from a simple interview to a whole lot more.

But for the first time in a long time, she was looking forward to tomorrow.

***

Piper was ready to go long before seven. In fact she'd barely slept since she'd arrived home after eleven, not sure what the day would bring. She'd dressed in jeans, hiking boots and T-shirt, and hoped Tai would consider that sensible clothing.

When there was a knock on her door, she poured her remaining coffee down the sink, grabbed her satchel and opened the door.

Tai stood there wearing black jeans, boots and a motorcycle jacket. In his hand he carried a helmet. He looked her up and down, and her body warmed.

"Got a thick jacket?" he asked.

"We're taking a bike?" she asked, not sure if she wanted to

be riding a motorcycle.

"Yep."

"I can drive us if you like," she offered.

"It's more fun this way." He grinned at her, his face lighting in mischief, and she forgot her concerns.

She had an old denim jacket in the back of her wardrobe that would have to do. She quickly fetched it and then followed him out to where a black sports bike was parked in the lot.

The helmet he handed her fit. She stood while he did it up, suppressing a shiver as his fingers brushed her skin.

"Tighten your bag so it doesn't flap about," Tai said as he mounted his bike.

She did as he suggested and waited while he wheeled the bike around.

"Hop on," he said.

Piper's doubts switched to nerves but she did as he asked, swinging her leg over the seat. Where was she supposed to put her hands? She had to hold on somewhere but there was no bar on the seat and she could hardly wrap her arms around Tai.

He glanced behind. "You've never been on a bike before, have you?"

She shook her head, the weight of the helmet making her feel like one of those bobble-headed dolls.

"All right. Slide in close, put your hands on my waist to hold on. There are foot pegs for your feet. Relax and feel the rhythm of the bike."

She shuffled closer and obeyed, reminding herself this was a business trip.

But it didn't mean she couldn't enjoy the warmth from his jacket or the hardness of his body.

Tai put his helmet on and turned the key. The low vibration between her legs wasn't entirely unpleasant.

"Ready?" he asked above the engine.

"Yes," she called back.

The bike took off slowly but once out of the parking lot picked up speed. Piper turned her head to watch the street go by. It was an entirely different sensation than being in a car. For starters the wind rushed by, which was pleasant because the day was already warm. She felt as if she could reach out and touch everything she passed. It was invigorating.

They stopped at a set of traffic lights near to the freeway.

"You're going to want to hold on real tight," Tai yelled to her.

She didn't like the sound of that. Were they heading onto the freeway? She shuffled closer; when the lights turned green, Tai accelerated quickly and she forgot about not getting too close. She wrapped her arms around his stomach, holding on for dear life.

If the city streets had been pleasant, this was terrifying. The world didn't meander past: it flashed by in an instant. She almost shut her eyes, but pride made her keep them open. It felt like they were flying down the freeway, but they were traveling at the same speed as the cars – a speed that had never been an issue when she'd been encased in a steel cage. Now the reality of it surrounded her.

Tai patted her hands and it was then she realized she had almost a death grip around his waist.

Piper loosened her hold a fraction.

Tai squeezed her wrists and she focused on relaxing one muscle at a time so her arms still circled him but were just resting against his jacket, ready to clench again if she needed to.

Tai pointed to something above them, calling out words that were lost by the wind.

Piper lifted her head and saw some kind of bird of prey, circling high above them. Did it feel terror in the rush of wind, or did it feel freedom?

Or were they the same thing?

Chapter 5

Eventually Tai turned off the highway and slowed the bike. They passed a sign that read *Queche Tribe of Texas.* They had reached the reservation. Tall pine trees lined the road, shading it from the morning sun.

Piper had never been on a reservation before – she had no idea what to expect. She doubted there would be tee-pees all over the place, but she wasn't certain.

They drove into a town with some municipal buildings and a school. Tai waved to someone, but continued through the settlement and took a narrow road leading deeper into the reservation. They rode into a clearing and he parked in front of a neatly kept brick house. He turned off the bike and took off his helmet.

Not sure what she should do, she dismounted, stretching out the kinks of the long ride, and took off hers as well.

An older woman came out of the door and called out something in another language. Tai grinned and responded, sweeping the woman up in a big hug. He was far taller than she was and he covered her.

Piper waited where she was, not wanting to interrupt.

The woman stepped back and noticed her. She said something to Tai and Tai beckoned Piper over.

The woman was in her seventies, with her graying hair braided all the way down to her hips. She had the same brown eyes as Tai.

"Piper, this is my grandmother, Eyota. Ka' sa', Piper is a reporter who is interested in doing a story on our people."

His grandmother glanced at him with questions in her eyes, but smiled and greeted Piper. "Come in. I've just prepared some iced tea."

The inside of the house was small, but clean and tidy. Piper took a seat at the round kitchen table and thanked Eyota for the tea.

"Tell me how you met my Tai," Eyota said.

"We met through a mutual friend, and then my boss asked me to interview him for a profile series we're doing on people of Houston."

"What type of profiles?" The question was innocent enough but there was suspicion in her tone.

"The series is supposed to be about what the people are doing for Houston, but many of them will have a political slant," she said, seeing no reason to lie. "Tai's profile will be about his restaurant and whatever else he'd like me to cover."

"I see." She turned to Tai. "How are your brother and cousin? They never visit me any more."

"Adahy is playing lots of gigs at the moment and he and George are getting ready to release his first single. Rayen is gearing up for college to start and I'm keeping her busy in the restaurant."

Rayen was one of the waitresses Piper had interviewed the night before. She hadn't realized she was related to Tai.

"Where are the kids?" he asked.

"They've gone into the forest to play, but I told them to be back in time, so they shouldn't be far."

What children? Was Tai married with kids? Piper acknowledged the pang of disappointment, but didn't feel like she had the right to ask for clarification. She wasn't entirely sure what he wanted her to see while she was here.

"Ka' sa' looks after a number of children on the weekend whose parents aren't able to for one reason or another." He watched her, waiting.

She got the feeling he wanted her to ask. "What kinds of reasons?"

"Some of the parents here work long hours; others have drug and alcohol addictions or suffer from depression."

Outside a mass of voices were shouting and laughing.

"Why don't you tell them you're here?" Eyota suggested.

Tai got to his feet and headed outside. Through the window, Piper saw him raise a hand in greeting.

"Tai's home!" someone yelled.

Other voices joined in and Tai was suddenly surrounded by a dozen children aged between six and twelve. Tai laughed and greeted them all.

Piper sat back in her chair. She never would have pictured him as a man who liked kids. But this man, here and now, was definitely a child magnet. Her heart warmed.

"You're surprised." It wasn't a question.

Piper nodded. "When I met Tai he was …" How could she put it nicely? "… reserved."

"Tai trusts slowly. He has been through much in his life and it has taught him to be cautious."

"Many people think reporters are an untrustworthy bunch regardless," Piper said and smiled at the woman.

The woman nodded. "What story would you like about our tribe?"

"The truth," Piper said. "When I was given the assignment to interview Tai I realized I knew very little about the Native American cultures. When I researched it, I learned each tribe was different and I was shocked to read about the levels of poverty and despair in some of the reservations."

"Statistics don't show everything. There are positive aspects too," Eyota said.

"That's what I thought. I would like to do a whole series of articles about the tribe, both the positive and the negative. I'm a firm believer issues can't be fixed until they are identified and discussed. Sometimes people in power don't pay any attention until enough people protest about it."

"Did you know that few of us identify as Native American?" Eyota asked.

Piper shook her head.

"I am of the Queche tribe on my mother's side and the Coushatta tribe on my father's. If you want to use a generic term, I prefer indigenous."

"Can I ask why?"

"Native American is too politically correct. All of the horrific things that happened to us happened to the American Indian, so the name glosses over that."

She would have to remember that. "Have you lived here your whole life?"

"Yes. I had to go off-rez for my schooling but I was ten before the government found me and took me away. My parents had already instilled the importance of my culture into me so the government's attempt to brainwash me didn't work. I pretended to go along with them, but kept remembering what my parents taught me, including my language."

Piper had read that during the nineteenth and twentieth centuries children weren't allowed to speak their native languages at school, or practice their culture, and if they were caught doing either, they were punished. They had to assimilate into the white culture.

"Do many people still speak the language?"

"Some do. It's mainly the older generation but some of the young ones are learning. I taught my children and grandchildren."

Eyota got to her feet and motioned for Piper to follow her out of the house. "Enough of this talk. Tai has a class to get to."

Surprised, Piper followed her. What class?

When the kids noticed Piper they stared, and one of them asked, "Who's she?"

"Piper's a reporter who's doing a story on me," Tai explained to them.

"Everyone in the pickup," Eyota called, and the children all scrambled into the tray of the pickup parked in the carport next to the house.

Tai climbed into the driver's seat and Piper and Eyota slid into the bench seat next to him.

"Where are we going?" Piper asked.

"School," Tai answered and flashed her a grin.

The cab space was suddenly too small.

The smile had taken up all the room.

He drove the short distance and led the way inside to a home economics room.

"Tai paid for this room to be upgraded," Eyota told her as they walked in, pride in her voice.

There was already a whole group of people waiting, ranging in age from six to sixty. The children took their places at different benches and Eyota showed Piper to a stool off to the side.

Tai greeted everyone and after a few moments, they quieted down and he began to speak. He captured the audience: that much was certain. His voice was clear, confident and friendly.

He was giving a cooking class. People in Houston would pay a fortune to attend a class taught by Tai and here he was doing it, she assumed, for free.

He showed them chef's tricks for slicing and dicing food and making it look pretty, but he also talked about nutrition and balance. They cooked one traditional meal, using only items he said had been on the land prior to the Europeans' arrival, and then two other easy, healthy meals for the busy person.

Tai was incredibly patient, going from station to station, helping people, teasing some, laughing with others.

Some of the kids cooked as if they had been doing it all their lives. Perhaps they had. Piper hadn't learned anything like it until well into high school, when she'd attended her own home economics class. Even now she preferred to buy something than make her own.

When the meals were prepared, they were carried out into a communal area where another group had gathered. The food was passed around and they all sat eating and catching up.

Tai came over and handed his grandmother and Piper a plate of food each. Piper was given the traditional meal, a fish stir fry that smelled delicious.

After she thanked him, she asked, "How often do you run these classes?"

"Every Sunday," he said.

How did he have the time? The restaurant had to keep him busy. "Do the same people come every week?"

"We have a roster so everyone who wants to gets a turn. Some make it every week and some can't."

An older man called Tai over and he excused himself.

Many of the adults who were there were overweight, and Piper remembered something else she'd read. "Does the tribe have a lot of trouble with heart disease and diabetes?" she asked.

Eyota nodded. "It's one of the reasons Tai holds the classes. He never cooks unhealthy or high-fat meals. He's keeping our culture alive with the traditional dishes, but he's also teaching them how they can improve their health. See the man over there?" She pointed. "He's lost twenty pounds since he started coming. The woman next to him now has her diabetes under control. Not everyone wants help, but those who do are getting it."

The cooking class was such a simple thing, but it was more than that.

"Does Tai ever take time off, time for himself?"

Eyota laughed. "This *is* his time for himself. This is what he loves."

Piper glanced over at Tai, who was laughing about something. He was definitely enjoying himself. "He was obviously brought up right."

Eyota smiled.

"How does he know the traditional dishes?" she asked.

"I remember some things my mother used to cook and some of the elders remember others. Then there are members of our tribe who spend time researching. It might not be one hundred percent accurate, but it's close, and better than nothing. Our ancestors realized it was safer to be seen to be assimilating with the white culture and so much was lost. There are some things we managed to keep hold of, though. Tai talks about doing a recipe book with it all in."

"That's a great idea. I'd buy a copy." Especially if it was anything like the food at the Wooden Spoon.

When the meal was finished, everyone pitched in to clean up and then went their separate ways.

"I'll drop you off and then take the kids home," Tai said to his grandmother.

"That would be great."

They all piled into the pickup again; and after Eyota got out

Tai and Piper were alone in the cab. The silence wasn't altogether comfortable, but it wasn't tense.

Refusing to be distracted, Piper focused on her job. "You're a good teacher."

He shook his head. "It's easy when they want to learn."

"What made you decide to run the lessons?" Had someone asked him, or had it been his idea?

"One too many bland communal dinners," he said lightly.

Piper didn't believe him. "Eyota mentioned people have had positive health effects from the classes."

"You are what you eat." He pulled up in front of a house and a couple of kids jumped down from the back and waved then headed inside.

Tai checked his rear-view mirror before pulling out.

"You've got a lot of kids in the class."

"You're never too young to learn."

He wasn't giving anything away. "Some of the kids have to fend for themselves, don't they?"

He glanced at her quickly, his hands briefly tensing on the steering wheel. "Some parents work long shifts, so the older children cook for the younger ones."

She was sure that wasn't the whole story, but she didn't push. Not yet. "You could make a lot of money running cooking classes in Houston."

"It's not about the money."

No it wasn't. "It's about culture."

Tai pulled up outside a house and didn't answer. This place had seen better days; the garden was full of weeds, the paint on the door was faded and peeling and one of the gutters was hanging on by a nail. Another couple of children hopped down, yelled their goodbyes and went inside.

"Eyota said you're considering writing a cookbook," Piper said, hoping to get a longer answer.

He frowned. "I'm thinking about it."

"What kind of recipes will it have in it?"

He scowled. "I'm not sure. I want to capture the traditional recipes but you can't get all of the ingredients easily."

Piper turned to him. "Why don't you substitute? Show the traditional recipe and then write what could be used instead."

He rubbed his chin as he considered the idea.

"Will you just do your tribe's food or collect recipes from others?"

He glanced at her. "I hadn't thought of other tribes."

By the time they reached the final stop they had traveled quite a distance from the main town.

"Does the school bus pick the kids up?" Piper asked.

Tai shook his head. "There is no bus. Some of the kids get lifts, others walk." He unstrapped his seatbelt. "I'll be back in a minute."

He walked the final child, a boy about eight years old, to the door of a little house, and the child waited while Tai went inside.

The child fidgeted with the bottom of his T-shirt and stared at his shoes. Finally he looked up as Tai came out with a man in his late fifties. The boy hugged the man, then Tai said something else and waved goodbye.

When he got back into the truck he was silent, his shoulders slumped, an air of sadness surrounding him. As he backed out and waved, the smile he gave the two was forced.

Piper wanted to ask what was wrong, but she stayed silent. Now wasn't the time. Any question could easily be misconstrued as a reporter digging for answers and she didn't want that.

She didn't want to intrude on whatever it was that was so painful for Tai.

Tai pulled off the road and parked the pickup in a clearing. "I've got to do something. Wait here." He didn't wait for her response, but got out of the cab and took a barely there path through the forest. It wasn't long before he disappeared from sight.

Piper stared after him, surprised and a little uncertain. He'd left her there, in the middle of the reservation, but surely he would come back soon. For all she knew he was going to visit a friend who didn't have road access to their house.

She got out of the pickup and sat on a fallen tree trunk to one side of the clearing. Something was bothering Tai, and she had an urge to soothe him, tell him it would be all right, but how could she when she didn't know what was wrong?

Why would Tai leave the boy outside?

Perhaps it wasn't his home. Perhaps the old guy was his

grandfather, and he was looking after him for the night, so Tai was checking he was there before leaving the child.

But then why was Tai so upset?

Was the older man an alcoholic and Tai had wanted to check his mood before he let the boy in? He hadn't seemed drunk, but then chronic alcoholics could sometimes hide the fact they'd been drinking.

No. The child hadn't looked scared about returning home, just worried.

Really she had no idea.

The ticking of the engine cooling stopped and silence descended. She was in the middle of a forest and there was no traffic, or people, or any of the usual city noises.

Instead she heard birds calling to each other, the swoosh of the wind through the trees and the occasional scurry of a small animal through the undergrowth.

Piper breathed in deeply: the air was sweet. There was no pollution, no smells of rubbish or food cooking – just the pine scent from the trees and the sweet fragrance of whatever flowers were growing nearby.

She put her hands behind her on the tree trunk and leaned back. It was peaceful. For the first time in she couldn't remember how long, she had nowhere to go, nowhere to be.

When had work taken over her life?

She'd liked going camping with her family, or heading down to the gulf for the day. Sometimes she'd go for a drive and see where she ended up. She hadn't done any of it, though, since she started at the *Houston Age* ten months earlier.

Before that she'd done a very brief stint as a television journalist, which she'd hated, and worked at community papers that were printed weekly rather than daily. There'd still been the deadline pressure but the number of stories she'd had to write per day was far lower.

But she'd wanted the daily job. It's what she'd dreamed of the whole way through college. A community paper wasn't going to give her the opportunity to do the investigative stories she wanted to do.

The *Age* could.

She'd been so sure that was why they hired her: they'd seen

the work she'd done on her blog, and they wanted her to do the same sort of writing for the paper. Perhaps her work on these profile pieces would show Geraldine she could handle the responsibility and she'd be able to write hard-hitting pieces – make readers sit up and take notice. Inspire them to want to do something to help. How could they do anything else when they were shown the truth?

Things would change. Her words would *cause* the change. The world would be a better place. Her frenetic pace now would be worth it when that happened.

She sighed.

And maybe she was kidding herself.

Her dream was a very long way off and right now she wondered whether it really *would* be worth it in the end.

***

Tai needed to get out of the suffocating little cab and breathe. Piper was too close and the situation with Jerry and Bradley was too fragile. He shouldn't have brought Piper with him. He should have left her behind with Eyota and done the drop-off on his own.

He strode down the little path into the forest to the place he'd run to when he was a child. He could breathe here, sort out his emotions and be at peace.

It had been a while since he'd visited and the boulder next to the little stream where he used to sit was covered in moss. He took off his boots, rolled up his jeans, and sat on the rock, careful not to disturb the greenery. He dangled his feet in the cool water.

Immediately it soothed him.

The soft gurgle of the water running along the stream told him to relax, that some things were the way they were, and that he couldn't control everything.

But damn, he wanted to try.

Jerry was the only responsible family Bradley had left. The kid's father was addicted to drugs, and his mother had left the reservation and wasn't coming back. But Jerry was struggling with his own demon. Depression was its name.

Ever since his wife's death, he'd refused to take the

medication he'd been offered, saying it messed with his head, and he refused too to take part in tribal activities that would keep him busy and connected.

Instead he stayed in his house, far away from neighbors, lived how he wanted to live and let the depression rule him.

Each Sunday when Tai dropped Bradley off, he went into the house first, to make sure Jerry hadn't given up, that depression hadn't won – that he was still alive. Tai couldn't be there every day when Bradley got home from school, but he held on to the hope that if Jerry ever did lose his battle, he would do it on a Sunday when he knew it would be Tai to find him, not Bradley.

Finding someone who had committed suicide haunted you for life.

He shut out the images and focused on the water, watched the patterns it made as it flowed down the stream, saw the bubbles in places and felt its calming caress.

Life was not fair.

He'd learned that from a very young age, but it didn't stop him from trying to tip the scales in a favorable direction.

There were days when he thought he was winning and then something would happen to remind him he wasn't in control. There were too many people wanting contradicting things.

Piper was proof. He hadn't wanted to do an interview, had said no, and somehow, despite his best intentions, she was sitting not so far away from him, in his home, in a place where he'd brought no one else. He'd thought he had control of the situation but he didn't.

He got to his feet. He wasn't sure how long he'd been sitting there and Piper was probably getting antsy. There was no cell reception and she'd be eager to get back to civilization. He put his boots back on, rolled down his jeans and walked along the path back to the truck.

At the edge of the clearing, he stopped and stared.

Piper was leaning back on a fallen log, her head tilted up, eyes closed, catching the few rays of sun that filtered through the canopy above. Her hair glistened gold and there was a slight smile on her face. Her whole posture was relaxed and calm.

She was beautiful.

He'd been expecting to find her pacing the clearing or writing something in her notepad. But not this. This was far harder to resist.

He shook his head. He couldn't stand there staring at her all day, though the idea held a strange appeal. Moving forward, he deliberately made his footsteps loud.

Her eyes flew open, she sat up straight and her hand flew to her chest when she saw him walking toward her. "You startled me!" She frowned when he said nothing, and got to her feet. "Are you all right?"

At that one simple question, he hesitated, stopped walking only a few yards from her. No one ever asked him that. He wasn't all right: he was angry, worried and confused, and he wanted to tell her, to share with her.

But that was ridiculous. She was a reporter. Reporters couldn't be trusted. He ignored the fact that if he'd brought her there he must trust her a little.

She walked over and put a hand on his arm. Her touch grounded him. His eyes were drawn to hers and he desperately resisted the urge to step closer, but she made her own decision, moved closer and wrapped her arms around him.

Chapter 6

Tai's arms moved on their own accord, circling her, bringing her closer and drawing from her the comfort he needed. He rested his cheek on her head, breathed in the sweet scent of her hair and let himself relax.

He couldn't remember the last time he'd let his defenses down this way. He was the strong one – but right now he needed the comfort more than he needed his barriers. She was warm in his arms, soft and soothing. Somehow it felt right, as if he'd known her for years rather than days. He should question it, but he didn't have the will.

Finally he stepped away, unsure what to say, what to do about his display of vulnerability.

He was never vulnerable.

All his barriers snapped back into place.

"We'd better get back," he said, and headed for the pickup, not looking at Piper. He didn't want to see her reaction.

She climbed into the cab with him. As he turned the key, he waited for her to comment, to ask a question, but she was silent.

The whole drive back was silent.

Piper looked out the window, but she didn't speak, she didn't ask what was bothering him. She was surprisingly quiet for a reporter.

He pulled up outside his grandmother's house and turned off the pickup. The silence grew louder and he got out of the cab, running from it. He'd never shown his vulnerability to anyone and of all the people for it to happen with, he had to do it with a journalist.

Inside the house, his grandmother asked, "Everyone get back safely?"

She knew about Bradley and Jerry. He nodded.

"Do you have time for a cup of tea before you go?" she asked.

"That would be lovely." It was Piper who spoke up. She'd followed him inside and now she took a seat at the table and asked, "May I ask you about the reservation?"

Tai tensed. He couldn't help it. It was his automatic response when people wanted to know about where he grew up. He braced himself for the usual ignorant questions, which would prove he shouldn't have trusted her.

"Of course you can," Eyota said, pouring the tea and placing a cup in front of Piper. She gestured for Tai to sit.

Reluctantly he did.

"Why is there no school bus?"

It was not the question he expected her to ask.

"We don't have the funds for a bus or the driver, not to mention the petrol and maintenance costs," Eyota told her. "Plus we don't have a lot of children on the rez."

"But education is so important. If the kids don't go to school, they'll never get ahead."

"Some don't believe they will anyway," Tai said.

"Why not?"

"They see their parents living hand to mouth, and their grandparents, and figure they can't expect any better."

"But of course they can change, with a little support," Piper said. "How much would a bus cost?"

Tai told her. He'd calculated it some time ago but hadn't managed to raise enough funds yet to make it happen. He agreed with Piper. Education was important, both their traditional education so the culture wasn't lost, and secular education so the next generation could choose what they wanted to do.

She was quiet for a moment before changing the subject; she asked a series of different questions.

When they finished their tea, Tai stood up.

"We should be getting back," he said. He wanted to get away. Piper was too comfortable in his grandmother's kitchen and she asked sensible and intelligent questions.

He was beginning to like her.

"Of course." Piper got to her feet, thanked Eyota and hugged the woman.

"I hope to see you again," Eyota said.

Piper smiled. "Me too."

Tai said nothing. It sounded like she meant it. He wasn't sure how he felt about that. It certainly hadn't been his purpose for bringing her here.

Outside, he hugged his grandmother and put on his helmet. "I'll see you next week." He got on his bike and waited for Piper to get on behind him. Her arms circled his waist, not as tightly as before, and her body pressed into his back.

Heat suffused him.

It was going to be a long ride back.

***

It was evening before they arrived at Piper's apartment. When Tai stopped the bike, she got off, taking off her helmet and passing it to him. "Do you want to come up for a drink?" She wasn't quite ready for their day together to end, even though she had work to do.

He shook his head, tucking her helmet into a section on the back of the bike she hadn't noticed. "I need to stop by the restaurant and do a few things."

Piper didn't let her disappointment show. "I'll have the interview written by mid week. I'll send you a copy to read."

He nodded, his face serious. The relaxed, friendly Tai who had let her in had been left at the reservation.

Piper stepped back, fiddling with the strap of her satchel. "Goodbye."

Tai turned the bike and rode off.

She sighed as he pulled out onto the street, and then turned and walked inside. Moggy ran toward her and she picked her up, stroking her fur as she went into the kitchen. It had been a confusing, exhausting day. She filled Moggy's bowl and put her on the floor and then took a frozen meal out of her freezer to heat up. When her dinner was ready, she sat down at her breakfast bar to record her thoughts.

The bike ride out to the reservation had been terrifying and then exhilarating. She hadn't felt that aware and alive in a long time. All her worries had shrunk to insignificant dots as the wind rushed by and she focused on holding on.

Then they had arrived at the reservation and it was a different world from what she knew. A quieter, less hectic world.

She got the impression she'd only scratched the surface with her visit. There had been a lot that had been unsaid – Piper could read between the words and she knew when she wasn't being told the whole story. But she also understood the Queches' reticence to open up. She was an outsider. More than that she was a reporter and, from the articles she'd found online, many reporters hadn't bothered to check their facts when writing about reservation life.

Tai's grandmother was lovely. She'd slipped Piper her phone number and told her she was welcome to call any time. Perhaps she realized her grandson might not be interested in continuing their contact after Piper had enough for the interview piece.

And that would be a real shame. Tai was an enigma. When she'd met him at the bar he'd been unfriendly – he'd as good as worn a sign that said, *back off*, but at the restaurant and then at the reservation he was a completely different person.

He was relaxed, friendly, encouraging and only when required was he stern.

Piper suspected his real personality was somewhere in between the two. She only had to consider the way he'd gone so quiet after dropping off the final child. There was something bothering him, but he didn't let it show in front of the children.

He'd looked so sad when he'd returned from wherever it was he'd gone. There was a heaviness to him, as if the whole weight of the tribe rested on his shoulders. She'd had to comfort him and she'd been surprised when he'd hugged her back. The strength of his arms around her body had also given *her* comfort she hadn't realized she needed. She couldn't remember the last time a man had held her like that.

She sighed. Perhaps he needed someone away from the tribe

to confide his troubles to. One thing she was certain of: she wanted to see more of him, wanted to get to know him and discover who he was. He fascinated her.

But first she needed to get the article out of the way. She didn't want him to think it was the only reason she was spending time with him. She would write it up, send it to him for review and then submit it to Geraldine.

Then she could really discover who Taima Woods was.

***

An hour later she had a bunch of notes, but nothing written. She had no idea what to focus on. If she wrote about the restaurant and how much his staff loved him, it was only one aspect – it ignored all the work he was doing for his tribe.

But did he want it highlighted? Surely if he'd wanted recognition, he would have done something about it before now. He could have invited any reporter to do a story. So what should she write?

She debated the whole situation for another ten minutes before getting annoyed.

This was ridiculous. Though it went against the grain, she needed to write what Geraldine wanted. She got typing.

It was getting late when Piper came up for air. She read through the article and frowned. It was good, there was no denying that, but it didn't show any of Tai's depth, didn't mention anything he was doing for his tribe. It was more like an ad for the restaurant.

She saved the article.

Unsatisfied, she wrote the article she wanted to write.

This time the words flew from her fingertips and the piece took her very little time.

Piper read through, pleased with the balance she'd achieved between restaurateur and tribal leader. She saved it and shut down her computer. She'd read them both in the morning and decide which one to send to Tai.

Still, she lay awake for a long time, thinking about him and the things she'd learned that day. She couldn't wait to see him again.

***

Geraldine called Piper into her office early on Monday morning. "I need the rest of those profiles by the end of the week," she said.

Piper gaped at her. "Why?" There was no way she'd be able to get them all done in a week. She still had five to interview plus two to write up.

"Keith's orders. I didn't ask why." Her tone invited no other questions.

"All right." Piper left her office, consciously trying to release the tension that had leaped to her muscles. It was a ridiculous amount of work, but she could do it. She managed to cajole the remaining interviewees into appointments before Thursday and then grabbed her notebook and laptop and headed out for her first story of the day.

While driving to interview Russell she mentally reviewed all the questions she wanted to ask him. She met him at his house, a large mansion with security gates in a very expensive neighborhood. The maid who opened the door directed Piper into a living room as big as Piper's whole apartment. It was decorated with basketball memorabilia and had a couple of oversized stuffed brown couches facing the biggest flatscreen television Piper had ever seen.

"Piper, thanks for coming."

Piper turned to see Russell walking toward her, hand outstretched to shake hers.

"Thanks for agreeing," she said easily.

He was wearing black basketball shorts and a Rockets' jersey. His cropped black hair was damp with sweat.

"Have you been training?" she asked.

"Yep. Gotta do my time every day if I want to get the minutes next season." He took the bottle of sports drink he was offered by the maid, who then put a glass of cold water in front of Piper.

"Thank you."

The woman smiled at her and left the room.

"Tell me about the training," Piper said to him. "How much do you do during the off season?"

He laughed. "Hours. I've been working on my mid range and ball handling. The association's competitive: if you don't work it, you don't stay long."

"But you still had time to run the camp for underprivileged kids," Piper pointed out.

"That's my passion. You gotta give back to the community."

"Why don't you tell me about it?"

Russell launched into the details of the summer camp, focusing largely on what he did and how much time he had spent down there, which, according to what Piper had discovered when she'd called the organizers, wasn't in fact more than an hour a day.

He was, from all reports, talking himself up.

Piper was used to it, but she couldn't help comparing him to Tai. Tai had barely said anything about himself, offered nothing more than she'd asked, and had let his staff and his actions speak for themselves.

Finally Russell stopped talking. Piper had more than enough for her article. She asked him a few more questions about what he liked to do in his spare time and where he wanted to go with his career and then said her goodbyes.

It was a relief to leave his house.

She took a deep breath of air and scrunched up her nose at the smell. It wasn't the fresh air of the reservation. It was more a damp, almost moldy scent, probably due to the high humidity. The heat rebounded off the driveway, cocooning her in its sticky embrace.

Inside her car she turned up her air-conditioner, made a few comments into her voice recorder and headed for her next appointment.

There she was left in a waiting area for three-quarters of an hour, so she used the time to type up her first impressions of her interview with Russell and outline the article she wanted to write. When Bob Randall's personal assistant finally led her into the oil and gas CEO's office, Piper was determined to keep the interview short. She now had only an hour before her next appointment and so his would have to suffer. He'd kept her waiting.

Bob Randall was Texan down to the bone. He was broad

shouldered and broad accented. He walked across the room, arm outstretched to shake her hand with vigor.

"Howdy, missy. Sorry to keep you waiting."

Piper managed not to roll her eyes. The CEO of an international company should know better than to call her "missy". She smiled and firmly shook his hand. "I'm Piper Atkinson from the *Houston Age*."

"Yes, yes. Sit down."

The large, lush corner office had glass windows looking out over Houston and toward the gulf. As she took the chair he indicated, he started talking, not even letting her ask a question.

It appeared Randall wanted to talk about the good his company was doing for the environment. Piper kept her disbelief well hidden until she asked, "How many of the average two hundred and eighty-five oil spills in Galveston Bay per year is your company responsible for?"

He blinked at her and then his expression grew firm. "Oil spills are an unfortunate side effect of doing business, but my company is doing what it can to reduce the number. Not all companies are as environmentally conscious as we are."

Piper didn't comment. Her father was the vice president of environment and sustainability at a competing company and they'd had many discussions about the industry. She knew how bad Dionysus's record was, but that wasn't what she was there for. Her managing editor, Keith, wanted a positive piece and it really galled her to have to portray this man in that way. He was in it to make as much money as he could for his shareholders – the environment be damned.

She stood. "Thanks so much for your time, Mr. Randall," she said, offering her hand again.

"I've got more to say. I thought this was going to be an hour's interview," Bob growled.

Piper kept the smile pinned to her face. "It was. We were scheduled to start earlier than we did and I unfortunately have meetings one after another today, so I can't stay later." That would teach him to keep her waiting.

"Keith is a good friend of mine," Bob said.

Piper recognized a threat when she heard it. "I'll be sure to tell him you said hello," she said. "It was lovely meeting you."

She shook his hand and left.

It wasn't until she got into her car that she started shaking. "Argh!" People like him made her blood boil. He thought he could walk all over her because he was in a position of power. Well, she wouldn't stand for it. The *Age* couldn't fire her for keeping to her schedule. She'd behaved professionally and hadn't shown her irritation.

Breathing in and out slowly, she tried to release the tension.

Checking the time, she started her car. She couldn't dwell on it now: she had to get to her next interview. Deadlines waited for no woman.

She'd just arrived at the next office when her cell rang.

"What the hell are you doing, cutting off Bob Randall?" Geraldine screeched in her ear.

Piper closed her eyes and put her best bright and perky voice on. "I would have loved to have stayed, but I'd already set up the meeting with Laurel. You want these interviews by the end of the week, don't you?"

"Yes, but Bob is an important man."

"I understand that. He kept me waiting for forty-five minutes."

Geraldine was silent for a moment, then she swore. "I'll explain to Keith."

It was as close to an apology as Piper was likely to get.

She hung up and focused on her next interview.

***

By the time she was finished with Laurel, the socialite charity queen, she'd had enough, but it was too early to go home. She still had articles to write. Unable to face the office and the conversation she would have to have with both Geraldine and Keith, she headed to Eat, Drink, Read.

Today she managed to get a seat at a table, and as she settled in she waved at Elle. Her friend came over to take her order. "What are you doing here?"

Piper grimaced. "I can't bear to go back to the office."

"Sounds bad. What happened?" She took a seat.

"Just one of the men I had to interview for the people of Houston profiles."

Elle waited for her to elaborate.

"He made me wait three-quarters of an hour and when I cut the interview short, he rang my managing editor to complain. I've had Geraldine on the phone already and I'm not ready for a face-to-face confrontation."

Elle shook her head. "Why would they listen to him?"

"He's a friend of Keith's and the CEO of Dionysus. He's a very influential man." She shrugged. "He's also a sexist pig who cares nothing for the environment and is about as insincere as they come. I wouldn't have stayed longer even if I didn't have back-to-back interviews today." Her words became angrier the more she spoke.

Her friend smiled at her. "Sounds like it's a good idea you don't go back to work."

Piper huffed out a breath and made an effort to calm herself. "Sometimes I don't know why I don't just quit."

"So why don't you?"

Her question made Piper stop. "Because I want to write articles that make people think."

"Aren't you already doing that on your blog?"

Elle was right. Was Piper too stuck on the idea that she had to work for a big paper that she wasn't recognizing what she already did?

"I think the articles you write are brilliant, and you said you've got thousands subscribing. Isn't that better than working on the paper where Geraldine can change anything she wants?"

"My blog doesn't pay anything."

"I'm sure there's a way you could change that." Elle squeezed Piper's hand and got to her feet. "I'd better get your lunch order in."

Piper absent-mindedly got her laptop out of her bag and set it up. Perhaps she should look into ways to monetize her blog. She'd heard about people doing it and, while it wasn't something she could make a living off immediately, it could be her long-term plan.

She'd have to think about it.

Elle's second-in-command, Nora, delivered her lunch, and Piper began typing, sending in her regular stories as soon as she completed them. By closing time, Piper still had a few more articles to write, but she didn't want to go back to the office. If she did, she'd get more work to do.

Remembering the articles she'd written for Tai, she sent him an email with them attached, explaining why she'd written two and asking which one he wanted her to run with. She'd let him decide.

Then she headed home. She could easily work from there.

By the time the day's deadline passed, Piper had all her stories in and was exhausted. She didn't want to have to write three more profiles but if she didn't do it, she wouldn't get the chance tomorrow.

She ordered Chinese delivery, poured a glass of wine and went back to the kitchen table. She'd start with Russell. He would be the easiest to write and right now she needed easy.

***

It was midnight before Piper pressed *save* on her final article. They weren't her best work, but her head just wasn't in it. She'd read over them again in the morning when her brain had refreshed, and polish them some more.

Her inbox pinged. It was an email from Tai: he wanted her to run the fluff piece.

The one decent article she'd written for the whole series, where she was actually proud of its content, and he wanted to go with the crappy version.

The anger that had been swirling around her stomach all day started a steady simmer. She dialed the restaurant number, not expecting it to be answered but needing to try.

"The Wooden Spoon," Tai answered smoothly.

"You really want me to run the fluff piece?" she asked him.

"Piper. I didn't think you'd still be up."

It was a good point. And it applied to him too – the restaurant would have closed reasonably early on a Monday night. "Why are you?" she asked.

"Couldn't sleep."

Her anger morphed into surprise at the admission. "Why not?"

"Things on my mind," he deflected smoothly. "What did you want?"

That's right, she was cross with him. "Why do you want me to publish the fluff piece? It says next to nothing about the good you're doing for your tribe."

"I don't need to brag about it," he said.

"But you deserve to be acknowledged. People need to learn about what is happening so things can begin to change."

"Piper, no one wants to know about it. If you publish the second article people will read it and make comments about the amount of hand-outs my people receive, about how it's about time we did things for ourselves and that there are starving children in Africa we should be focusing on." His voice was firm and confident.

"How do you know?"

"Check out these websites," Tai said and named them. Piper wrote them down and typed the first one into her search engine.

It was an indigenous American blog calling for the removal of racist stereotypical sports-team mascots. She speed read the first post which was really interesting and then got down to the comments section. Her heart sank. The amount of vitriol directed at the blogger was astounding.

"Do you understand now?"

"Yeah." But surely it had to change and the only way it would was if people kept talking about it. "Don't you believe we can change things?"

He sighed. "Not tonight."

There was sadness in his tone that made Piper forget her anger. "What happened today?" she asked.

He was quiet. "One of the tribe died." There was grief in his voice.

Piper gasped, her hand coming to her chest. "I'm so sorry. What happened?"

Another long pause. "Do you remember the last house we stopped at yesterday?"

"Yes."

"The grandfather, Jerry, died."

Piper's heart went out to Tai and to the child. "How's the boy?" He'd been a sweet thing.

"Devastated. He's staying with Ka' sa'."

Eyota would take care of him: Piper was sure of it. "How

did he die?" He'd looked healthy enough yesterday, but heart attacks came with little warning sometimes.

The answer came as a tortured whisper. "Suicide."

The shock was sharp. Was *that* why Tai had gone into the house first?

Piper had no words, nothing to comfort him with, but his pain came through her phone. He shouldn't be alone with this. He was suffering.

She grabbed her bag and locked the door behind her. "Do you want to talk about it?" she asked, keeping her tone gentle as she started her car, and switched to hands free.

"There's nothing to say. Bradley came home and found the note and, instead of going for help, went to find him." There was a little bit of anger in with the grief. Whether it was for the grandfather or the boy, she didn't know.

The little boy had found his grandfather. She didn't ask what method of suicide Jerry had chosen – it didn't really matter. He was dead and an eight-year-old had found him.

She pushed the accelerator closer to the floor.

"The note was meant for his counselor, who was due this afternoon, but the counselor was running late. Bradley skipped the afternoon classes and arrived first. It was the counselor who found Bradley with the body."

Piper eased into a parking lot in front of the Wooden Spoon. She switched her phone over and hurried around to the back entrance. She knocked on the door.

"There's someone at the door," Tai said, sounding confused.

"It's me. Let me in."

"No. I'm fine. You didn't need to come."

"Open the door, Tai." She kept her voice steady, and spoke with authority, hoping he would do as she asked.

A dial tone buzzed in her ear and she hung up, waiting, watching the door.

Chapter 7

She breathed a sigh of relief as the locks clunked. The door opened and Tai stood there, his eyes red and shadowed, his shoulders hunched. Her heart clenched as she stepped forward and wrapped her arms around him.

He hissed in a breath, shutting the door, and then he hugged her back, his body shaking.

Piper's heart broke for him as he began to sob. She ran a hand up and down his back, soothing him the best she could. This sensitive man was carrying so much on his shoulders.

They stood there for five minutes or more before Tai pulled back. He wiped his eyes with the palms of his hands and stared at her as if coming back to his senses. He looked horrified.

Piper gave him a small smile, patted his back and then walked into the kitchen, giving him some space to recover. He didn't like to show he was human.

The kitchen was a mess. There were pots simmering on the stove and the ovens were on. Aromas filled the air and there was enough food to feed an army.

"It's all for the wake," he said as he glanced around the kitchen, running a hand through his hair.

Piper filled a glass with water and handed it to him. He took it without a word. It was way too bright in here; the lights were glaring. She went over to the stove. "Is it done?"

He nodded.

She turned it off and then took his hand, leading him into the restaurant, which was dark except for the dim security lighting. She pulled out a chair and gently pushed him into it. "Feeling any better?"

"I'm not sure." He was cautious, confused. "I didn't mean to …"

"But you needed to." Piper said. The grief was eating him up.

"He *knew* I visited every Sunday. He *knew* I went in before Bradley."

That was why Tai had left Bradley outside – because he knew Jerry was a suicide risk. Tai's selflessness was amazing. It would be horrific to find someone who had committed suicide.

"Perhaps he didn't want you to find him either," she said. "You were his friend."

"But I've done it before." His eyes widened and he clamped his mouth shut.

He'd done what before? Found someone who had committed suicide? She lowered herself onto the chair next to him. It was hardly a common occurrence, but he'd clammed up again, so maybe it was true. She couldn't even fathom it. She squeezed his hand. "Perhaps Jerry wanted the counselor to find him so he didn't hurt you or Bradley."

"The poor kid."

"Eyota will be caring for him," Piper said.

"She knows what to say."

How could she? How could anyone *really* know what to say to a person who had found a body?

"Are you going home?" she asked.

"I'll drive there tomorrow with Adahy and Rayen. I need to call Kath first and clear it with her."

From what Piper knew of the sous chef, it wouldn't be an issue. "Is there anything I can do?"

"I don't know if there's anything anyone can do," he said. "I've been trying so hard." He wasn't talking about this one death.

"And you've been succeeding." Her words were so inadequate, but she had to make him understand. "You have a great turn out at your classes and everyone loves you." She cupped his face. "Not everyone wants to be saved." She said it as gently as she could, keeping her gaze on his. She wanted to kiss him better, and make all the bad things go away.

Giving in to temptation, she leaned forward and brushed her lips against his, lightly, gently.

He tasted like coffee and his lips were surprisingly soft. She'd expected them to be hard and demanding, unyielding, but they relaxed and he kissed her back.

An oven timer beeped loudly in the quiet night.

Tai broke the kiss, his eyes wide. "I can't do this, not now." He sounded as sorry as she felt.

Her body was incredibly warm, but she stood up. "You're right," she said. "I'm sorry."

Tai smiled for the first time that evening and it lifted Piper's heart. He stood up. "I'm not, but I need to get home. Adahy and Rayen might need me."

Of course they would. This death would affect them all. Piper took his hand and they walked back out to the kitchen. "Do they know where you are?"

"Yeah. I needed to be alone." He turned to her. "Thank you for coming." He squeezed her hand.

She pressed up on her toes and kissed him. "Any time." She wasn't quite ready to say goodbye yet. He was definitely brighter than he had been, but the sorrow was drifting back across his face. "Can I give you a lift home?"

"I've got my bike." He turned off the timer and took the meal out of the oven. The smell was warm and comforting.

"Should you be driving right now?"

"I'll be fine." He transferred the food into plastic containers, sealing each and carrying them to the coolroom. "You should go," he said when he turned on the tap to run water in the sink. "It's late."

It was, but she wasn't going to leave him there by himself so he could sink down low again. Plus the rest of the kitchen needed cleaning. She grabbed a dish towel. "If I dry we'll be faster."

He hesitated and then agreed.

They worked as a team, dishing the food into containers and then cleaning the pots and pans. When the kitchen was once again spotless, Tai went into his office; he turned off his computer and the lights on his way out.

He was quiet again. Piper didn't want him to be alone. She waited for him by the door as he did his nighttime checks, making sure everything was turned off and locked up.

"Maybe you should go to Adahy's so you're not alone."

Tai gave a small smile. "Adahy and Rayen live with me. They'll be home when I get there."

"Oh." It was a relief to know he wasn't going to be by himself.

Outside after he locked up, he asked, "Where are you parked?"

"Out front."

"I'll walk you out," he said, taking hold of her hand.

She smiled and let him walk her to her car. At the door he kissed her again.

"Call me if you need anything," she said. "Even just to chat."

He nodded. "I'll be thinking about you even if I don't get a chance to call."

Her insides went all squishy. She slid into her car and waved goodbye. Pulling out of the parking lot she watched him in her rear-view mirror until he turned and walked back toward his bike.

Their relationship had definitely changed.

***

Tai woke with a weight in his mind, but reasonably refreshed. He'd fallen into a deep sleep when he'd finally got to bed the night before after assuring his brother and cousin he was all right.

And surprisingly he was.

He grieved for Bradley, and alternatively felt anger and grief for Jerry, but Piper had soothed some part of him that needed to be soothed. When he was with her, he didn't need to carry the weight of his tribe on his shoulders. When he was with her he didn't need to keep up a pretense of being strong. With her, he could just be.

It was an incredible gift.

He called Kath and told her what had happened.

"Take as many days as you need. We'll be fine here."

Tai was lucky to have her. He had no doubt she would take care of everything. "Thank you."

"No problem, Chef. Call me if you need anything."

He hung up and moved through to the kitchen to turn on the coffee machine. Rayen and Adahy weren't up yet: as he walked past his brother's room snores echoed through the door. There was no need to rush to the reservation, nothing was going to change, but he wanted to be there for Bradley.

He knocked on both doors. "I'm heading out in thirty minutes," he called and received groans in response.

He made three mugs of coffee, leaving Adahy's and Rayen's on the table, and took his own out to the back garden.

When he'd decided to buy a house, he'd searched until he found one with a big garden. He needed space and he needed to surround himself with trees. This yard had a lot of trees, blocking him from his neighbors' views, and he'd added some of his own which would take years before they were fully grown. Eyota had potted up some of the plants found on the reservation and had planted them for him as well. It was enough to remind him of home, and keep from missing it too much.

He sipped his coffee, walking slowly through the yard, brushing some leaves with his hands, bending down to smell the flowers. He needed to prepare himself for the day. It was going to be hard, it was going to be emotional, and he needed to keep himself together. He shouldn't have stayed up so late, though he didn't regret it. If he'd left earlier, Piper never would have come.

No, he'd needed time to process, and he'd been fighting it, by cooking for the wake, and answering all his emails so he didn't need to think about what had happened, about the life that had been lost.

Then Piper had called, all mad about his decision to go with the fluff piece, and somehow she'd known something else was wrong. He hadn't meant to tell her, but it had slipped out. And she had cared enough to come.

He sighed, finishing his lap of the garden, and walked into the kitchen where Rayen and Adahy were nursing their coffees.

"Your phone beeped," Adahy said, gesturing to where it sat

on the bench.

Tai picked it up. A message from Piper.

Thinking of you. xx

He tucked his phone into his pocket.

"What was it?" Adahy asked, his expression suspicious. "You're smiling."

"It's from a friend, and none of your business," he said. "I'm going to call Ka' sa'."

It stopped Adahy prying further. He didn't want to tell anyone about Piper yet. He didn't even know what there was to tell.

He dialed his grandmother's number. "How is he?" he asked when she answered.

"He's gone quiet. When will you be here?"

"We're getting ready now," Tai told her.

"Good."

He hung up. Adahy and Rayen had already got to their feet. Rayen headed for the shower while Adahy cleaned the dishes.

"Bad?" he asked.

Tai shrugged. "Bradley's not talking." It wasn't necessarily a bad thing. Sometimes he didn't feel like talking either. "We need to stop by the restaurant on the way out to pick up the food."

"That's what you were doing last night?" Adahy asked.

"Yes."

"Well, we won't have to worry about starving." His brother smiled and Tai knew it was his attempt to lighten the mood.

He wiped down the table. When Rayen came out again, her eyes were red. She'd been crying. He opened his arms for her and she dove in.

"It's not fair, Tai. I don't understand why he did it. He was Bradley's only hope."

Tai refused to believe it. "Ka' sa' will watch over him."

"But to have to live with his father ... The man doesn't know where he is half the time, and he lives twice as far away from the school. Bradley can't walk that far."

It would all depend on whether Bradley's father claimed his right to be Bradley's guardian. There wasn't a lot they could do if he did.

"We'll work something out." He added it to his never-ending list.

Adahy came into the kitchen. "Ready to go?"

They all piled into Adahy's small hatchback and, after stopping at the restaurant, made their way to the reservation.

***

When they arrived at Eyota's house people were already gathered to give their condolences to Bradley. Bradley sat on the couch with his arms crossed, staring at a spot on the carpet, and said nothing.

Tai went to his grandmother first. "Anyone told Carl yet?" he asked.

"Scott went out there first thing this morning. He wasn't very lucid."

Meaning Bradley's father was still on a high or coming down from his latest one.

"I'll go out there if he hasn't shown up by lunchtime." He walked over to the couch and stood in front of Bradley. The boy was only eight and he appeared smaller, skinnier than he had on Sunday, as if he'd drawn in on himself, as if he were protecting himself from the world.

Tai knew that feeling. "You want to go for a walk?"

Bradley's mouth opened and he scrambled to his feet.

Tai ignored the others who were gathered there. They weren't talking to Bradley anyway. If anything they were talking *at* him.

He walked into the forest with Bradley by his side, and when they came to a fork he let Bradley choose which way to go. They walked slowly, Bradley kicking sticks on the path or running his hands over plants that grew close. Tai was content to walk. Bradley would talk when he was ready.

They'd been walking for at least half an hour before Bradley asked, "How did you know?"

Not sure what the boy was referring to, he said, "Know what?"

"Know Grandpa was going to kill himself." There was accusation in his gaze.

"I didn't."

"You must have, that's why you always made me wait

outside when I got home." His voice wavered.

"Let's take a seat." Tai led the way over to the same fallen tree that Piper had sat on and leaned against it. Where did he start?

"You know Jerry had depression," he said.

Bradley nodded.

"My dad had depression as well. When it gets bad it's really hard for them to see any purpose to life." As he'd got older he'd researched more and more into the illness, trying to figure out why his dad had chosen death over being with his children. In some cases depression could be genetic and he was scared he or Adahy could one day suffer from it.

"Did he kill himself as well?"

"Yes." The pain of it was still a dull ache after all these years.

"How?"

It wasn't a morbid question. It was a child seeking to understand.

"He shot himself."

"Who found him?"

If he closed his eyes he could still picture it. "I did."

Bradley reached out and grabbed Tai's hand. "Then you know. I couldn't wake him. I tried so hard but still, he wouldn't wake up."

Jerry had chosen to slit his wrists, giving his blood to the earth. It was a tidier way to kill himself than blowing off the back of his skull.

"He didn't mean you to find him," Tai told him.

"I wanted to talk with Grandpa's counselor. I was worried about him, but Grandpa wouldn't let me stay at home."

"So what happened?" Tai asked. It would be good for Bradley to talk about it.

"I got home and found the note on the table. It was meant for the counselor with instructions on who to call and where he was." He looked up at Tai. "I didn't know how long I had."

He understood. If he'd been in the same situation he would have run to find Jerry instead of calling for help.

"He was in his favorite place, where he went to think. He was leaning up against a tree like always and I thought I was in time." The boy's voice broke.

Tai put his arm around the boy's shoulder.

After a minute Bradley continued. "There was so much blood on his wrists and I couldn't wake him. He wouldn't wake."

Tears ran down his face and he sobbed, holding Tai tightly.

Tai's heart broke.

He hadn't been able to help. All the things he'd said to Jerry to convince him life was worth living, that Bradley needed him, were for nothing.

Piper's words came back to him. *Not everyone wants to be saved.*

Not everyone *could* be saved.

But damn it, he couldn't see why not. Why was everything he was doing for his tribe still not enough?

He hadn't been able to stop this child going through the exact same thing he'd been through nearly twenty-two years earlier.

They lost so many of their tribe through preventable causes: suicide, heart disease, diabetes. The Queche tribe was dwindling and not enough of the children were breaking the cycle.

Bradley lifted his head. "Do you think Grandpa's soul is stuck here?" he asked, his eyes wide and fearful.

It was a question he'd asked himself as he'd got older about his own father. "We'll give him a proper funeral, we'll dance like we've never danced before and he'll dance with us to the ancestors."

"Are you sure?"

"Yes. I'll even bet your Ka' sa' will come down to fetch him, and dance with him." Bradley's grandmother had died a year earlier – she had always been so full of life and had loved to dance at the celebrations.

Bradley smiled. "She will, won't she? We'll make it the best celebration ever." He got to his feet. "Let's go back."

Tai followed him back along the path to Eyota's house. There were still people coming and going, bringing food.

"Tai, can we go back to my house for the lunch?" Bradley asked.

It was traditional to have a wake of sorts the day after the person died, at their house. "Sure. I'll let everyone know."

It didn't take long to pack the food and start the calls to tell everyone the lunch would be at Jerry's place. Tai drove the pickup with Eyota and Bradley, and stopped to pick up those who needed a lift.

At the door to the house Bradley hesitated, took a deep breath and pushed it open. Tai followed him in and waited by the door while the child looked around.

"I kind of expected him to be here," he said in a small voice.

"I know."

The boy walked through the few rooms and then back out to Tai. Tai stayed where he was by the door to give him space. In the kitchen Eyota was arranging the food.

"OK, I'm ready. Do we need to heat stuff up?" Bradley asked.

He wanted to be in charge and so Tai let him. "A few things."

"Let's get to work then."

The boy was using the lunch as a distraction. Tai recognized it just as he supported it. There was too much for him to take in for one day. The grieving would go in stages.

Together Bradley and Tai heated the food and spoke to the people who came to pay their respects. During the lunch, people told their own stories of Jerry – some stories of the trouble he got up to in his youth and others to do with his marriage and his children. Bradley listened to them all, smiling and asking questions.

Mid afternoon Eyota came over to Tai. "Carl hasn't turned up."

Tai had noticed, though he wasn't sure whether it was a good thing or not. It really depended on what Carl had in his system. "I'll find him," he told his grandmother.

After telling Bradley he'd be back shortly, Tai drove out to where Carl had his trailer.

He knocked on the door.

Carl was a couple of years older than Tai, but they knew each other from school and around the reservation. Carl had got involved in drugs at an early age and progressively moved to stronger and stronger ones in order to get his fix. It was a miracle he hadn't died of an overdose already.

When no one answered, Tai tried the door and found it open. He walked inside and called, "Carl, are you home?"

As his eyes adjusted to the dim light inside he made out a body on the couch. With a hideous sense of déjà vu he rushed over and shook the man, checking his pulse.

"I'm alive," the voice grumbled.

Tai stepped back, relief coursing through his veins. He sat down on the chair opposite and waited for the man to sit up.

"What are you doing here?" Carl asked.

"I came to see if you're all right."

"Why wouldn't I be?"

Tai was sure his grandmother had said someone had been out to tell Carl about his father but perhaps he didn't remember. "Your father died yesterday." His voice was gentle.

"Killed himself more like it," Carl said, screwing up his face in anger. "The selfish bastard said he'd take care of Bradley, and now he's gone and done this." He glared at Tai. "What am I supposed to do with him now?"

Anger stirred in Tai's veins too and he reminded himself Bradley was better off without his drug-addicted father. "There are others who will care for him."

"Good."

"Do you want a say in the ceremony?"

"No. Do what you want." Carl reached for a bottle of bourbon on the table and Tai knew it was time to leave.

"Take care of yourself," he said and walked out.

He took some deep breaths as he walked outside. He didn't want Bradley left with his father, though his mother wasn't a great option either. Eyota was trying to track her down anyway, and someone had called Carl's sister. She was on her way from Austin.

It was tough. At least when Tai's father had died he'd been surrounded by family. There was never any doubt he'd have Eyota by his side, even as his mother had withdrawn from him.

Well, he'd never let any doubt enter Bradley's mind either. He would look after the child himself if it came to that. Though with his nighttime work, he wasn't sure how he'd manage it.

He drove back to the party and, when he pulled up, a car pulled in after him. He recognized the woman, though it had been years since he'd seen her. It was Carl's sister, and Bradley's aunt, Teresa.

"Teresa," he said and she glanced at him.

"Tai, how is he?"

"Bradley's doing all right. He was enjoying stories of his grandfather when I left."

"And my brother?"

"I've just come from there. He's planning on getting drunk." He stepped forward. "How are you?" Teresa had left the reservation as soon as she'd been old enough. She'd got a scholarship to college, and after she graduated, she'd moved to Austin where she'd married. She came back to the reservation for weddings and funerals but that was it.

Her eyes filled with tears and she blinked them back. "It was probably inevitable. Dad let go of life when Mom died."

He hated that she accepted it. Hated that no one thought they could stop it. Now wasn't the time to go into it though.

"Do you want to come with me?" he offered instead, and led her through the gathering to Bradley.

Tai stood back, watched the exchange, the perfunctory hug. Teresa was virtually a stranger to the boy. A glamorous stranger who turned up for special occasions, but didn't stick around for long enough to get to know.

She greeted some others and sat in the circle. Eyota handed her a plate of food and Teresa thanked her.

His heart was so very heavy in his chest. In his tribe there were two types of people: those who felt trapped and escaped the moment they could and those who were happy to embrace their culture.

He turned away, wanting to go for a walk, when another car pulled up.

The woman who stepped out was someone he hadn't seen in months, hadn't even spoken to. A woman who hadn't really been part of his life. A woman who belonged in the first category.

"Hello, Mom."

Chapter 8

Piper wished there was a way she could mainline coffee. Then she might have a chance of staying awake.

She'd got about three hours' sleep after leaving Tai before her phone rang, and she had to head out to a breaking news story. That didn't stop her from sending Tai a text, and wondering how he was.

Now however, she was desperately trying to seem interested and alert at an opening for a new public library. She swallowed a yawn and took some photos to go along with her article.

The politician who was doing his speech was rambling, going on and on about his vision and about how important reading and literacy were for the community.

She'd believe him if his party hadn't tried to close three libraries on the outskirts of Houston six months back.

Hypocrite.

She wrote down a couple of quotes, and after all the speeches were done she interviewed some of the community members who had attended. They were all really pleased about the building and Piper was happy for them.

She then escaped and headed over to Eat, Drink, Read to get another coffee.

Elle served her, then sat down across from her. "Are you all right?"

"Too little sleep last night," Piper said and yawned.

"What on earth were you doing?" Elle held up a hand. "Or don't I want to know?"

Piper laughed. "Mostly writing articles. Geraldine wants all ten interviews by the end of the week."

"And she's not dropping any of your other stories?"

"Of course not." She sipped her coffee, hoping the caffeine would hit her system.

"I didn't expect to find you here," a voice said.

Her friend Libby was standing next to the table, carrying a laptop bag. Piper shuffled over so she could take a seat. "Coffee break."

"What happened to you? You look awful." Libby hugged Elle and then sat and put her hand over Piper's.

Well, obviously the makeup she'd put on this morning wasn't doing its job.

"No sleep," Elle told her. "She's been working on those profile interviews."

"And I can't figure out if they're garbage or not," Piper said. Every time she tried to read them, the words blurred. Either she was incredibly tired or they were incredibly boring.

"Let me read them," Libby said. "I'll tell you."

Libby was an author, and she'd be able to tell if the writing itself was any good. Piper brought up the articles and slid her laptop over the table. "Go for it."

She leaned her head on her hand and closed her eyes.

***

"These are excellent," Libby said when she was done.

Piper opened her eyes.

Elle nodded. She'd been standing behind Libby reading over her shoulder. "I really like the ones of Tai. Why are there two?"

Piper sat up straight. "Damn, I shouldn't have shown you those."

"Why not?"

"Tai doesn't want it known that he does those things for the reservation. He wants me to run the piece focusing on his restaurant."

"He seems really private," Elle said. "I imagine it's personal."

"It is." Piper checked the time, wondering if she should call him.

"How much time have you spent with him?" Libby asked.

Piper was reluctant to share her feelings about Tai. Perhaps it was because they were so new. They hadn't even been for a date. It had all been business – well, almost all. "A bit."

Libby frowned at her, but Piper ignored it. "I need to get back to work."

"Have you got plans Saturday night?" Libby asked. "We could have a girls' night. Talk weddings." She glanced at Elle. "You haven't done anything about organizing yours yet."

Elle smiled. "There's no rush. It won't change our relationship and I need to find out when my family can get to Houston. Besides, April might be a nice month for it."

Piper checked her calendar. "I can do something after seven." Helping Libby organize her wedding had been fun and she was thrilled her other friends were getting married now.

"George is going out, but why don't you come to dinner at our house?" Elle said.

"Great. I'll call Imogen and confirm," Libby said.

Piper packed away her laptop and got to her feet. She had three more interviews for the series and next week her life would go back to normal. She hugged her friends and left, desperately hoping the caffeine would hit her system soon.

***

By the time Piper dragged herself into her apartment that evening, she was ready to collapse. She'd lost count of the number of coffees and sugary cola drinks she'd consumed. She still had the interviews to write up but she needed sleep more. She set her alarm for an hour, pried off her shoes and fell onto her bed.

When the alarm went off, she struggled to open her eyes. It felt like she'd only just closed them. Slowly she dragged herself out of bed and went into the bathroom to splash water on her face. The cold helped to wake her up. She had to get at least one article written before she could go back to bed.

Getting some snacks out of the cupboard, she sent Tai another text.

Hope everything is all right.

It was a stupid thing to say. How could things be all right when a grandfather had committed suicide? She hoped Tai would understand what she meant.

Tai would be surrounded by family at the reservation, she was sure of that. He would have the support he needed.

She hoped.

Munching on her snacks, she got to work.

***

"I came as soon as I could," Tai's mother, Jackie, said. She insisted on being called by her Americanized name.

Tai tried to suppress the instant disappointment he always felt when faced with his mother. She'd always put work in front of family, so why should now be any different?

He nodded and kept his distance. "How's work?"

"Busy," she said.

She'd worked her way up to manager at a local Walmart. He was proud of her, she'd worked hard for it, but as a child he'd resented her absence.

"Adahy and Ka' sa' are in the crowd," he said.

"Are you leaving?"

"Taking a walk," he said and didn't wait for her response. He needed to be by himself. He walked away from the noise and the laughter as they celebrated Jerry's life and headed for the place where Jerry had chosen to die.

It was a pretty little spot, though the light was fading. Someone had already laid flowers over the place where Jerry had sat. Tai stared at the spot wishing he could conjure Jerry's spirit, wishing he could ask why, ask what he could have said to convince him to keep living.

He'd thought he'd been making progress on Sunday, thought perhaps he was about to get through to him, but he'd been so very wrong.

And now Bradley was going through the same pain he'd been through. At least he'd had Eyota, but Bradley's mother had left, his father didn't want him, and, unless Tai was very much mistaken, his aunt didn't either.

He needed to talk to Ka' sa' about what they could do for

the boy. Eyota was getting too old to look after all the kids who needed a kind word and a helping hand. Maybe he could raise funds to build a youth center, somewhere the kids could go after school or if their parents weren't around. He'd need to find someone to staff it too. It would take some of the burden from his grandmother and she could have Bradley live with her.

Piper's face came to his mind, which was completely ridiculous. He needed someone who knew the culture and understood all the issues they faced.

Yet still the thought of her eased some of the trouble in his heart. He wished she were there, so he could let down his defenses in the protection of her arms. He only needed a minute before he'd rebuild them stronger than they were before.

He frowned. Since when had he relied on anyone? Since when had Piper become the person he turned to? They were virtually strangers.

He pulled out his phone and checked the reception. Nothing. He put his cell back in his pocket. Stranger or not, it would have been nice to hear her voice.

Should he be worried that she'd snuck in under his radar so quickly?

She fascinated him with her contrast of professional journalist and compassionate soul. Why she'd come to him last night, he didn't know, but when she'd said she was outside the door, he could have wept.

Well, he did weep, but he couldn't feel any shame in it. He'd felt so much stronger afterward, especially after they'd kissed.

He smiled. The kiss had been so sweet and he'd wanted to deepen it but the oven timer had brought him back to his senses.

Footsteps behind him made Tai turn around. Adahy stood there, looking at the flowers.

"Is this where …?"

"Yes."

"Tai, are you coping? This is so similar to Dad—"

"I'm fine." The words came out a little sharp. "Really, little brother, I just needed a few minutes of quiet."

"Mom's here."

"I saw her when she arrived." Adahy had a better

relationship with their mother. He was six years younger than Tai, and had been only a toddler when their father died. He was too young to remember their mother had been largely absent from their lives for the first few years after that. She'd been working long hours to provide for the family, and never got home until after Eyota had got them both to sleep.

Neither Adahy nor his mother knew Tai had thought she'd blamed him for his father's death and how her absence had been his punishment.

He walked over and put a hand on his brother's shoulder. "Are you all right?"

"Yeah. I feel sorry for Bradley. That kid is going to have some tough times ahead."

Tai would do what he could to smooth the road. "Why don't we head back and you can add some music to the celebrations?"

"Sure."

Tai followed him back to the house, building up the walls he needed as he went.

***

It was Thursday evening before Piper heard from Tai.

He called her cell phone as she was sitting down to another dinner of snacks she'd found in her cupboard.

"I only just got your text," he said. "Cell-phone reception is sporadic at best on the rez. I'm in Houston to get some things for the funeral."

"When is it?"

"Saturday."

"How are you?" She'd been worried about him.

"Fine," he said.

She wasn't sure he meant it, but she let it go. "Have you got time to drop around?" If she could see him, she could tell how *fine* he was.

"Yeah, if you're not busy."

She had her final article to write, but she might be able to knock it out before he arrived. "I'm not busy."

"All right. I'm at the restaurant. I need to deal with a couple of things and then I'll be there. Have you had dinner?"

Piper glanced at the snacks on her table. "Not if you're planning on bringing something from the Spoon."

He chuckled as she'd hoped he would. "Any preference?"

"No."

"See you soon."

Piper smiled as she hung up. He sounded OK. There wasn't as much heaviness in his voice as when they'd last spoken.

She couldn't wait to see him but she really should get the article finished before he arrived.

***

There was a knock on her door as she was reading through the final paragraph of the article. She got up to answer it, and glanced around her apartment. She groaned. She hadn't tidied for days. Her table was strewn with notes and snack packets, her satchel was dumped on her couch with its contents spilling out and the washing she'd done the other day was still heaped in a basket on her coffee table, with Moggy lying comfortably in the middle of it. She'd have to wash it again.

She opened the door to find Tai on her doorstep holding a bag of takeout containers. He was wearing a blue shirt today and blue jeans, but no motorcycle jacket.

"Don't you have the bike today?" she asked as she let him in.

"I borrowed Adahy's car."

He stepped closer and she tilted her head, reaching up to kiss him. It was a simple welcome kiss but she felt it all the way to her toes.

Before she got carried away she turned and walked into the kitchen. "Can I get you a drink?"

"Some juice if you've got it."

"No wine?" she asked, holding up the bottle of white she had in her fridge.

"I don't drink."

She didn't need to ask why. With the amount of substance abuse on the reservation it wasn't surprising. Her friend Adrian didn't drink either because his father had been an alcoholic who had abused him and his brother.

"Juice it is." She put the bottle back and poured two glasses of apple juice.

Tai put the bag of food on the counter and looked at the snack wrappers still littering her table. "Don't tell me that's your idea of dinner."

"I was writing," she said. "Deadlines wait for no one."

He turned, concerned. "I can go if you like."

"No, it's fine. I finished just as you arrived. I only need to read it over and it will be good to go."

"Why don't you do that while I dish up?" he suggested.

She gave him some plates and sat in front of the computer. It was strange how they had gone from complete strangers to this comfortable friendship in such a short period of time.

Not willing to examine it closer, she read through the article and saved it with the others, making a backup copy to her USB stick, which she'd later transfer to her personal laptop.

Tai placed a delicious-smelling turkey dish in front of her, garnished with some berries. Somehow he'd got the presentation perfect, despite the fact it had been transported in take-out containers. She slid her laptop out of the way and cleared a place at the table.

"This is your last chance to change your mind about which article I use," she said to him. She was still hoping he would reconsider.

"I didn't think they were due for another couple of weeks."

"Geraldine suddenly wants them all tomorrow," Piper told him. "It's been a busy week."

He pursed his lips together. "Let me read them again after dinner."

Piper bit into the turkey dish and moaned. "I do not know how you do it, but everything you make is sensational."

He grinned. "It's all about the spice."

"Maybe I should attend one of your cooking classes. Though then I'd need the time to cook and there never is any."

"I'll teach you a couple of quick and easy ones," he told her.

She liked that idea. Liked the thought of Tai standing in an apron and not much else while teaching her how to cook. It definitely had merit. "You're on."

"How's your week been?" Tai asked. "You look tired."

She shrugged. She was sure hers hadn't been anywhere near

as draining as his. "As I said, Geraldine told me on Monday that she wanted all the articles by Friday. That's a hell of a lot of extra work, with the research, then the interview and finally writing the article. I'm so glad we did yours on the weekend."

"So am I." His gaze sent a lovely shiver down her spine.

She shoved a forkful of food into her mouth before she could say something stupid. She'd never been so aware of someone before.

Wanting to change the topic and to make sure he was coping she asked, "How's Bradley?"

"I'm not sure." Tai paused. "He seems to be doing OK. He's staying in Jerry's house with his aunt, and he's insisting on helping to organize the funeral and making sure all the traditions are followed." There was pride mixed with worry on his face. "But no decision has been made as to who he'll live with afterward. His father and his mother don't want him."

"What about other aunts, uncles or cousins?"

"Jerry only had two kids. Teresa lives in Austin and doesn't have any children. I don't think she wants that to change. Carl isn't fit to look after Bradley even if he wanted to. Ka' sa' is the next closest relative, being Jerry's aunt. That makes her Bradley's great great aunt."

"Would Eyota take him in?"

"Of course. The only problem is, she has so many kids who rely on her after school and on weekends. I'm worried about her health. We need some kind of youth center to lessen her load. Then she would be able to have Bradley live with her."

"You'd need staff then, wouldn't you? That would be good for the community."

"Only if we could pay them, and I'm not sure if we could. I'll have to search for available grants and funding. The tribe relies heavily on the government for money as it is." He sighed. "Some people would volunteer, so we might get enough from them."

Piper had led such a sheltered upbringing. She'd had two parents who loved her and each other; the family had had a stable income and a lovely house. All children should be able to live like that. "Could we raise some money?" She spoke her thoughts out loud. "We'd need to find out how much a center would cost, check to make sure the tribal council approved it, find some land and work out staffing. We may even be able to find some people willing to volunteer their time to help build it." George's father, Hank, came to mind immediately.

"The elders support it. They've spoken about something like this for a few years but it's the money that's a problem."

"I'm sure we can come up with something," she said, her mind racing. "Let me get through the rest of the week and submit the articles, and then I can focus on it."

"This isn't your problem, Piper," Tai said.

She frowned at him. "Of course it is. There are underprivileged kids out there who need help – they need a proper education and support. That's everyone's problem."

Tai was quiet for a long moment before he said, "You're amazing." He leaned over and kissed her.

She smiled. "Thank you. I'm not sure what I did to deserve that, but I'll take it."

"The number of people I run into who believe my people have it easy, living on handouts from the government, and that we all just like to complain, far exceeds the number of people who really understand."

"So we need to do something about it. We start by submitting the article about your work on the reservation."

"Let me read it again," he said.

She brought up the two articles and cleared their plates while he read through them.

"All right," he said finally. "Submit the one about the rez. It's worth a shot. It might raise some discussion."

Piper grinned. "Thank you." At least one of her articles would have some substance behind it. That was better than none.

He got to his feet and walked toward her and straight away her article was the last thing on her mind. Tai stood in front of her. "I'm glad you don't give up easily," he said and smiled. Then he lowered his head and kissed her.

Piper wrapped her arms around him and kissed him back. She'd been waiting for this, this passion, this strength behind his kiss.

Her head went light and her body warmed as the kiss

deepened. She ran her hands over his back, down to his butt, cupping his cheeks. She wanted him closer.

His tongue parted her lips and she was tasting him, the spicy flavors of his dinner and the taste that was exclusive to him. Sensations swamped her body. She wanted him, more than she'd wanted anyone before.

Tai stroked her breast and she leaned into him. She ran her hands up underneath his T-shirt, and a surge of satisfaction ran through her when he moaned. "This way," she said and led him through to her bedroom.

She hadn't made her bed that morning but it made it all the easier to fall into.

"Piper," he said, and for a moment she thought he was going to refuse, to say he wasn't interested.

"I want to take it slow," he said.

She grinned. Slow was good. "Come here then."

Chapter 9

It was some time before Piper summoned up the energy to move. Her body was well and truly sated. Tai was lying across her where he'd collapsed after cleaning up. As far as she was concerned, it was the best place to be, lying underneath a sexy, intelligent man who'd just given her the best sex of her life. His fingers continued to trace lines over her skin and his breath was warm on her neck.

She didn't think she could possibly be aroused again but damn, his hands did something to her.

His whole body did.

Reaching out, she ran her hand over his side, down to his butt. He shifted to look at her and his gaze was so intense that her insides squeezed.

"You want to go for round two?" he asked.

She laughed. "You're insatiable."

"I was thinking you were."

She shook her head in disbelief. "I have no words." She kept touching him and he stirred, shifting a little so she had better access.

"I said I wanted slow," he said with a wicked grin that made her heart beat so much faster.

"You did," she admitted. And she would never complain about slow again in her life. But they hadn't gone slowly when it came to his pleasure. And really that was hardly fair.

She rolled over, surprising him, and used her advantage to straddle him. "It's my turn," she said and bent down to kiss him.

***

Sometime later they came up for air. Piper lay in the crook of Tai's arm, her arm across his chest, more content than she had been in a long time.

"Slow is good," she said.

He chuckled. "Slow is great, but had I realized how torturous it is to be on the receiving end, I might have been a little faster."

No one had ever reciprocated the favor? Piper couldn't comprehend it. This man's body was a playground for exploring.

"Keep it in mind next time," she said. She was looking forward to next time very much.

He kissed her forehead and slowly moved out from under her. "I should go."

Disappointment zapped through her. She wasn't ready for him to leave. She wanted to fall asleep with him next to her.

She sat up, surprised by the thought. It was the first time she'd wanted someone to spend the night. What was she thinking? She ran a hand through her hair. "Are you heading back to the reservation tomorrow?"

He nodded, his face suddenly serious. He stood up and got dressed.

"Is there anything I can do to help?"

"No." He turned away and Piper frowned. He was cutting her out.

Tai swore under his breath, and turned back. "Yes," he said, moving over and pulling her to her feet. "You help just by being here."

The admission soothed her. The way he gazed at her, the way he held her in his arms, told her she meant something to him.

"I'm glad. Call me if you need me." She slipped on a T-shirt and followed him to the door, kissing him once more before he left.

Shutting the door behind him she leaned back against it, pressing a hand against her chest. Her body felt amazing and she couldn't wipe the smile off her face.

In such a short space of time Tai had come to mean so much to her. She wished the next time she would see him wasn't so far away. Were they moving too fast? If she wasn't careful, she'd be in danger of losing her heart to him.

She tapped her palm on her chest, keeping time with her heartbeat.

Was she already too late?

***

On Saturday evening Piper drove around to Elle and George's house. She'd had a brief phone call from Tai yesterday but he wasn't going to call her today. Today was the funeral and there would be rituals and celebrations lasting into the evening.

She was glad to be meeting her friends. She needed some girl time, some space to figure out what to do about Tai.

Piper was the last one to arrive and Toby was saying good night to everyone. He requested Imogen read him a story, so she went with him while Elle poured Piper a drink and led her to a comfortable chair in the living room. Piper sank into it gratefully.

"Hard day?" Libby asked.

"The usual, but this week Geraldine wanted everything yesterday." She was more than ready for her day off.

"Did you get the articles done?" Elle asked.

"Yeah, and Tai agreed to the article about the reservation."

"You saw him again?" Libby asked, an eyebrow raised.

Piper flushed. "We're kind of seeing each other," she admitted. Surely she could say that. They hadn't discussed it, but they'd slept together, and Tai had said she helped him.

"Get out!" Libby exclaimed. "That's amazing. Why haven't you told us sooner?"

"Told us what?" Imogen asked as she walked in. To Elle she said, "He was out like a light."

Elle smiled and said, "Piper's dating Tai."

"Wow. I never would have guessed it. He's not your usual type."

Annoyance flittered through Piper and she smoothed out her frown. "What's my normal type?"

"Fun-loving, casual. Tai strikes me more as a serious guy."

"Serious can be good." Her skin warmed as she remembered their night together. She cleared her throat. "He's a lot of fun as well."

"Tell us more about him," Libby said. "I don't think I've ever heard you talk like this about any guy."

The rest of her friends waited expectantly.

Piper sighed. "He's different. He's so dedicated to his tribe, and he cares so much. He's passionate about his cooking and when he focuses on me ... well, I lose all *my* focus."

Imogen grinned. "It sounds serious."

She shrugged. "We haven't discussed it."

"Do you want it to be serious?" Libby asked her.

"It's too soon to tell. We've only known each other a few weeks." She didn't really want her friends digging too deep, not when she wasn't sure herself. "Anyway we're not here to talk about me: we're here to talk about weddings."

Imogen grinned. "I've got a date," she said. "The caterer Tai recommended was really great and had a cancellation in October."

"That's only six weeks away," Piper pointed out.

"Seven, actually," Imogen said. "I've already sketched out my wedding dress and one of the fashion photographers I know wants to branch out into weddings so she's going to do mine." She paused. "I'm getting the invitations printed next week and I'll order the extra furniture we need as well."

"Sounds like you've got it all under control," Libby said.

"Well, I've been through yours so I knew what I needed to do and what I wanted."

"Can we help you with anything?" Elle asked.

"Is there anything I've forgotten?"

Together they brainstormed and checked the internet, discarding things they didn't like and adding to the list the things Imogen wanted.

"Are you going to have a theme?" Libby asked.

"How about a cowboy theme?" Elle said. "Toby would love that."

Imogen laughed. "I'll leave that for you. Speaking of which, we should plan your wedding too."

"You're right. I might as well write down some ideas," Elle said as she answered the door to the delivery guy.

"What kind of wedding do you want?" Piper asked her.

Elle toyed with her wine glass. "I've always wanted the traditional wedding: white dress, pretty venue, great music. I gave up those dreams when I was with Dean."

"He's out of the picture now," Libby told her. "I know George will go with whatever you want. He just wants to get married."

Elle's smile was full of love. "I know. I do too. Maybe we should pick a date as well."

"Choose your venue first. Their availability will dictate when you can get married," Imogen advised.

She and Elle leaned in, searching on the laptop for a suitable venue, while Libby tapped out a search on her tablet. Piper sat back and watched her three best friends planning the next stage of their lives and there was a twinge in her heart. She was perfectly happy as an independent woman, but part of her wanted what her friends had: a best friend, companion and lover who she wanted to spend the rest of her life with.

Was Tai that man?

It was too early to tell. All she knew was she'd never felt this strongly about anyone else.

***

Within a couple of hours they had a list of places for Imogen to call on Monday and another of things Elle wanted for her wedding.

"You girls are great," Imogen said. "Next time I need an event planned, I'm coming straight to you."

"I'll say. I had no idea where to start," Elle added.

Piper sat up. "What do y'all know about fundraising?"

"I've taken part in fundraisers in the past," Imogen said. "But I've not organized one."

"What do you want to raise funds for?" Elle asked.

Piper explained what was happening on the reservation. "Tai wants to raise funds to build a youth center and I can't help thinking if the kids had a bus to pick them up and drop them off each day, they might not miss so much school."

"Some authors auction off characters in their novels for fundraisers, but it won't raise the amount you want," Libby said.

"Maybe we could do an auction with a lot of things. Papa would donate an outfit if I asked him, and so would Chantelle," Imogen said, mentioning her current employer. "I'm sure a few more designers would donate as well."

"What about a concert?" Elle asked. "George knows enough people to put one together."

"And Adrian would sing. He can relate to those kids. I'm sure he would have loved a refuge when he was a child," Libby added.

That's exactly what the youth center would be – a refuge.

A rush of excitement flowed over Piper's skin, making her shiver. Maybe they could pull this off. "We'd need a venue for both the concert and the auction," she said.

"How about an online auction?" Libby said. "Get people to tweet their bids and you might find it sparks a frenzy."

It was a great idea and would reduce costs as well.

"I'll talk to George about the concert when he gets home," Elle said. "I'm sure this is something he'll support. He always wants to help and he can make anything happen."

He really could. Piper couldn't wait to talk to Tai about it. A concert headlining Kent Downer was sure to be a success, and she was certain Adahy would play as well. It could raise enough money for both the center and the bus.

"I'll talk to Tai when he gets back."

"Wouldn't it be great to get something like this off the ground?" Imogen asked. "I've always wanted to be more hands-on helping people in the community."

Piper smiled. So had she. This wasn't just writing about something to drive change – it was actually doing something.

Tai needed to spend more time with her friends. Then he would see not everyone thought about Native Americans in such a negative light – that there were people out there who wanted to help.

She'd show him he had a right to be optimistic.

And they'd help the tribe.

***

The next day, Piper slept most of the morning away. She was woken by her phone ringing near midday. It was George.

"Elle told me about your fundraising idea," he said. "Adrian's on board and I've got the arena interested. They might not do it for free, but they'll at least give us a discount. I'm going to chat to a couple of my contacts and see which other acts we can get on board."

Piper's mouth dropped open. "How the hell did you arrange that already? It's Sunday!"

"I've got contacts," he said.

She laughed. "Thanks, George. This is amazing."

"It's the least I can do. Adahy told me about the funeral and the circumstances surrounding it."

"Did he say when he'd be back?" she asked. She hadn't wanted to ask Tai in case it sounded like she wanted him to hurry home.

Which she did because she missed him, but he didn't need to know.

"Probably tonight. We've got a meeting tomorrow. Adahy mentioned Tai had something he had to do on Sunday."

That would be the cooking class. She wasn't sure whether they would skip it or want things to go back to normal as soon as possible. "Thanks. I'll call Tai tonight and tell him what we're planning." She hung up and jumped out of bed. It was already an amazing day and she was keen to get planning.

Making herself some toast, she sat down to brainstorm what else they needed to arrange for the fundraiser.

***

Tai woke on Sunday morning with his head throbbing and his body aching. He'd done a lot of dancing the night before and was paying for it now. Quietly he got out of the bunk he'd been sleeping on for the past few days, careful not to wake Adahy or Bradley in the other bed, and went into the kitchen to make coffee. As he waited for the machine to heat up, he glanced out the window and saw his grandmother sitting cross-legged under a tree, her head bowed.

He walked outside to talk to her. There hadn't been any chance to do so alone during the week: there had always been someone else around.

"Ka' sa'," he said as he got closer, so as not to startle her.

She looked up at him, tears streaming down her face.

Shock speared through Tai. He dropped to his knees, gathering her close. He'd never seen her cry. Not once, with all the things that had happened, not when her son had died, or her brother.

She hugged him fiercely, her hands shaking. "We're losing, aren't we, Tai? We're losing this fight to save our people." The pain in her voice was all too real. "I thought we had a chance with Jerry. I thought Bradley would be enough to keep him here, but it wasn't. It never is. How can we save each other if people don't want to be saved?"

Tai had no answers. It was terrifying to see the woman he considered a rock brought down by this. He'd thought her faith was all encompassing, all empowering – he'd always got his determination from her.

He'd thought she was invincible.

"We're trying, Ka' sa'. That's got to count for something."

"What about poor Bradley? His mother wants nothing to do with him. She doesn't even want to admit she's Queche. Luckily Bradley has his roll number and tribal citizenship." She sighed. "I've told him he can stay with me, but I'm getting too old for this. He should be with someone young, someone who will run around with him, who has other children he can play with."

The problem was many such families were already struggling. Another mouth to feed and body to clothe could push them over the edge. "I'll come down as often as I can." Maybe he could even foster the boy – though he'd have to have a stable routine for that to happen. He couldn't have Bradley hanging out in the restaurant every evening.

But perhaps he could step back from the restaurant. His heart panged. He truly loved cooking, but he could do that on the reservation. Kath was capable of running the Spoon on her own, as she'd proven over the last week. He could divide his time between here and Houston. He could even run cooking retreats on the rez.

It would also mean less time with Piper.

The thought was equally painful, which worried him. He

hadn't wanted to leave her on Thursday night, but he'd needed to get an early start. He'd stolen enough of her sleep over the past week, and she needed it.

Suddenly what Eyota said about Bradley's mother reverberated in his mind. She wasn't acknowledging her heritage. If Bradley hadn't already been part of the Queche tribe it would have affected him because tribal membership was passed down through the mother.

Piper wasn't one of the tribe. If they stayed together and had children, their kids wouldn't be Queche. He wasn't willing to deny his children that, which meant what he and Piper had couldn't go too far.

He rubbed at the pain in his chest. Maybe he needed to cool things with Piper. Or explain why it couldn't go any further than it had. She'd caught him when he'd been most vulnerable and that was surely the only reason they'd become so close so quickly.

"You can't do everything my boy," Eyota said, patting his knee. "You already do beyond what you need to."

He put his thoughts of Piper aside. "I can't help it, I was taught by the best," he said.

She gave him a small smile. "You should have been too busy playing to notice," she said. "But you always did want to learn everything I could teach you."

"Someone will have to take over from you one day," he said. "It's my heritage too."

"It is. That is why we keep trying." She wiped her eyes and sighed. "Sometimes it all gets too much." She groaned as she got to her feet. "I should prepare breakfast for the others."

Tai stood up. "You'd better let me: I'm the better cook."

She rewarded him with a chuckle, as he'd hoped she would. "I taught you everything you know."

"That's why I'm so good." Pleased she had brightened somewhat, Tai put his arm around her and headed inside.

He couldn't let his grandmother down. When he got back to Houston he would focus his energies on other ways he could help his people.

He would never give up.

***

It was later than he'd hoped when they arrived home.

"It's good to be home," Rayen said as she got out of the car. "I need a little bit of quiet."

"Tell me about it," Adahy agreed. "I'm not going to pick up my guitar at all tomorrow."

Tai smiled. His brother had been playing music almost non-stop over the week and had enjoyed himself. In fact he'd even arranged to give lessons on the reservation regularly. As much as he complained, Tai knew his brother loved it.

Still it was quieter in Houston, which was a rare thing. On the reservation there had been gatherings and people dropping in non-stop over the six days. The only time he'd had to himself was that night with Piper.

The thought of her made him want to back the car out and drive over to her place but it was late. It wouldn't be fair to disturb her.

"You coming?" Adahy asked. "Or are you going to let us carry everything inside?"

Tai got out of the car, grabbing his bag from the trunk.

"Are you going to the restaurant?" Rayen asked.

"I'll head in early tomorrow," he told her. "Kath will have everything under control."

"I'll grab a lift if I can," she said. "I need to check my roster before I head over to the college to sort out enrollments."

"Sure."

His younger cousin was so determined to finish her degree. He was proud of her and pleased he could help. Her parents both lived on the rez and between them earned a reasonable income now that her father had finally got his addiction under control, but it wasn't enough to support Rayen living in Houston. She lived with him rent free and had a secure job that would pay for her day-to-day college needs.

He had another spare room in his house but the two girls from the reservation who were going to college this year both had scholarships that included board.

He'd have to find out whether others were looking for an apprenticeship or training to improve their job prospects.

Heading for the kitchen, he found Rayen and Adahy at the table eating the fast food they'd picked up on their way home. Tai shook his head. The food was crap. It was so full of grease and fat with no flavor at all

Taking a couple of eggs and a few other ingredients from the fridge, he whipped up an omelet. The simple process soothed him as he took his time to beat the eggs until they were light, adding a dash of milk and a few of his favorite spices, before pouring the mixture into the warm pan. Working quickly now, he added the filling – a little bit of smoked salmon and some dill – before flipping the top over and sliding the omelet onto a plate. He joined them at the table.

"Did Piper ever do that interview of you?" Adahy asked.

Surprised to hear her name, Tai said, "Yes. She showed me the profile on Thursday."

"Any good?"

"Very. She highlighted the issues at the rez with sensitivity and accuracy."

"Wow, that's a change," Rayen said. "She must be half decent."

"She's very decent," Tai retorted, annoyed on Piper's behalf.

Adahy and Rayen looked at each other and raised their eyebrows.

"Somebody's got a crush," Adahy sang.

He refused to comment. What he did in his own time was his own business and he wasn't ready to talk about it yet. He focused on his dinner.

Rayen scrutinized him. "I think it's more than that."

Adahy blinked. "Really? Are you dating Piper?"

He didn't know what to say. They'd not discussed the details of their relationship. He shrugged.

"What's that meant to mean? Are you seeing her again?" Adahy pushed.

"Yes." As soon as he could, though tomorrow night he had to be at the restaurant. He'd taken too much time off as it was.

"Way to go, bro. She's so hot."

Tai glared at his younger brother who held up his hands palm outward. "I'm just saying."

There was so much more to Piper than her appearance.

"She seemed nice when she was at the restaurant," Rayen said.

"She is."

"You should invite her around for dinner some time. Then we can get to know her properly."

It was always difficult finding a time when the three of them were at home together and it was a big step. "Maybe." He stood up and put his dishes in the dishwasher. "I'm going to bed."

He left without waiting for a response.

***

Monday morning Piper positively danced into work. She'd had a wonderful, restful day yesterday, brainstorming ideas for auction items and the concert, and planning the auction website. She'd also updated her blog, writing a couple of posts about the upcoming election and the tactics that both parties were using to fool voters into supporting them. Having finally written something of substance she was now ready to face the week. With the profile interviews completed, it would have to be a less stressful week and she was looking forward to the change in pace. She'd even put together a comprehensive pitch for the investigation she wanted to do into the state of the reservations in Texas and what could be done to help the indigenous people of America. She hoped Geraldine would change her mind when she saw Piper's notes. She'd have to.

Piper called good morning to a couple of colleagues, turned on her laptop and sat down to start the day. Her phone rang.

"I need you in my office," Geraldine said.

"Be right there," Piper told her and picked up her take-out coffee cup and the pitch she'd printed out.

Walking into Geraldine's office she was surprised Leslie from human resources was in there.

"Close the door behind you," Geraldine said.

Confused and a little nervous, Piper closed the door and sat at the small meeting table in the room next to Geraldine and Leslie.

"The newspaper has recently been reassessing its structure and the requirement for staff reporters," Geraldine began.

Surprise hit Piper first. She'd not heard any rumors about

changes.

"Our readership has decreased and the paper is struggling to make ends meet."

Nausea began to swirl in her stomach.

Geraldine was very matter-of-fact. "We've had to carefully review each role. Unfortunately yours has been identified as surplus to our needs and you are therefore being laid off."

Chapter 10

Piper's mouth dropped open. What? She was losing her job? This could not be happening.

It had to be a joke.

She'd worked so hard for them.

She'd kept her mouth shut when she disagreed with the changes Geraldine made to her articles.

Mostly.

"Is this about Bob Randall?" she asked. The CEO hadn't been happy she'd cut his interview short.

Geraldine shook her head. "It's about what's best for the paper."

Piper didn't believe her. "I write great articles for the paper."

"And inappropriate blog posts," Geraldine said. "We can't have that associated with the *Age*. I'm sorry, Piper. You don't fit the paper's values and mission statement and it's best you go now, before you cause any trouble."

Cause trouble? Hell, she'd toed the line for months. Her blog was her *only* outlet to say what she wanted.

"In lieu of notice, the *Age* will give you two weeks' pay," Leslie said.

"Effective when?" she managed to ask.

"Today," Geraldine answered. "I'd like to thank you for your work and your dedication." She passed over her business card. "If you need any references, you can call."

Both women stood.

Piper sat there, staring at them. They couldn't be serious. She'd busted her gut writing a huge number of stories each day and with the additional work like the profiles. No wonder Geraldine had wanted them done by the end of last week. She'd known this was coming.

"If you come with me, I'll escort you to your desk and you can collect your things," Leslie said.

Piper got to her feet. Her throat burned, but she was lost for words. Numbly she shook Geraldine's hand and followed Leslie out to her desk.

Automatically she went to pack up her laptop and Leslie stopped her. "That's the company's laptop."

Of course it was. She wasn't thinking straight. But she had notes and article ideas on there she wanted to delete. She didn't want to give them any of it. "May I get my personal files from it?" she asked.

"No. You shouldn't have saved anything personal on it."

Piper swallowed. Damn it.

One of her coworkers asked, "What's up, Piper?"

She stared blankly at him. "I've been laid off." Her voice wavered and she swallowed. There was no way she was going to break down and cry here. She wouldn't give them the satisfaction.

He swore and ran a hand through his hair. "I'm sorry to hear that. Are many going?" He directed the question to Leslie.

"Everyone who is affected will be told before lunch," she said.

He went pale.

Piper packed up her things. She didn't have a lot of personal items – just a photo of Libby, Imogen and herself on Libby's wedding day, a coffee mug and a few training and reference manuals, which she tucked into her satchel.

She followed Leslie to the elevator and down to the ground floor, where she handed in her security card.

"Good luck in the future," Leslie said and shook her hand.

"Thank you," Piper replied.

She walked outside. The sunlight and heat hit her in a wave. She blinked and then pinched herself.

That had really happened. She'd really been laid off.

What the hell did she do now? She had rent and bills to pay, and the number of full-time journalism positions were rapidly on the decline. But she couldn't stand here in the sun. Her mind a jumbled mess, she headed for her car.

She'd worked so hard.

She'd been so sure Geraldine was going to give her a chance to branch out. She'd been working toward investigative journalism from the moment she set foot through the *Age*'s door. Sure, she hadn't been happy, but she was sure it was a step in the right direction on her career path.

Her vision became blurry and it was hard to swallow. At her car she stopped, wiped her eyes.

She shouldn't be surprised.

She'd never felt she was a valued member of the team.

Geraldine hadn't respected her skills.

Sliding into the driver's seat, she couldn't stem the tears. She leaned her head against the steering wheel so no one saw, and cried.

***

After she'd cried herself out, she wasn't sure what to do. Normally at this time on a Monday morning she was deep into the stories she had to get done for the following day's paper.

Now she had nowhere she had to be. It was unsettling. She was used to her routine, to always being busy. She should probably head straight home and start searching for a new job, but her head wasn't in the right space. Surely she could afford a single day's grace.

But she also didn't want to be alone. Her thoughts were too sad and she didn't want to be with them right now.

Maybe that was how Tai had been feeling the other night. He would be at the restaurant now, catching up on the week he'd been away and preparing for the lunchtime rush.

Libby would probably be at home. As an author, she had a home office, but she was likely to be in the middle of writing or editing, or some other thing writers did as part of their working life. Piper wasn't going to be one of those people who expected Libby to alter her routine just because she had need of her. She had to treat it as if it were any other day job.

So that left Imogen, who would also be at work, and Elle, who may or may not be at the café. It was nearing the mid-morning lull so Piper put her car into gear and drove to Eat, Drink, Read, parking not far from the front door.

Inside, the café was humming with people but there were a few spare tables. A little shimmer of relief went through her as she saw Elle taking an order. Piper waved and moved to the bookshelves.

She couldn't remember the last time she'd read a book, so she browsed until she found a romantic suspense that appealed, and went to the counter to pay. Then she ordered a cappuccino and a humongous slice of chocolate cake, and took a seat at one of the tables.

Elle brought her order over to her. "What are you doing here so early?"

"They sacked me," Piper said. Her words were bitter.

Elle gaped at her and slid into the seat closest to her. "What?"

"I was laid off," she explained. "Geraldine called me into her office first thing this morning and gave me the news."

"Oh, honey. I'm so sorry." Elle hugged her. "How are you feeling?"

"Pretty crappy. I don't know what to do with myself. My world has suddenly shifted. I have no job, no income and no idea what I'm going to do next."

"I know how you feel. When I left Dean, each day was like stepping into a dark room. I didn't know what was ahead of me."

Piper sighed. Her situation was nothing like what Elle had gone through. She'd left an abusive partner with only two hundred dollars in her pocket and a five-year-old boy to care for. It put Piper's own life into perspective.

"If you need a job until you find a permanent one, I can find you a few shifts. Some of my regulars are busy getting the kids ready to go back to school."

"Thanks." Piper smiled at her friend. "That would be great. Call me if you need me." She'd pitched in and waitressed for Elle when the café had been understaffed, and didn't mind the work on an occasional basis. Besides she couldn't afford to be choosy.

They chatted for a few minutes more before Elle had to get back to work. Piper opened her book and resolved to immerse herself in another world.

***

When the lunch rush began, she said goodbye to Elle and moved to a park down the road, freeing up her table. She sat underneath a big shady tree and kept reading.

A few hours later, she closed the finished book.

She sighed.

If only life guaranteed a happily-ever-after.

She rubbed her eyes, which were sore after the crying jag and several hours of reading. It was time she went home.

Her phone rang as she walked back to her car. Checking the caller ID she discovered it was her younger brother, Tom.

"What do you want?" she said with a smile. Her brother was not one to call out of the blue, or really at all.

"Mom's invited us for dinner Sunday night," he said.

They hadn't had a family dinner in a while, but usually her mom would call. "Sounds good."

"She wants me to bring my new partner."

"I didn't know you had one. What's his name?"

He paused. "Casey."

There was definitely more to it.

"What do you want me to do?" she asked.

He sighed. "You know how Mom gets. She's always so interested it's like she's giving them the third degree, and I don't want her to scare Casey off."

That was new. Usually her brother brought boyfriends to their parents for just that reason. "Is he special?"

"Kind of," he admitted. "I don't suppose you've got someone you could bring? Someone to split Mom's focus."

Tai would definitely get his share of their mother's focus. It had been a long time since she'd brought a guy home for dinner. It would depend on whether Tai was working. "Maybe."

"Really?" He was surprised. "That would be great."

"I'll let you know."

She hung up. The idea of introducing Tai to her family was exciting, and that was as unusual as her brother being serious about a guy. Deciding now was as good a time as ever to catch Tai, she dialed his number.

"Piper, I was just going to call you." His voice sent warmth through her body.

"I hope you're not busy," she said, suddenly nervous about asking him to dinner at her parents' place.

"Not for you."

"Well, listen, do you want to come to dinner at my parent's place on Sunday night?" When there was nothing but silence, she added, "You probably have to work, and I have to warn you Mom is usually overly enthusiastic about getting to know her guests, but my brother Tom is bringing his boyfriend for the first time too, so you wouldn't be alone." She was rambling. Shutting her mouth tightly, she ran a hand through her hair and waited for his response.

Perhaps he didn't consider them a couple and she would scare him off.

"I'd like that. What time?"

Relief poured through her. "About six." That would give them time to talk before dinner.

"Great. I can pick you up if you like."

"I'd better drive. Mom's got a thing against motorcycles."

"All right, I'll come to your place about five-thirty." He paused. "What can I bring?"

"You don't need to bring a thing."

"I'd like to."

She remembered what he'd said at George's place about always bringing food. "My mom loves chocolate mousse," she said.

"Done," he said. "Are you working late tonight?"

Piper laughed. "No. That's not going to be happening for a while. I was laid off today." This time instead of tears, anger stirred inside. She'd been loyal to them.

He exhaled loudly. "That sucks. I'm sorry. Do you want to come by the restaurant and talk?" His tone soothed her.

She did. "Not if you're busy."

"I've got an hour or so before it will start to get busy."

There was no decision to be made. "I'll be there soon."

***

She drove straight to the Spoon and went in the back entrance. Kath was heading out, her street clothes on.

"Nice to see you again. He's in his office," she said.

Piper walked through and found him at the computer. He rose when he saw her and came around his desk to give her a hug. Then he kissed her and some of her worries faded.

"Are you all right?"

She shrugged. "I've had better days."

He glanced over her shoulder.

Piper turned and found one of the waitresses staring at them. She searched her memory – Rayen. "Is she your cousin?" she asked.

"Yes." He waved Rayen in. "You've met Piper before."

Piper shook her hand. They had met, but before she was kissing Rayen's cousin. Would she have a problem with that?

"How are things?" Rayen asked.

"Fine. Were you planning to study before work?" Piper asked, indicating the pile of textbooks Rayen was carrying.

"Some pre-class reading I want to get ahead on. One of my units has a mountain of reference material. I'll catch you later." Rayen disappeared into the room next door.

"I'm not sure she was happy with us kissing," Piper commented.

"Probably surprised is all," Tai said. "I can see who I want."

Piper turned to him. "Is that what this is? Are we exclusively seeing each other?" She really wanted to clear it up.

"Yes." He shuffled his feet. "I wanted to—"

At that moment Jared walked in. "Hey Chef, Louis just called in sick."

Tai swore. "Thanks. I'll sort it." He turned to Piper. "I'm sorry, we'll have to take a rain check."

The disappointment was instant, but she understood. "No problem. I'll get out of your way. I should probably be looking for work anyway."

"Use Kath's computer," he said. "If you want to stick around a bit longer that is. I'll provide dinner." He said it with a smile.

She would have stayed without the dinner, but that was icing on the cake.

"I'd love to."

He showed her to the other computer and left to deal with the absence.

With a sigh, Piper typed in the usual employment search websites and trawled through the results. There wasn't a lot. A couple of communication jobs wanting a journalism degree, sure, but nothing for a newspaper journalist.

Nothing for someone who wanted to use her writing to make a difference in the world.

Perhaps freelance was the answer. She knew a couple of people from university who had gone on to make successful careers from freelancing. She'd never really considered it because she'd been so focused on her initial dream of newspaper work, but so much had changed in the last five years with the rise of online news sources. Perhaps she'd been too narrow-sighted. She was sure she could find journals and newspapers whose editors wanted the type of articles she wanted to write. There were even blogs which would pay for well-written pieces.

The problem was it would take her time to establish herself and she wasn't sure she could afford it.

Maybe she could start running advertising on her blog. She didn't like the idea, but right now she had to consider every option that would bring in an income.

She changed her search queries and delved into the world of freelance and online advertising.

She only surfaced when Tai brought two plates of steaming food into the room.

"Time for a break?" he asked. He had changed into his chef's uniform, which was now decorated with a few splotches of sauce.

"Yes please," she answered, and turned away from the computer, rubbing her back.

"Any luck?" He passed her the cutlery and sat down across from her.

"A few options. I'll call a couple of contacts tomorrow

morning and find out if anyone's hiring, but I suspect they aren't. Fewer people are getting their news from newspapers these days. It's all online content, so papers don't want full-time staff." She'd considered herself so lucky when she'd got the job at the *Age* last year.

"What will you do?" he asked.

She shrugged. "I don't know." She didn't really want to talk about it. Her whole financial world was crumbling. She no longer had the security of regular pay and it was scary. Two weeks' pay wouldn't last long and there weren't any jobs out there.

Searching for a change in topic, she realized she hadn't spoken to Tai about her fundraising ideas. She grinned at him. "I've figured out how to raise money for the youth center."

His eyes widened. "What?"

"I meant to tell you earlier. I had dinner with Elle, Imogen and Libby on the weekend and I was telling them how we need to raise money. They came up with some great suggestions. We're going to do an online auction with items donated by Libby and Imogen. Both were sure they would be able to get some more people on board. You could donate a private cooking lesson – that's sure to raise some dollars." She paused but before he could speak said, "But the big one is a concert, headlining Kent Downer. George is all for it and he thinks he can hold it at the arena. He's going to ask around for other performers to donate their time. Adahy would sing, wouldn't he?"

Tai sat there staring at her for a long time, an unreadable frown on his face.

Had she done something wrong?

"Say something," she said. "Did I get carried away? I thought you wanted this." Maybe she'd misread the whole situation.

"I do," he said. "I never considered anything on such a scale. Do they realize it's for the rez?"

"Of course."

He shook his head. "Something like that could raise thousands."

"It could. Maybe we could stream the concert live on the

internet," she added as the thought occurred to her. "We charge a small fee, like five or ten dollars, so people can watch it as it's happening."

He stood up and pulled her into his arms. "Thank you. Even if it doesn't work out, thank you for thinking of it. Thank you for trying."

He was overcome. It humbled and concerned her that he would be so surprised people would want to help the kids on the reservation.

"It'll work. I'll make sure of it." She wasn't sure it was a promise she could keep but she would do her best.

He ran a hand through his hair. "I've got some friends who will probably donate to an auction. I'll ask around."

"Great idea. I'm sure there are plenty of people who would pay to have a chef cook them a private meal, or to win dinner at a five-star restaurant."

He nodded. "I'd better get back to work."

He left the room and Piper turned her attention back to her job search.

***

At closing time Piper wandered out of the office with her satchel over her shoulder. Tai wanted to go home with her, but he had to give Rayen a lift. It would take him an hour to drop Rayen off and return to Piper's and by then it would be too late.

For the first time since moving to Houston he wished he lived closer to the center of town.

"Heading off now?" he asked, stopping and wiping his hands on a dish towel.

"I can wait if you want to come home with me," she said.

He kissed her. "I have to take Rayen home."

"Oh."

Rayen stopped next to them. "I can catch a cab."

"No." He was responsible for her and he wasn't going to let her get into a stranger's car at this time of night alone.

"I'm a big girl, Tai," she said. "If you want to go home with Piper, I'll be fine."

"You could take my car," Piper offered.

He and Rayen turned as one and stared at her. Why would

she offer to lend her car to someone who was effectively a stranger?

"What? Is she a bad driver?"

He shook his head.

"Doesn't she have her license?"

Rayen said what he was thinking. "You don't know me."

"You're Tai's cousin," Piper said. "You'd vouch for her, wouldn't you?" she asked, turning to him.

He was still surprised. "Of course."

Piper took the car key off her keyring and held it out to Rayen. "I'll meet you here in the morning." She turned to Tai. "Unless you don't want to stay?"

"Take the key," he said to Rayen, and earned a laugh from them both.

"If I've got my own wheels for the night, I'm off. Have fun." Rayen leaned over to kiss his cheek and whispered in his ear, "She's a keeper. We're going to talk about this later."

He smiled. "Drive carefully, little flower."

Piper showed Rayen to her car and Tai sent Jared to watch out for them while he did his checks. Then finally he was able to lock up and take Piper home. She wore Rayen's helmet and it was a blissfully short ride to her apartment.

Once inside, she dumped her satchel on the table. "I'm beat."

She did look tired, and he hadn't been able to give her the attention he'd wanted to tonight. She must be worried about losing her job.

They hadn't had a chance to really discuss what she was going to do. But it was too late to start in on that now. He wanted her to forget about it for the night and relax. In the morning, when she'd had a chance to rest, they would find a solution.

"Is your shower big enough for two?" he asked.

She grinned at him. "Might be a bit of a squeeze but I'm sure we can make it work."

***

They definitely made it work.

He washed and massaged Piper's short hair, and her moans

of appreciation led to other kinds of moans. They were forced out of the shower when the water ran cold and stumbled to her bed, where they made love, fast and hard.

He'd never been so consumed by someone before. He'd thought he'd figured her out when he'd first met her, but he'd been completely wrong.

She'd floored him with her fundraising ideas. He'd expected she would forget all about it, but instead she was doing her best to ensure it happened, to get the kids a chance at a better life. He couldn't express what it meant to him in words, which was why he had to show her with his body.

When they settled down for the night he pulled her close to him and she cuddled in. He'd never have picked her as a snuggler, but he was glad she was. He wanted to hold her through the night, to make sure she didn't disappear like a dream.

"Night, Tai," she said, sleepily.

He kissed her forehead. "Night, Piper."

He lay there, listening to her soft breathing. Earlier in the evening he'd started to tell Piper about his tribe's laws, telling her that although they were exclusive, it couldn't be serious, but Jared had interrupted and he'd had to rush off and deal with the restaurant. Afterward he hadn't wanted to spoil the evening by mentioning it. Piper had enough on her mind at the moment. Plus there was a part of him that was afraid she'd stop seeing him if he said anything. Perhaps that was unfair of him, but he didn't want to address the future yet. He just wanted to enjoy being with her.

Shutting the thoughts out of his mind, he too fell asleep.

***

In the morning when Tai woke he had no idea where he was. There were traffic noises outside the window and he was alone in a bed that wasn't his. He glanced around and recognized Piper's bedroom.

He threw on his clothes from last night before going to find her. She was in the kitchen burning toast.

"Morning. I was cooking breakfast," she said. Her hair was standing up in a million different directions and she was wearing a pink stretch tank top that clung to every curve. She was adorable and sexy at the same time.

"That's actually called burning breakfast," he said as he brought her close to him and kissed her.

"Oh, don't – morning breath," she said, taking a swig of orange juice and then holding her hand over her mouth to check.

He grinned, took the glass from her and took his own mouthful. "Shall we try again?"

"Absolutely." She met him with an enthusiasm that made him want to drag her back to bed again. But he didn't have time.

The toaster popped, revealing the toast as inedible. "I can cook an omelet," he said, opening her fridge.

"Don't—" She reached out a hand to stop him, but she was too late.

He stared at the contents of her fridge in horror. A pint of milk, a couple of jars of ready-made sauces, some jelly and a limp bag of carrots that were long past their use-by date. It wasn't a fridge: it was a disaster zone.

He turned to face her. "We can't see each other any more," he said, only mostly kidding.

She shut the fridge door and stood in front of it. "I eat out a lot."

"I hope so," he answered. If not, she was subsisting on air. "I'm going to have to make those cooking lessons a priority."

"Or you could just keep cooking for me," she suggested. "I may have lost my job, but there are other ways I can pay you." She winked and slid her hands around his waist, kissing him slowly.

He took the kiss she offered and then moved away. "Everyone needs to know how to cook," he said. He checked how much bread was left, adjusted the toaster settings and put two slices down. "Ka' sa' made sure we all knew the basics."

"I know those – I just never have time to go to the grocery store," she said. "Half the time I grab lunch or dinner while I'm at work."

"You need to take care of yourself. Your health is so important." He'd seen too many examples of what happened when people didn't watch what they put into their bodies.

"It's usually healthy stuff."

The toast popped up and he spread it with jelly, handing her the slices. "What are you doing today?"

She shrugged. "I don't know. It's weird not having a routine. I feel a little lost."

She looked it as well. He put some more toast down and turned to hug her. "You're welcome to hang out at the restaurant." He liked having her around.

"I might for a little while. I need to pick up my car from Rayen anyway." She sighed. "I really need to figure out what I'm going to do next. Two weeks in lieu doesn't give me a lot of time to find another job."

He knew nothing about the media business except for his own dislike of it. "Have you got colleagues you can call?"

"Yeah." She wasn't all that enthusiastic.

"Do you want to continue with journalism?" he asked. "Maybe you should try something different."

"I've always wanted to help people," she said. "It seemed people sat up and took notice of issues reported in the media. If it wasn't there, no one noticed. I was certain I could use my skills to highlight injustice in the world." She sighed. "But the *Age* wasn't interested in anything that didn't suit their target market. And you know what really grates?" she asked, whirling around to face him. "I was working so damn hard for them. I busted my gut getting stories that were different, offering suggestions, working *way* past the hours I was paid. Then they laid me off."

Lost Piper was gone, replaced by angry Piper. She stood with her hands on her hips, her eyes flashing.

The toast popped up and he spread it, keeping his eyes on the fiery woman who had appeared before him. "They didn't appreciate what they had," he said.

"Damn straight," she agreed. "Keith doesn't know diddly-squat about news. He's only interested in keeping the owners happy and they've got an agenda as big as Texas."

He took a bite of his toast and let her continue to rant.

"It amazes me readers don't complain about the bias, but maybe they don't notice it."

"So who would publish the stories you want to write?" he

asked.

She shrugged as the fight left her. "Some of the online newspapers have good coverage of facts," she said. "I need to do more research."

"Do you enjoy finding the stories, the research and the writing? Or do you want to help people?"

Actions spoke louder than words.

The question made her squint at him, thinking. "I like digging up facts, researching things."

"Are there many jobs for researchers?" he asked. Perhaps she could use her situation to change her direction in life, if that's what she wanted.

"I don't know." But she was considering it. She stared at the table, her attention elsewhere.

He swallowed the rest of his toast. "I need to go. You going to come with me?"

"Yeah. Let me grab my bag."

While she did that, he tidied the kitchen, putting the last two slices of bread in the cupboard and wiping over the bench top.

"You don't need to clean up," she said.

"I ate too." Plus he hated a dirty kitchen. It was ingrained into him. Everything had to be clean when cooking.

He took his helmet off the counter, waiting while she locked up her apartment then handing her Rayen's helmet.

It was a short drive to the restaurant and it was nice to be the first one there, to enjoy the quiet of his place. Piper had brought her laptop and set it up in the break room while Tai went through his morning routine. Rayen was rostered on at lunchtime so it would be a couple of hours before she arrived.

As he sat down at his computer to go over the figures, he sighed. This was his least favorite part of his role as head chef. He would have much preferred to have left the business side to a manager and just cooked. Perhaps it was something he needed to explore further. Particularly if he wanted to spend more time at the reservation.

It was also time he thought seriously about expanding his business. He'd had a few ideas but he needed to review them critically to see if they were viable.

There was the cookbook he'd spoken to Piper about,

opening another restaurant, or doing cooking classes. He'd like to know Piper's opinion.

Tai finished reading the report, made some notes and stretched, getting to his feet and wandering next door. Piper sat at the table, her laptop in front of her and her fingers flying over the keys. She continued to type as she looked up. Seeing him she smiled. He was impressed. He wasn't a slow typist but he had to look at the keys when he did it. "Any luck?" he asked.

"One of my friends put me onto a couple of freelance websites where writers post they're looking for work, and companies leave details of jobs. There's a lot there."

She didn't seem enthusiastic. "But nothing that excites you?"

She shook her head.

"What about research jobs?"

"They're all for scientific roles I'm not qualified for. Plus, I'm not sure if that's what I want to do." She hunched over her laptop.

It was the first time he'd ever seen her defeated. He wasn't sure how to help. He couldn't tell her what to do with the next stage of her life. "If you could do one thing and income and qualifications didn't matter, what would you do?" he asked.

She frowned. "I'd help people less fortunate than me."

"So have you considered charity work?"

"No, not really. I've never had much time to volunteer, and it doesn't pay." She shrugged. "I need to earn a living."

He understood completely. When he'd finished his apprenticeship, he was living on the meals he got as part of his job. He'd been staying in a dingy one-bedroom apartment within walking distance of work. He'd rented the bedroom out to an apprentice, had slept on the lumpy fold-out sofa and had no luxuries like a television. It had been hard but he'd made it work because he wanted to succeed.

It was one of the reasons he always had a spare couch or bedroom in his house for anyone who needed it.

"And you still mainly want writing work," he said, mulling it over. He grinned: he'd found the solution. "Maybe you can help me. I want to write a cookbook but I haven't got the time to put it together. You could – what do they call it? – ghost write for me." He liked the idea. It would get one of his business ideas off the ground and he could help Piper. "I can provide the recipes easily enough; it's the other bits I need help with."

"What else is there except recipes?" Piper asked.

He'd forgotten she did very little cooking. She probably had no idea what celebrity chef cookbooks were like these days. "I want to include a history of the food and my culture, how things were prepared and hunted."

"That's a great idea."

The idea excited him. "I've made some notes already – come and have a look." He returned to his office and pulled up the document with his very brief notes. Showing them to Piper he said, "If you're interested, tell me what price is reasonable. I don't know what the going rate is."

"Neither do I," Piper admitted. "But I can do this for you in my spare time."

He shook his head. He wasn't going to take advantage of her. "There could be a lot of work in this," he said. "I don't have a clear idea of what I want – or whether there's a publisher who will want it. Give me a price and we'll draw up a contract to make it official."

The more he considered it, the more he liked the idea. He could highlight both of his passions in one book: his culture and his food. "You might need to take trips to the rez to talk to Eyota and other elders about the history."

Slowly Piper nodded. "All right. I'll do some research today, review other cookbooks, find out what the going rate is and get back to you."

He grinned. The thought of working with Piper and getting his idea off the ground was thrilling. He would show the world they weren't a forgotten people.

And it would give Piper extra time to sort out what she wanted to do. Plus it would give him an excuse to spend more time with her – it would be business.

He wrapped an arm around her waist and pulled her close, kissing her.

Chapter 11

"Ugh, would you two stop that?" Rayen stood at the door to the office, holding Piper's car key.

Tai smiled at his cousin. "No."

Rayen tossed Piper the key. "Thanks for the loan."

"No problem." Piper turned to Tai. "I might as well get started. I'll give you a call later."

He was sad to see her go. He liked having her around, which was strange. Normally he liked his own space, his own company. Piper was changing that. Or maybe he wanted more of her *because* she gave him the space he needed.

He kissed her again and she left.

Rayen stood in the doorway. "What's she getting started on?"

"I've asked her to help me with my cookbook," Tai told her. "I don't have the time at the moment and she does."

"That's great. I keep telling you you need to write one."

"Don't get too excited. Nothing may come of it."

"So this thing between you and Piper is serious," Rayen said, completely changing the subject.

"It can't be serious. She's not part of the tribe." Tai shrugged. "But we are seeing each other."

"What does it matter if she's not part of the tribe?"

It wasn't something Rayen had to worry about. "If I want my children to be part of our tribe, their mother must be

Queche. Membership is passed down the maternal line."

Rayen frowned. "Are you serious? You'd let that stand in the way of your feelings?"

Tai was silent. Their traditions were almost the only things they had left.

She raised her eyebrows. "Does Piper know?"

He shook his head, the guilt hitting him. It was a difficult topic to work into conversation.

"Then you need to tell her," she said pursing her lips. "Are you taking her to meet Ka' sa'?"

"She's already met her." He smothered a smile as his cousin's eyes bugged out of her head.

"What?"

"Piper came to the rez as part of the interview she did," Tai reminded her. "She met Ka' sa' then."

"That was before you were seeing her."

"I'm going to ask her to come with me on Sunday," he said. "Then I'm going to her parents' place for dinner."

"Wow. Do they know you're Queche?" she asked.

He shrugged. "I didn't ask." He was hoping it wouldn't be an issue.

"Meeting each other's family is a big step."

He didn't want to consider that too deeply. He changed the subject. "She's organizing a fundraiser for money to build a youth center at the reservation."

Rayen's mouth dropped open. "Did you ask her to?"

"No. I mentioned the youth center last week and she decided to do something about it."

"You should marry her now," Rayen advised, with a grin. "She gets you and I'm not sure even Ada and I get you all the time."

Tai took a step back, his hands up. "Don't get carried away." His heart pounded at the very thought. It wasn't possible. What was Rayen thinking?

She grinned at him. "OK, that's a relief. You're acting normally now." She gave him a hug. "I'm going to do some reading before my shift starts."

After she left he added a couple more notes to his cookbook document and closed it. He had no idea what the going rate was for ghost writing, so he did a quick search and made note of the huge range. It wasn't that he didn't trust Piper to tell him the truth; rather he wanted to make sure she charged enough.

Then, reading a little bit more into it, he wrote up an outline of what he wanted to achieve.

***

"Chef, are you ready?" Kath's voice interrupted his typing.

Tai checked the time and swore. He had a whole lot to do before their first customers arrived. "Of course." He saved his work and followed her into the kitchen, where Kath had already started preparations.

"I really appreciate your help last week," he said. He'd thanked her before but he needed to say it again.

"Don't sweat it. The Spoon is my baby too."

Tai hadn't thought of it that way. Before leaving to open his own restaurant, he'd spoken to Kath and Jared about coming to work with him and they'd both agreed. As soon as he'd set up, they'd given their notice and moved to the Spoon, helping him with the menu and with sourcing the right suppliers. Perhaps she would take over as head chef, or if he branched out to another restaurant, she could be head chef there. There wasn't anyone else he'd trust more. She knew his recipes, knew his style and knew how to treat the staff. He'd have to chat to her about it when they got a minute.

But now, he needed to cook.

***

Piper headed to Eat, Drink, Read. Elle had a stock of cookbooks and Piper wanted to check what was being published.

It had taken her by surprise when Tai asked her to write it for him. Ghost writing wasn't something she'd had any interest in, but if it helped Tai she was happy to. Plus it was income when she desperately needed it.

The cookbook would be a chance for her to learn more about Tai and about his tribe. It was such a great idea to really highlight where the tribe had come from and explain its history.

She didn't think Tai realized how much work he put into the reservation and helping his people: it was just something he did – it was part of who he was. She hoped they recognized and appreciated it.

Elle wasn't at the café, so Piper waved to Nora and grabbed a couple of the cookbooks from the shelves. She took them over to her table and flicked through them, taking notes of what each chef had done, how the pictures were laid out and how much extra information was in them aside from the recipes.

It varied from chef to chef. There were a couple of ideas Piper liked so she wrote them down and recorded where she'd seen the idea. They could twist it somewhat and make it fresh and new.

When she was finished with her notes, she returned the books to the shelves and outlined how she envisioned the book. Tai might have a completely different vision but at least she would have something to present to him.

Then she researched the tricky topic of payment. Tai would insist on paying her and while she appreciated it, she wasn't sure if she was comfortable with it. It felt a little bit like charity. He had only briefly mentioned a recipe book and now that she needed work he was suddenly all enthusiastic about going ahead. But she was unemployed and couldn't afford to let pride get in her way.

Piper checked the hourly rates, read a recommendation that ghost writers should treat each project separately and make sure they had a good understanding of what was involved before quoting, and then the advantages and disadvantages of a per hour or per word rate. When she was finished she had a ballpark figure in her mind that should suit both of them.

Then Piper called Libby. She had only a vague idea of how the publishing industry worked, but Libby would know a lot more.

"I was just going to call. Adrian told me you were laid off. Why didn't you call me?" were Libby's first words when she heard who it was.

Piper winced. "I didn't want to disturb you during your writing day," she said. She realized that was exactly what she was doing now – but it was for Tai, not for herself.

"You know I would stop everything to help you," Libby said.

"Sorry." She did know that. She'd been feeling sorry for herself.

"What are you going to do now? Are there many jobs available?"

"Not a lot. I'm trying to figure it out, but in the meantime, Tai wants me to help him with a cookbook. It's why I called. Do you know how to get them published?"

"It depends on the publisher. Some require you to submit via an agent, which means you need to find an agent first. Though if George spoke up for Tai it might count. I'm sure if he mentioned he was Kent Downer's manager he'd get an audience at least.

"For non-fiction they usually want an outline and maybe a couple of chapters, though for a recipe book it might be a little different. The publisher's website usually tells you what they want. I can ask my editor if you like."

"That would be great."

"So what are you going to do when you've finished the book?" Libby asked.

It was something Piper wasn't ready to think about. "I don't know." Tai's question that morning about whether she really wanted to be a journalist had stumped her. For so many years she'd associated journalism with being able to tell the world about injustice so it could be addressed, but now she stepped back and thought about it, she wasn't so sure.

She'd done nothing of importance at the *Age* and before that hadn't been able to change the world working on a local level. The only thing she was proud of was her blog.

It had been her dream to win an award like the Pulitzer, to be recognized not only as a good journalist but also as a good citizen of the world. Which was incredibly self-absorbed and ridiculous – it didn't matter whether she got recognition, what mattered was she was doing something worthy, and she hadn't done anything worthwhile yet.

"I need to think about it."

"Well, I'm here if you need a sounding board."

Piper smiled. "Thanks. I'll talk to you later." She hung up.

Perhaps the fundraiser would be her start. She would raise so much money Tai would be able to build his youth center. If she became a freelance journalist, she might even be able to help out there regularly. As long as the tribe were happy with a white woman on the reservation. She'd love to be there as someone to talk to. She would have to chat to Tai about it.

***

By the end of the week, Tai and Piper had put together a comprehensive outline for the cookbook. They'd agreed on a price for Piper's work and she had written a proposal to the non-fiction editor at Libby's publisher, who had been excited about the idea.

Piper sat in Tai's office, watching the Friday-night hustle and bustle of the kitchen. It had become a habit over the past few days for her to bring her laptop or a book and spend the evenings with Tai, even if he was mostly working. It was nice to be among the action, something she'd never expected to miss from the paper.

She'd picked up a couple of freelance jobs through contacts and was also working on monetizing her blog. Neither would be an immediate solution to her lack of income, but it was a start, and Tai's project would keep her going for a few more weeks.

Rayen stuck her head into the office. "Hey, Piper, I've got the night off tomorrow. Do you want to come to Adahy's concert with me?"

Despite Tai's cousin being six years younger than Piper, they'd struck up an easy friendship. Rayen often took Piper's car when Tai went to her apartment.

"Sure." She needed to make an effort to get out. She was in danger of becoming a complete hermit. She'd only been at the restaurant or her apartment all week.

"Great. Why don't we meet here at six? Tai can make us dinner before we go." She grinned.

"Sounds good." Tai wouldn't mind. He and Rayen were as close as siblings and he had a thing about making sure they both got fed.

Rayen left and Tai ducked his head in. "What are you two planning?"

"We're going to Adahy's concert tomorrow night."

"Oh good. I was worried she'd want to go alone."

"Doesn't she have any friends?"

"She's got a few but none of them were free." He checked over his shoulder and then came closer. "After the concert, why don't you stay at my place? That way we can head to the rez early."

A little thrill went through Piper. It was the first time he'd invited her to his house. "Sure."

He bent his head and kissed her. Piper closed her eyes and savored it. He tasted like the barbeque sauce that went on their special ribs, one of her favorite meals. "Yum."

He grinned. "I'd better get back to work."

Piper watched him go, her heart beating faster than it should. There was something about the man that made her jittery, that made her want, that made her love.

She frowned.

Why the hell had love entered her thoughts?

She'd only known Tai a few weeks. That wasn't enough time to fall in love. She had to be mistaken. Just caught up in the idea of being in a relationship like the rest of her friends.

She shook her head.

The idea would disappear soon enough.

***

On Saturday night Piper took her time getting ready. The club Adahy was playing at was dressier than normal so she wore a black skirt that ended mid-thigh and a red shimmery top. To finish the outfit she wore a pair of earrings that dangled to her jawline and a black pair of stilettos she only wore on special occasions.

She arrived at the restaurant a little earlier, hoping to catch Tai before he got too busy. She'd become a regular face in the kitchen and so no one minded when she used the back door. Once inside, she greeted Jared as she searched for Tai.

Jared whistled. "Well, don't you clean up real nice?" he said, giving her the once over.

Piper laughed. "Thanks."

Tai was on the other side of the kitchen, showing one of his apprentices how to flip food in a fry pan. Piper stayed where she was, out of the way. The kitchen had its delicate dance and she wasn't going to mess it up.

Tai instructed the boy, demonstrated what he meant and then handed the fry pan to the apprentice. The apprentice tried and failed, slopping food all over the stove. He turned to Tai apologetically. Tai smiled, handed him another fry pan and told him to try again.

The third time it happened it was obvious the apprentice was getting more nervous. Tai put his hand over the kid's and showed him what he meant. The food flipped properly and the apprentice beamed. Then Tai let go of the pan and the boy did it by himself, whooping when he succeeded.

It was one of Tai's gifts. He was so incredibly patient with his staff. He didn't get angry: he just demonstrated what he meant again.

Tai clapped the boy on the back and turned. His eyes met Piper's and even across the room she saw them darken. The way he walked toward her, slow and stalking, his eyes never leaving hers, made her body heat.

He stopped only inches away from her. "I've never seen you in high heels before," he said, his voice smoky.

She glanced up at him through her eyelashes, pretending to be coy. "Do you like it?"

"I do." He ran a hand down her arm before grabbing her hand, and pulling her into a storage room.

Heart beating wildly, Piper found herself pushed up against some boxes.

Then his mouth was on hers.

Fierce, hot longing swept through her as his mouth plundered hers and his hands slid up her shirt, caressing her breasts. Her body was going to erupt, so intense was the heat.

"Chef! Chef!" a voice called – the sound vaguely entered the periphery of Piper's consciousness.

"I think you're wanted," she managed to say.

"I *know* you're wanted," Tai answered and kissed her again.

The temptation to ignore the call was strong but Piper placed a hand on his chest and forced herself to push him away rather than pull him closer like she wanted to.

He stopped kissing her and frowned.

"Someone's calling you," she said. Though her heart was still beating rapidly, she looked around and found some paper towels. She wiped his lips, which were now covered in the lipstick she wore.

"Chef!"

Tai swore. "Don't move." He strode out of the store room.

Piper's heart rate slowed and she used the opportunity to straighten her top and pat down her hair. If Tai had been wearing half her lipstick, she must look a mess. She dug into her clutch bag for the little compact mirror and pulled out her lipstick. She fixed her lips and checked the rest of her appearance. It was good enough for her to leave the room and find a mirror in the ladies' bathroom to check the rest of the damage.

As she walked out, Tai was deep in conversation with two of the line chefs. The conversation was very heated on one side. He saw her leave the room and scowled at the men who were talking. They shut up.

Piper smiled. She'd forgotten what pissed-off Tai looked like. She ducked into the bathroom. The damage wasn't so bad – once she'd brushed her hair back into place and adjusted her skirt a little more, she was entirely presentable.

She walked out into the kitchen as Rayen arrived. Her friend waved and walked over to her.

"You look gorgeous," Piper said. She'd not seen the younger woman out of her waitress uniform before. Rayen wore a gold strappy top and a deep blue handkerchief skirt that ended at her knees. The heels she wore didn't quite rival Piper's in height but gave her another inch and a half. Her long brown hair was in a messy pile on top of her head. It must have taken her hours to style it like that.

"Thanks. I don't get a chance to go out much, so when I do, I make the effort. I love your earrings."

Tai finished talking with his line chefs and walked over. He greeted his cousin and murmured in Piper's ear, "You were meant to wait."

His breath made her shivery.

"You stop that," Rayen said. "Piper's mine tonight. You can

have her back when we get home."

He glanced at her and then back to Piper. "I'll look forward to it." It was a promise of so much more to come.

Piper wished the night was already at an end.

"I've reserved a table in the restaurant for you," Tai said as he took a step back.

"You didn't have to," Rayen said. "We can eat in the kitchen."

"You're having a night out. You deserve to be spoilt. Order whatever you want on the menu."

Rayen beamed at him and kissed his cheek. "Thanks, Tai." She moved toward the restaurant.

"Take care of her tonight," Tai said to Piper. "And take care of yourself."

"We'll both be fine, don't worry." Piper kissed him. "Thank you for dinner." She walked out into the dining area.

"This is great," Rayen said as she sat at the table Tai had reserved for them. "I've never eaten out here before." She ran her hands over the tablecloth.

"Haven't you asked Tai if you could?"

Rayen shrugged. "No. I'm usually working and I need the money more than I need a night out. Besides, in the kitchen I can wear what I want. It takes hours to look this good." She grinned.

Piper looked around the restaurant. It was still relatively early so they had their waiter's undivided attention. He was a young guy called Lance and he seemed sweet. After he took their drinks order, she turned to Rayen.

"He's cute," she said.

Rayen blushed. "He's so nice as well."

"Why don't you ask him out?"

Rayen gaped at her. "If he said no it would be awful. I'd still have to work with him every day."

"But if he said yes, you'd get to see him all the time."

Rayen shook her head. "It's too much of a risk, plus we never have the same day off."

"I'm sure if you had a word with Kath she could arrange it," Piper said.

Lance came back with their drink order. "Cocktails for the

beautiful women." He winked at Rayen as he placed her glass in front of her.

She blushed. "Thank you."

"You're *more* than welcome." He left.

"He was totally flirting with you," Piper said, and grinned as Rayen's eyes widened and she glanced at Lance who was taking a new table's order. "No, he wasn't. He's like that with all the women he serves."

Piper was pretty sure it was more than that, but it wasn't her place to say any more. It *would* be awkward if they broke up later and had to work together.

She changed the subject. "Has college started yet?"

"I've got a couple of workshops to attend next week and then it will start full-time."

"You're doing elementary school teaching, aren't you?"

"Yes. I'm hoping if I can interest children in learning early, they'll continue as they get older. We get so many drop-outs on the rez."

"So you plan to teach on the reservation?"

"Of course." She said it as if it were a given.

Lance came over to take their food order then while they were waiting for dinner Rayen and Piper chatted about all sorts of things. Piper enjoyed getting to know Tai's cousin. She was as proud of her heritage as Tai was and as determined to help her people.

"You and Tai have the same morals. Eyota must have taught her children well," Piper said.

Rayen narrowed her eyes. "Ka' sa' taught us well," she said. "She didn't have so much success with our fathers."

Piper hadn't spoken to Tai about his parents and was a little hesitant to ask Rayen. It was Tai who should be telling her.

"I'm told my father was a great member of the community until Uncle Derek died. Then he took comfort in the bottle. That was the only side I saw of him growing up. He's getting better now."

Piper stopped with the fork halfway to her mouth. "How many children does Eyota have?"

"Two."

Piper put her fork back onto the plate. "Tai's father is

dead?"

Rayen's eyes widened. "I thought you knew."

She shook her head. "How did he die?"

"You should ask him about it," Rayen said, pursing her lips together.

She wasn't going to say. Piper didn't mind. She was right. She changed the subject but it stayed in her thoughts. There was a lot she didn't know about this man.

***

The concert was being held in a classy, dimly lit nightclub. There was a huge dance floor in front of the stage with a few discreet booths and tables to the sides. Most of them were full except for the table reserved for George. The music was loud.

"I'll buy you a drink," Piper said as they approached the bar. "What do you want?"

Rayen named her drink and waited next to Piper as she ordered.

"Hey, Pocahontas. I'll be your John Smith." The voice came from the other side of Rayen and Piper turned as a Hispanic man ran his hand over Rayen's shoulder.

She shrugged him off, but didn't turn.

"Come on now, baby. Don't play hard to get."

Rayen's face set hard, staring straight ahead.

Piper leaned over and said, "Get lost."

"Don't be jealous, sweetheart. There's enough of this to share." He pointed to himself. "The three of us can have some fun."

She couldn't tell whether he'd been drinking or if he was just an egotistical asshole. Either way it didn't matter. "Not in this lifetime," she told him, and handed Rayen's drink to her. Then she let the younger woman walk ahead to where George's table was. She ignored the quick butt squeeze she received when she turned her back on the jerk. It was tempting to throw her drink in his face, but she didn't want to waste it or cause a scene. The quicker they got away from him the better.

Rayen reached the table first and took a seat. As Piper arrived a staff member was saying to her, "You can't sit there. It's reserved."

Rayen glanced at Piper.

"This table is reserved for George Jones, isn't it?" Piper asked.

The guy nodded.

"We're George's guests, Piper and Rayen. You can check with him if you like."

The guy looked at the two of them and then backed off. "I will."

"I'm glad you're here," Rayen said. "He would have kicked me off no matter what I said."

"That's not true," Piper said, hoping she was right. "He backed down when we mentioned George's name."

Rayen looked at her with pity. "If I had said that, he would have told me to stand somewhere else until George arrived."

Piper didn't know what to say. She had no experience with racist behavior before, but it was obvious Rayen had. And there was Piper thinking they were living in the twenty-first century.

They sat listening to the music until Adahy was introduced. The crowd applauded loudly as Adahy hit the stage. A few minutes later George joined them.

"Ladies, you both look gorgeous tonight. I'm glad you could make it."

George was one of Piper's favorite people.

Rayen blushed. "Thanks for letting us sit at your table."

"Any time," he said.

They listened to a couple of songs before Rayen said, "I love this one. Do you want to dance?"

"Sure." Piper got to her feet and followed her onto the dance floor. She hadn't been dancing for months and she closed her eyes, getting into the rhythm of the music. Adahy certainly had great beats. The music was easy to dance to and made her want to move her body.

Opening her eyes again she noticed the Hispanic guy from earlier spot them and dance his way over.

Piper groaned.

Why did some people not know when to give up?

Before Piper could warn her friend, he was behind her, grinding up against her back. Rayen turned, saw who it was and moved away.

Piper glared at him, but he paid no notice, instead following Rayen around the dance floor. Rayen yelled at him to go away but he stuck close. In the end they both returned to the table.

Rayen's face was troubled.

Piper squeezed her hand. "I can ask the bouncer to have a word to him."

"There's no point," Rayen said. "Let's just listen to Ada."

Piper was upset for her friend. She had a right to dance unmolested and that jerk was ruining it for her.

George ordered them more drinks. He hadn't seen what had happened; he'd been watching Adahy's performance.

A few songs later Rayen stood. "I'm going to the bathroom."

"Do you want me to come?" Piper asked.

Rayen shook her head. "No, I'll be fine."

Piper watched her walk through the crowd toward the bathrooms, then she noticed the Hispanic guy follow her. Her instincts went on high alert. She stood. "I'll be right back," she said to George.

Going through the dance floor was the most direct route but it was crowded. Piper pushed her way through, yelling apologies as she did. It took forever to reach the other side and she checked the signs for the direction to the bathroom.

It was down a corridor. The women's bathroom had a short line outside it but Rayen wasn't there. Piper pushed into the room and called her name but she didn't answer.

Worry hit Piper in her stomach.

Where was Rayen?

She moved to the men's bathroom, calling her friend. A man came out of the room.

"Can you check if my friend Rayen is in there?" She might have been desperate for the toilet.

The man shrugged and went into the room, calling Rayen's name. He came back a moment later, shaking his head.

Had Piper missed her as she came off the dance floor? Perhaps Rayen had spotted someone she knew and was talking. Piper hurried down the corridor past an offshoot hallway with an emergency exit sign on its wall. There was a crack of light coming from the doorway.

Without hesitation, Piper turned that way.

Chapter 12

Piper turned down the corridor, her heart beating rapidly, and pushed through the door out into the alleyway. "Rayen!"

"Help!"

Piper's heart leaped to her mouth as she turned and saw Rayen against the wall. The bastard who had followed her had his hand up her shirt and she was struggling to push him away, sobbing.

Fear and rage intermingled in Piper and her reaction was instant. She ran to the guy, grabbed the back of his hair and yanked him back, kicking him in the back of one knee as she did so. Rayen pushed him too, and he lost his balance and fell backward onto the ground.

Piper pressed her stiletto against his windpipe. "Move and I'll break it," she growled. Her heart pounded in her chest and her breath came in gasps.

The guy swore and struggled.

She pushed her shoe harder against his throat. "Just try me," she dared, almost not recognizing the flat, cold voice that came out of her mouth. She wanted to hurt him.

The guy's eyes widened and he stopped struggling.

"Are you OK?" Piper called to Rayen.

Her friend was slumped down against the wall, hugging her knees and crying. Piper wanted to go over and put her arms around the girl, but she wasn't letting this asshole get away.

Piper pulled her cell out of the clutch purse hanging over her shoulder and called George. It would be a miracle if he heard his phone in there. She huffed out a breath when he answered.

"What's wrong?" George asked.

"I need you to go out the emergency exit near the bathroom," Piper said. "I need your help."

"Be right there."

That's what Piper loved about George. He didn't ask any unnecessary questions. She hung up and called the local police station. She had it on speed dial from when she'd worked at the local paper in this area. She recognized the voice of the guy who picked up.

"Piper, I haven't heard from you since you left the paper."

"Chuck, can you send a police car to Whitewash? Alleyway down the side: there's been a sexual assault."

"You OK?" he asked.

"Yeah, but my friend isn't."

"Should be one there in five."

Rayen was staring at the ground. Piper hoped George would hurry up.

George exited the nightclub, took one look at the situation and swore. "What the hell?"

"This guy forced himself on Rayen," Piper said. "I've called the cops."

George glanced at Rayen and then at Piper. "Let me take over," he said and hauled the guy to his feet, throwing him against the wall. The guy slid down to the ground, no fight left, and George stood over him.

Piper rushed to Rayen and pulled her into her arms. "I'm sorry, sweetheart. I should have been faster."

Rayen clung to her and pushed her head into Piper's chest.

Now the danger was over, Piper's heart rate returned to normal and the guilt flooded in. She should have gone to the bathroom with Rayen. That guy had been bothering them all night.

She could have stopped this from ever happening.

Rayen shuddered as the police car pulled up in front of the alleyway and the officers jogged down. The creep wasn't going to get away. Piper kept her arms around Rayen and let George explain what he knew of the situation.

The officers cuffed the guy.

"That bitch is crazy. She tried to kill me. She said she'd break my wind pipe," the guy cried.

"Well, if you'd assaulted one of my girls, I would have done a hell of a lot worse," one of the officers said.

The guy paled. "I didn't do it. She wanted it."

One of the officers read him his rights and took him to the police car while the other took down their details.

"We're going to need statements from y'all. Do you want to come down to the station?"

Rayen hadn't said a word.

"I'll take Rayen down," Piper said.

"I need to tell Adahy," George said. He checked his watch. "He should be almost finished. We'll be there after."

The police officer nodded.

Piper helped Rayen to her feet. She didn't resist, but walked silently next to Piper as they were accompanied by the officer out of the alley and to their car.

Worry washed through Piper. She needed to get Rayen to talk.

On the drive over to the police station, Piper said, "Do you want to tell me what happened?"

Rayen shook her head.

Piper was at a loss as to what to say or do.

She pulled up in front of the station and together they walked in. Chuck was at the front desk.

Piper gave him a small smile. "We need to make statements."

Chuck came around the desk and escorted them into a small room. "Can I get you a crappy coffee?" he asked.

Piper glanced at Rayen. "Maybe a couple of glasses of water."

"Sure."

A few minutes later a female police officer entered the room, carrying the glasses of water. "We need to take your statements separately," she said with an apology.

"Can we wait until Rayen's cousin arrives?" Piper asked. "I

don't want to leave her by herself." Piper's phone beeped and the text from George said, *On our way.* "They won't be long."

"Sure. When we're done here, we'll take Rayen to a doctor," the woman said. "She'll need to be examined and we'll need to take photos of any damage."

"He didn't rape me," Rayen said. "Piper stopped him in time." She shuddered.

"That's good, but there might still be some bruises we need to record. There are other types of sexual assault and they can have as much of an effect on their victims," the officer said.

The door opened and Adahy rushed in. He'd come straight from the stage.

"Little flower, are you all right?" He wrapped Rayen up in a hug and she started crying again. She clung to her cousin.

"How about you take my statement first?" Piper suggested. It would give Rayen more time to work through her emotions.

"All right." The officer took Piper through to another room.

Piper spoke about the evening, starting with the pick-up line at the bar and ending with her discovering Rayen in the alleyway. The officer recorded the interview but took notes as well, asking questions, going over points until she was satisfied. "I'll get this typed up and you can sign it. It's good you were taking care of your friend."

It was then Piper remembered Tai. She'd promised to look after Rayen and this had happened. She should have called him immediately but she'd been too concerned about Rayen to remember. Some girlfriend she was.

She left the room and saw George in the corridor. "I need to call Tai."

"Adahy did. He's on his way," George told her.

Piper was relieved, but she wasn't looking forward to explaining how she hadn't been able to care for his cousin like she'd promised.

She closed her eyes. She should have listened to her instincts earlier.

The officer went into the room with Adahy and Rayen. A minute later Adahy came out.

"Rayen wants Piper in the room with her," he said.

Piper walked in, not sure whether she was supposed to be

there.

"We have your statement now," the officer said when she asked. "And Rayen wanted you here rather than her cousin."

Piper sat next to Rayen and squeezed her hand.

Rayen began slowly. Explaining how the guy had approached her, then danced too closely next to her, and wouldn't take no for an answer. "He said he'd had women of all different races but he'd never had an Indian before," she said.

Piper felt sick.

"I went to the bathroom, but before I got there, he grabbed me and dragged me down the corridor. I yelled but either the music was too loud or people didn't want to help. He pushed me up against the wall in the alleyway and kissed me. He tasted like alcohol and cigarettes.

"I tried to push him away but he was too strong. He groped my breasts so hard it hurt, and then he shoved his hand up my shirt ..." Rayen squeezed her eyes shut as if willing the image away. "That's when Piper came out, grabbed him by his hair and threw him to the floor." She looked at Piper then. "How did you do that?"

"Mom insisted Imogen and I took self-defense lessons before we were allowed to go out at night," Piper said. She would thank her mother for it at dinner tomorrow.

"Your mother's a smart lady," the officer said. "Then what happened?"

"Piper put her foot on his throat so he wouldn't get away, and rang for help. I'm not really sure what happened after that."

The officer took Rayen through her story, asked more questions and got her to repeat what the guy had said. When the officer was satisfied, she explained they needed to go to the local hospital to have a doctor examine Rayen, and then let them leave.

Outside the room Adahy, George and Tai waited.

Piper's steps faltered. She wasn't ready to face Tai yet. Bracing herself she met his eyes, expecting accusations, but all she saw was relief. He swept Rayen up in his arms after checking her over and she clung to him for a moment.

"I'm OK," Rayen said.

She was calmer than she'd been earlier. Maybe talking about

it had helped. Adahy put his arm around her and led her to a chair.

George entered the room to give his statement.

Tai turned to Piper. "What about you?"

Piper wrapped her arms around herself. "I'm fine. I should have got there sooner." She shouldn't have let Rayen go to the bathroom by herself.

"Hey. It's not your fault that asshole tried something," Tai said.

"He'd been bugging us all night. I should have known." If she'd been quicker she could have stopped him from dragging Rayen outside. If she'd gone with her in the first place, he wouldn't have tried anything.

"You can't blame yourself." Tai pulled her into a hug.

Tears pricked Piper's eyes as the composure she'd been holding on to crumbled.

When she'd pressed her foot on the guy's windpipe, she'd been so angry she really could have killed him, and the idea terrified her now.

"It's all right," Tai soothed. "You're both OK."

He rubbed her back and she focused on the sensation. It was silly to be so upset. She wasn't the one who had been assaulted.

George came out of the interview room with the police officer. "Can we leave now?" he asked.

The woman nodded. "Rayen needs to go to the hospital. There's a doctor waiting to examine her and take the necessary photos."

"Do you want me to take you?" Piper asked.

Rayen nodded.

"We'll come as well," Tai said, speaking for himself and Adahy. The guys weren't going to let Rayen out of their sights for a while.

"I'll head home, if you don't need me," George said.

Piper hugged him. "Thank you for coming so quickly."

"Any time. You call me if I can do anything."

Tai and Adahy hugged him as well, and Rayen smiled shyly.

***

It was very early morning by the time they all got back to Tai's house. Both Adahy and Tai fussed around Rayen, making her a hot drink and tucking her into bed. Piper waited in the kitchen, not wanting to get in the way, but she could hear Adahy was crooning what sounded like a traditional lullaby.

She sipped her tea and looked around the kitchen. She'd been excited about visiting Tai's house before everything had gone wrong and now it didn't seem so important. It was a family kitchen, much like the house was a family house. It was large and had all the mod cons she'd expect a chef's kitchen to have. The dining table was fit for a banquet, with long bench chairs – it was big enough to seat at least twelve. Did he entertain here often?

He lived much further away from the restaurant than she'd expected. It was on the outskirts of Houston in an area where the blocks were big and the neighbors weren't close. She wanted to wander through the house and get a feel for who Tai was when he was home, but it wasn't an appropriate time.

So she sat and sipped her drink and considered how differently the night could have turned out if she'd acted sooner. If she'd insisted on telling the bouncer the guy was bothering them, or if she'd accompanied Rayen to the bathroom, or if she'd squashed the guy's windpipe. Her mind was a crazy, nasty loop of what ifs and her skin was tight.

Tai came into the room. "She's asleep now."

Relief swept through her.

He held out his hand. "Let's go to bed."

Making an effort to block her thoughts, Piper took the hand he offered and followed him through the house to the master bedroom with its adjoining bathroom. They showered together and then climbed into bed. Piper was too tired to pay any attention to what the room looked like.

Tai pulled her close to him. "Thank you for being there for Rayen."

Piper didn't want his thanks. She didn't deserve it, but she drew comfort from his arms.

It was long after Tai's steady breathing indicated he was asleep that sleep finally claimed Piper.

***

When the alarm screeched them awake, Piper felt as though she'd just shut her eyes. It took her a second to place where she was and to remember what had happened the night before. She squeezed her eyes shut, hoping it was all a dream.

Tai stirred next to her, ran a hand over her hip and pulled her close. "Morning," he said, kissing her neck.

"Is it really?" Piper asked. "Can't we wind back the clock a few hours and pretend it's not?"

He chuckled. "I wish we could. It'll take an hour or so to get to the rez. I'll drive and you can sleep in the car."

It was hardly fair. He'd worked all night and then come to the police station. He'd barely had any sleep himself. She forced herself out of bed and padded to the shower. What she needed was hot water and then a strong coffee and she'd be all right.

Hopefully.

When they went out to the kitchen they found freshly brewed coffee and Adahy and Rayen sitting out on the back porch, chatting.

"What are you two doing up?" Tai asked as he and Piper joined them. Piper clung to her mug, worried about their reaction. Would they blame her today for what had happened?

"We thought we'd come to the rez," Adahy said.

Piper looked at Rayen. She appeared rested. She hoped she'd slept deeply. When the girl glanced at Piper, she surveyed the backyard, not ready to face her yet.

It was a large space with tall trees and shrubs that blocked the neighbors' view. Birds flitted back and forth, calling out their morning song. Piper took a deep breath in and let it out. She understood why Tai lived here. It was just far enough away from the city that he'd be able to relax and not have to listen to the constant sound of traffic.

He'd brought some of the peace of the reservation with him.

"Great. Why don't we take your car?" Tai suggested to Adahy. "It's bigger than Piper's."

"Sure." Adahy glanced at his brother. "Now, we've been sitting here waiting for our breakfast, and I don't see you at the stove. Rayen wants pancakes." He was teasing, as if it were a long-standing joke.

"With maple syrup and berries," Rayen added.

Tai laughed as he got to his feet. "Who made you king?"

"I did," Rayen joked.

Piper was glad Rayen was up to joking. She must be feeling a little better.

Not wanting to be alone with them, Piper followed Tai inside. "Can I help with anything?" she asked.

He already had all the ingredients out and was measuring the flour.

"I've seen your kitchen. It's best if you just sit down and keep me company."

Piper stuck her tongue out at him to keep the mood light. Perhaps it was the lack of sleep but she couldn't find any positivity and enthusiasm. She wanted to go back to bed and curl up in a ball and pretend last night hadn't happened. She'd been so stupid.

Tai added a pinch of something to the batter and stirred, before adding a pinch more. His focus was absolute. She doubted he'd hear her if she spoke. He nodded in satisfaction and stopped stirring. Turning, he lit the stove and placed a fry pan on top.

He was so confident with his movements, so sure of what he was doing – he didn't hesitate. Everything flowed like clockwork.

The smell of cooked pancakes wafted in the air, bringing back memories of her childhood and sitting at the kitchen table watching her father make a batch. She smiled. Tai dished up two, drizzled them with maple syrup and topped them with berry compote. He poured more batter in the pan and presented the plate to Piper. "Bon appétit."

"Thanks." She wasn't hungry, but the smell was enticing. She bit into the first pancake and flavor burst on her tongue. She closed her eyes and allowed herself to enjoy. It was impossible not to.

"I love watching you eat," Tai said and she opened her eyes. He was staring at her, his eyes dark. "You get such enjoyment out of it."

"It's your cooking," she said. "It has to be savored."

He beamed at her and dished up the next serve. "Breakfast's ready," he called outside.

Rayen was first inside. She grabbed the plate and sat down next to Piper. "Yum."

Piper gave her a small smile.

Adahy grumbled, but made a second cup of coffee while waiting for his.

When they were all seated around the table there was little conversation. Everyone was too busy eating to talk.

Piper was relieved. She didn't know what to say about the night before, didn't know the best way to apologize for not being there. They finished, and she helped Tai clean up while Rayen and Adahy got their things together.

During the drive to the reservation, Piper slept. She hadn't meant to but somehow she closed her eyes for a second and then they were pulling into Eyota's driveway. She was glad Adahy and Rayen were there to keep Tai company. She couldn't figure out how none of them were as tired as she was.

Piper hung back while they greeted their grandmother, who was thrilled by Adahy and Rayen's visit.

"Ka' sa', you remember Piper," Tai said when they'd finished hugging.

"Of course."

"Piper's Tai's girlfriend," Rayen said in a singsong voice.

Piper's face burned. "It's lovely to see you again," she said, not sure if she should shake her hand.

Eyota came over and hugged her. "Likewise."

The children who had been there the last time came out and greeted everyone. Bradley was there, but he hung back from the others.

"Time for class," Tai called and gestured to the pickup. The kids all clambered up. "You coming?" he asked Adahy and Rayen.

"I might steal Piper for an hour," Rayen said. "Show her around a bit."

Nerves fluttered in Piper's stomach but she nodded her assent. Maybe Rayen wanted to talk about last night.

"There's food on offer, so I'll come," Adahy said. "Ka' sa', are you coming?"

Eyota shook her head. "I'll be down later. There are a couple of things I need to do here."

Tai walked over to Piper. "Come by the school at midday. I'll save you a plate." He kissed her.

One of the children in the pickup said, "Tai kissed the white girl." A lot of murmuring ensued.

It hadn't occurred to her that her skin color might cause an issue for Tai.

Tai turned and called, "I kissed my girlfriend." He grinned at her and left.

Piper clutched her hands together, not sure what to say to either woman.

"I'll show you the lake," Rayen said.

"Not before you have a cup of tea and tell me why you came today," Eyota said, looping her arm around her granddaughter.

"We wanted to visit," Rayen said.

"That's one reason," Eyota agreed. "But there's another. The only time the three of you come together is if something's gone wrong."

Rayen glanced at Piper.

As far as Piper was concerned it was up to Rayen to tell her grandmother if she wanted to.

"Come inside," Eyota said.

They sat at the kitchen table while Eyota made tea and then joined them. "What happened?"

Rayen sighed. "Piper and I went out last night to watch Adahy play. While we were there, a man groped me, but Piper stopped him from going too far."

Eyota's eyes narrowed. "Define grope."

Piper had to give Eyota credit for reading between the lines.

Rayen closed her eyes. "He dragged me into an alleyway, squeezed my breasts and put his hand up my shirt."

Eyota's mouth dropped open and then she placed her hand over Rayen's. "My baby girl. Are you all right?"

Rayen nodded. "I am. I'm better than I expected, because it could have been a lot worse. Piper's not coping as well."

Piper's breath hitched and she stared at Rayen. How could

the girl be worried about her when *she* had been assaulted? It didn't matter how Piper was feeling.

"She blames herself for not preventing it."

Eyota turned to Piper. "Bradley feels the same way about Jerry."

They were two entirely different situations. "There was nothing Bradley could do," Piper said. "Jerry was depressed and he was determined."

"It sounds as if this man was determined as well," Eyota said.

Piper shook her head. How could she even compare them? "If I'd stayed with Rayen he wouldn't have had the chance."

"Maybe not this time, but perhaps the next time he saw her in a club with less thoughtful friends."

Logically Piper understood what Eyota was saying, but emotionally it was much harder. She'd promised Tai she would take care of Rayen.

"I want to organize self-defense classes at the school," Rayen said. "All the girls should be able to defend themselves like Piper did. If I'd known some moves, perhaps I could have escaped him on my own."

Piper hadn't thought about it, she'd just reacted, but she couldn't deny the classes had helped.

"Good idea," Eyota said. "Let me know when you find an instructor. The tribal council might be able to pay for it." She gathered up the empty teacups. "Why don't you go to the lake now?"

Rayen excused herself to go to the bathroom.

Eyota smiled at Piper. "My babies always stick close to each other after a bad experience," she said. "It's how I know something has happened. It makes me so happy they have each other."

"You raised them all, didn't you?" Piper said, remembering what Rayen had told her.

"Yes."

"You should be proud. They're all wonderful people."

She patted Piper's hand. "And you're a lovely woman. Now go to the lake and find your peace."

***

Together Rayen and Piper walked through the forest to the lake that lay in the center of the reservation.

"The camp grounds are over there." Rayen pointed to the other side of the lake. "Others are allowed to camp with a permit and we get people through in summer. Not so many now school is going back."

"Is that how the tribe gets an income?"

"One of the ways," Rayen answered. "I come here a lot when I need to think," she said. "It's quiet and I wander along the shore or go for a swim. I need a swim today." She stripped off to her swimsuit. "There's a shady spot through there you might like. It's peaceful."

Rayen waded into the water and then dived in, using long strong strokes to swim out into the center of the lake.

Perhaps Rayen was right. Perhaps she needed to find some peace. She walked along the shore, keeping an eye on her friend until she stopped swimming and turned over to float on her back.

Finding the spot Rayen had pointed out, Piper sat down. She closed her eyes and focused on her breathing. She was still so tired from the night before that her brain didn't want to think, so she fell into the breathing rhythm easily.

Piper wasn't ready to go over the attack yet, so she let her thoughts drift.

She liked Rayen's idea of getting a self-defense teacher, liked that Rayen was doing something to fight back against her assault, liked that she was trying to help others too. She was a strong woman.

When Piper considered her own life, she realized she didn't spend any time actually helping people, even though that was what she'd got into journalism for. Instead she'd been caught up in the day-to-day grind of finding the next story.

And her dreams had gone on the back burner.

When she'd helped Libby plan her wedding and helped Imogen renovate her house, she'd felt so invigorated. It had been amazing to work with her friends to achieve what they wanted. And she'd felt awful when she hadn't been there to clean up Elle's café.

Maybe Tai was right. Maybe she should find a job where she could help people directly. It had to be more rewarding than her job with the *Age* had been.

She could still write articles, continue her blog, maybe even use it as a way of promoting social justice and charity. If she went to freelance journalism she could pick her jobs, make sure she had time to do the type of charity work she would enjoy. The colleagues she'd spoken to made a good income with their freelance work.

The idea stirred her blood. She could expand her blog community, encourage others to work for a better world, lead by example and write the type of stories she wanted. She wouldn't have to worry about being edited or censored because some newspaper tycoon didn't agree with her views: it was her chance to say what she wanted to.

Some twigs cracked nearby and she opened her eyes.

Bradley stood in front of her, staring, tears on his cheeks. He turned to go.

"Wait." Piper didn't want to get in his way. "I'm sorry. Is this your place?"

He hesitated, wiping the tears from his face, and then nodded.

"I can leave if you like."

"What are you doing here?"

"Rayen and I came down to think. She went for a swim." Piper scanned the lake and saw her still floating lazily in the water.

"What do you need to think about?"

"Lots," Piper said. "I've lost my job, so I need to decide what I want to do next in my life." She debated telling Bradley about the attack and then remembered what Eyota had said about Bradley blaming himself. "Then last night, Rayen and I went to watch Adahy perform and she was attacked by someone."

Bradley's eyes widened.

"It was scary and I blame myself because I said I'd look after her and she got hurt." The admission still stung, but after her conversation with Rayen and Eyota, it was less painful.

"What happened?" he asked, coming over and sitting next to her.

Piper didn't want to go into detail. Bradley was too young. "There was a man who kept bothering Rayen and when she went to the bathroom, he dragged her outside. I should have gone with her."

Bradley frowned. "She should be safe going to the bathroom by herself. It was inside, right? And there were lots of people around?"

Piper nodded. "But I knew the man had been bothering her all night."

"So Rayen got away though?"

"I saw the man follow her and I stopped him."

"Wow. That's neat."

It wasn't. "I should have been quicker, then she wouldn't have been hurt at all."

Bradley was silent for a long moment. "It's the same with me and my grandpa," he said.

How much should she admit to knowing? Finally she asked, "What happened?"

"My grandpa wasn't well. He had depression." Bradley looked at her to see if she understood what that was.

Piper nodded. "I'm sorry to hear that."

"I thought if I was really good and told him I loved him every day, then he'd get better, he'd be happy."

"Depression doesn't work like that," she said, gently. "It's not that simple."

He shrugged. "I had to try." He was silent for a long moment. "He was really sad one day and I didn't want to go to school, but he made me. I was so worried that I came home early to talk with his counselor and instead I found this note." He screwed up his face as if he didn't want to say anything else. "I followed his directions and found him in a clearing, but I couldn't wake him up and there was blood everywhere." Tears streamed down his face. "I shouldn't have gone to school. I shouldn't have left him."

Piper's heart broke for the little boy. "I think if you'd stayed, he would have chosen a different day," she said. "The illness took over and there was nothing you could do to stop it. Just like I … I couldn't stop that man from attacking Rayen."

"But if he really loved me, he wouldn't have done it," Bradley whispered.

"That's not true," Piper said, putting her arm around him and pulling him closer. He leaned in to her. "I'm sure he loved you very much, but the illness didn't let him think straight, it kept his mind clouded and occupied with other thoughts."

"Now I have no one," he said, sobbing.

"You have Eyota and Tai." She paused, not sure of his friends' names. "And you've got me."

He blinked at her. "You?"

"I'd like to be your friend, if you'll have me," she said.

He squinted at her, assessing, and must have seen she meant it: he threw his arms around her and hugged her.

She closed her eyes and her chest hitched. This poor little boy was so fragile and in so much pain. She wanted to take it all away from him.

Letting out a shaky breath and squeezing back the tears, she opened her eyes.

And saw Tai staring at her from across the clearing.

Chapter 13

Tai had finished the cooking class and neither Rayen nor Piper had arrived for lunch. When Eyota had told him they had gone to the lake, he'd walked down.

The last thing he'd expected to see was Piper holding a crying Bradley in her lap. The way she comforted the boy and held him tight hit him right in the heart.

What would it be like if the boy she was holding was their own?

The idea rattled him. He shook his head. It wasn't a possibility. Not with the tribal laws. He pushed it away and focused on what was happening now.

Eyota had said Bradley hadn't cried since the funeral. Wouldn't speak about what had happened to anyone. She'd been worried and wanted Tai to talk to the boy today.

But Bradley had found his own confidant.

Piper opened her eyes. He saw the surprise and her tears.

His heart swelled.

Not wanting to interrupt the moment, he put a finger over his lips and moved away. He would wait until they came out, wait until Bradley had finished crying and talking, and then he would show himself.

In the meantime he had to get his heart under control. He walked along the shore, noting that Rayen had begun to swim back. He shouldn't be thinking about children and Piper in the same sentence. Sure, their relationship had progressed quickly, but they weren't at that stage. They could never be at that stage.

It was just that she'd had Bradley in her lap and it was such a nurturing image that of course he'd seen her as a mother figure.

But only temporarily.

Piper might have become a part of his day and he enjoyed the anticipation of seeing her, but that was normal in a new relationship. But it was still casual. He barely knew anything about her family or her childhood, and they had only touched on her reasons behind becoming a journalist.

Sure, there was the way his body reacted to her.

Last night was the first time he'd seen her in a skirt and stilettos. He smiled as he remembered how his blood pressure had skyrocketed, and how he'd dragged her off to ravage her.

He'd never felt that level of intensity for anyone before. He wanted to know *everything* about her.

No. That wasn't what their relationship was about.

It couldn't be.

Water splashing behind him made him turn around. Rayen was walking out of the lake. "Hi, Tai. Is it lunch already?"

"Yeah." She had bruises on her wrists from where the bastard had held her back, but aside from that, she appeared fine. "Did you enjoy your swim?"

"Very much," she said. "I feel fabulous."

It was her way of telling him she was fine. "Good."

Piper and Bradley came out of the forest holding hands. "Did I hear lunch mentioned?" she asked.

Bradley's eyes were bloodshot but otherwise Tai wouldn't have been able to tell he'd been crying.

"Yeah. I saved you all a plate." Bradley had left in the middle of the class and Tai had put food aside for him.

"Are you hungry?" Piper asked Bradley.

He nodded.

"All right. Lead the way," she said to Tai. He smiled at her and headed back toward the school. He wanted to find out what Bradley had said to her, but it would have to wait until later. Right now, he'd just enjoy being with his family.

At the school others were hanging around, chatting and swapping news. Tai took the plates out of the oven where they were being kept warm and gave them to Piper, Rayen and Bradley.

They went outside and sat together, Bradley choosing to sit next to Piper. Something she'd said had obviously resonated with him.

Adahy joined them at the table. "Have a good swim?" he asked Rayen.

"Yeah. Did you take a cooking lesson?"

His eyes widened in mock outrage and Tai chuckled. His younger brother didn't like to cook. "No, I caught up with a couple of friends."

Eyota gestured to him so Tai excused himself and went over.

"I noticed Bradley walked in with Piper," Eyota said.

Tai nodded. "I found them both in that spot by the lake. Bradley was crying and Piper was comforting him."

"Oh, good. I've been so worried about him. Hopefully they were able to help each other."

"Each other?" Tai asked.

"Piper blames herself for what happened last night," Eyota told him.

He frowned. "What do you mean?" What had Rayen told their grandmother?

"Rayen told me about the attack."

"Then you know there's nothing for Piper to feel guilty about." She'd helped Rayen, not hurt her.

"Our emotions are not always sensible," Eyota said. She changed the subject. "Rayen is going to organize self-defense lessons at the school."

He should have thought of it, should have made sure his cousin could protect herself. He was glad Piper had been there with her.

"Both girls look happier now, but keep an eye on them for me," Eyota said. "It would have been a traumatic experience."

It hadn't occurred to him that Piper might be affected as well. He would watch out for her.

"Are you going to stay for dinner?" Eyota asked.

"No. We've got to leave a little earlier today. I'm going to Piper's parents' place for dinner."

"She's a lovely girl." Eyota wouldn't pry.

He shrugged. "I like her." His grandmother knew it couldn't be more than that.

Eyota smiled at him. "I'm glad you're happy." She glanced over her shoulder. "I need to talk with Stan." She left him.

Tai looked around the gathering. People of all different ages had come together to share food and stories. They were a community who helped each other. Which reminded him: he needed to introduce Piper to a few people who would be able to provide information for the cookbook.

He was so pleased he'd decided to go ahead with it and that Piper understood exactly what he was going for. He wanted to have tribal stories about hunting, gathering, ceremonies and celebrations at the beginning of each section, and he trusted she would be able to get the information she needed from the people here. The elders loved to share their stories.

By doing this, he would teach others about his culture, help them understand the tribe's perspective. And the profits would bring income into the tribe.

Wandering over to the table where she sat, Tai said, "Can I steal Piper for a minute?"

Bradley frowned.

"I need to introduce her to a few people. You can help me, if you like."

Bradley brightened and stood up. "Come on, Piper."

Piper smiled at Bradley. "I'm a bit nervous – can I hold your hand?"

"Sure. They're not scary."

Tai took her around and introduced her. He explained about the cookbook and told them Piper was going to help research it. Most people were enthusiastic but he overheard one person say, "He could have hired one of us. What would a white girl know?"

He ignored it. He'd chosen the best person to do the work, he was certain. He'd seen how good her research and writing skills were.

When he was finished he checked the time. "We'd better go if we're going to be on time to your parents," he said to Piper.

Bradley's face fell. "Do you have to?"

Piper walked over to the table where she'd left her bag and took out a piece of paper and pen. "Here's my number," she said writing on the paper and then handing it to Bradley. "You call me any time. And I'll be back during the week to do the research for Tai's cookbook, so we can catch up then."

Tai's respect for Piper grew. That would mean so much to the boy.

Bradley took the paper, read it and tucked it into his pocket. "Any time?"

"Sure."

He hugged her. "Thank you."

"Thank *you* for helping me."

They shared a smile.

Tai's heart warmed.

After saying their goodbyes, they piled into Adahy's car.

"Bradley sure took a liking to you," Rayen commented to Piper as they drove out of the reservation.

"He's so sweet. He's feeling lost and alone right now, and blames himself for Jerry's death. We talked about how it wasn't his fault."

"Just like the attack last night wasn't your fault. If you hadn't been there that guy would have raped me." Rayen said it so matter-of-factly that Tai gripped the steering wheel tighter. They hadn't mentioned the "r" word.

"You saved me and I will always appreciate it. I don't blame you at all. I told you not to come with me. I should have been more aware of my surroundings. But I won't be the victim again. I've spoken with the school principal and he's agreed to let us use the school grounds for the self-defense classes. I just need to find an instructor."

Piper was quiet. Tai glanced at her and her forehead was rumpled.

"It's difficult. I ignored my instincts. I won't do it again." She paused. "I might still have the name of the self-defense instructor I went to. I'll send it to you."

"That would be great."

They chatted for the rest of the journey home.

Piper fit in with Adahy and Rayen easily and they both liked her. The conversation was casual and flowed as they spoke about Rayen's study, Adahy's music and the restaurant.

He hoped his introduction to her family would be as smooth.

He wiped his suddenly sweaty palms on his shorts. It was no wonder he was nervous. He generally wasn't the best at meeting new people; he couldn't help thinking they were judging him. So many times it had been true that it was a hard thing to shake.

But Piper's brother was bringing a new partner so not all the attention would be on him. He was glad. He never relaxed until he got to know people a little more. But maybe the dessert he was bringing would help to sweeten them up.

***

After dropping off Adahy and Rayen at his house, and grabbing his things, he followed Piper to her place, where they showered and got ready.

"Tell me again, who is going to be there?" he asked as they got into Piper's car.

"My brother, Tom, and his boyfriend, Casey. I haven't met him yet. Then there's just Mom and Dad."

"What do your parents do?"

"Dad's the senior vice president of environment and sustainability at an oil and gas company. He makes sure the company is upholding its environmental responsibilities and explores ways to reduce its impact. Mom's a personal assistant to the owner of a chain of sportswear shops."

So both were high-paid individuals with a lot of business know-how. How would they feel about their daughter dating a chef?

He owned his own business, though, and it was doing well. He was branching out too.

It was the first time he'd been worried about what people thought of him in a long time. Their opinion mattered because Piper mattered.

Guilt prodded him. He really needed to tell Piper about the tribal law.

He tapped the doorframe of the car as Piper pulled up in front of a large two-story house in an affluent suburb. The gardens were neat and the house was in good repair.

It was a far larger place than he'd grown up in.

He ran his hand through his hair. Perhaps he should have braided it, to keep it off his face. Would Piper's mother believe men with long hair should have it cut?

He shook his head at himself and got out of the car, grabbing the bowl of chocolate mousse he'd made the day before.

Piper took his hand, squeezing it. "Ready?" she asked, as if she sensed his nerves.

He nodded.

Piper knocked on the door and then entered. "We're here," she called.

The hallway was immense; stairs led to the next floor and there was a huge wooden hallstand that held shoes, umbrellas and a mirror.

An older version of Piper walked down the hallway, smiling. "Hi, sweetheart. It's so long since I've seen you." She hugged Piper and turned to smile at Tai.

"Mom, this is Tai. Tai, my mother, Ashlin."

"Lovely to meet you," she said and kissed his cheek.

Taken by surprise at the genuine greeting, he said, "Likewise."

"What have you brought with you?" she asked.

"Chocolate mousse. For dessert. I'm a chef." God, he felt like he was sixteen again.

"Oh, you didn't need to do that," Ashlin said, taking the bowl from him. "I'll put it in the fridge."

"Tai owns the Wooden Spoon," Piper said.

Her mother stopped and turned to him, then looked at the bowl in her hand. "Is this your triple chocolate mousse with Kahlua?" she asked.

Surprised, he nodded. "Yes."

She hugged the bowl to her chest and sighed. "I might not tell anyone you brought it and keep it for myself. I had it when I went there for work and I wanted to lick the bowl." She grinned at him. "Thank you."

Her grin was so much like Piper's, so warm and mischievous, Tai found himself grinning back. "You're welcome."

Ashlin walked down the hallway and they followed. Piper glanced over her shoulder at him. "Told you," she mouthed and grinned.

They walked into a large open-plan living space. There was a kitchen with dining table next to it, a set of sofas in another section and floor-to-ceiling windows overlooking the manicured garden.

Three men sat on the sofas drinking beer.

One of the men stood up. He had the same blond hair as Piper, but was a couple of inches taller.

"Hey, Pippy," he said. He wiped his hands on his jeans and then said, "I'd like you to meet my boyfriend, Casey."

Piper gave her brother a quick hug and then stepped forward and shook Casey's hand. "Nice to meet you." She turned back to Tai. "This is my boyfriend, Tai." She gestured to each person in turn. "My father, Michael; my brother, Tom, and Casey."

Tai shook their hands, waiting for any indication they were judging him. He found nothing but genuine friendliness.

"Can I get you a drink?" Ashlin asked. "Beer, wine?"

"A glass of water would be great," he said.

"Are you sure?"

"Tai doesn't drink alcohol, Mom," Piper said. She sat down on the sofa across from Tom and Casey and Tai sat next to her.

"Oh, all right."

He was used to people considering him weird for not drinking alcohol and it didn't bother him.

"So what have you been up to?" Piper asked her brother.

"Mostly work. Casey and I are planning a vacation in October. Thought we might check out New York."

"Sounds great. Have you been to New York before, Casey?" she asked.

He shook his head. "No, it will be our first time." He exchanged a glance with Tom and they smiled.

There was a lot of love in that look. Did Piper see it as well?

"What about you, Pippy? They still burning you out at the *Age*?" Tom asked.

Piper sat back. "Ah, well. No, I was laid off on Monday."

"What?" Piper's mother, father and brother said it in unison.

"My position was no longer needed so they gave me two weeks in lieu and sent me on my way."

"Why didn't you tell us?" her mother said.

"I've been busy."

"Doing what?" her father asked.

"I'm helping Tai with a project for the next month or so, and figuring out what I want to do next."

Ashlin handed Tai a glass of water and sat down on one of the chairs. "You don't want to do journalism any more?"

"I'm not sure."

"But you always wanted to be a journalist," Tom said. He turned to Tai. "She used to write stories about us when we were kids."

Tai smiled. He could imagine Piper doing that. She would have been an enthusiastic kid, interested in everything.

"I realized recently it's not quite what I thought it would be," she said. "So I'll use the extra time that working on this project will bring, and decide if I want to go in a different direction."

"What's the project?" her father asked.

Piper glanced at Tai. He answered for her. "It's a cookbook. I've wanted to do one for a while. Piper's going to do some research for me and I'll do the recipes."

"Will the chocolate mousse recipe be in there?" Ashlin asked.

"Maybe. I haven't decided yet." His focus was on his tribe, but he supposed he could add some of his restaurant's other recipes.

"It's going to explore the Queche tribe's history and traditional food," Piper said.

"That will be fascinating." Michael said.

He was genuinely interested. Perhaps Piper was right and people would be intrigued.

A timer in the kitchen went off. "That will be dinner. Why don't you all sit up to the table?" Ashlin said, heading to the kitchen.

Tai followed Piper to the table and sat between her and Michael and across from Casey.

"It's shrimp bake," Piper's mother said as she placed it on

the table. "I'm sure it's not as good as you'd make," she said to Tai, scrunching up the dish towel she used to carry it to the table.

He'd never had someone nervous about his opinion before. It was sweet. "I'm sure it will be delicious." And if he wasn't he'd still clear his plate and say it was. People often overcooked shrimp so he didn't have high expectations – one of the reasons he cooked so regularly at home was to ensure he ate something edible.

They dished up and conversation turned to the day to day.

Tai tasted the shrimp bake. It was actually pretty good. There was a flavor in it he couldn't quite place, but which added a lift to the whole dish. He had to ask. "Ashlin, this is great. What did you put in it?"

She waved him away and flushed at the compliment. "A bit of this and that."

"There's a spice I can't pick."

"Oh, that's my secret ingredient," she said.

"Mom doesn't tell anyone her secret ingredient," Piper told him.

He really wanted to know. He tried another mouthful. "Maybe we can do a trade. Your secret ingredient for my mousse recipe."

She beamed at him. "Sold."

Piper put down her fork and stared at her mother. "I've been asking you for this recipe for years," she said.

"But you don't cook," Tai said, amused at her reaction.

"Doesn't mean I can't," she said.

"Sometimes mousse is thicker than blood," her mother joked.

Tai smiled. He liked her. She reminded him of Piper.

Piper leaned over to him. "You need to pass that recipe on to me," she whispered.

He shook his head solemnly. "A chef guards his recipes carefully and a shared secret must be respected."

She gaped at him, outraged, and he chuckled. "You have to paddle in the shallows before you can swim in the deep."

"Are you saying I'm not a good enough cook for the secret?"

"If he doesn't, I will," Tom said. "Mom always said she'd tell you if you held a dinner party and cooked it yourself."

Piper pouted and Tai wanted to kiss the pout right off her face. He'd never seen this side of her and it was adorable. Who would have thought such a smart, confident woman would sulk when it came to her family?

He glanced up and noticed Casey was staring at his plate, eating slowly. The poor guy was probably feeling left out. It was the first time he'd met Tom's family as well. "Where do you work, Casey?" he asked.

Casey looked up. "I'm a marine biologist. I'm currently studying the sea-grass meadows in Galveston."

Tai had no idea what that entailed, but the guy lit up when he spoke. "What do you need to study?" he asked.

Both Tom and Casey beamed at him. Casey launched into the details of his latest study, which related to pollution levels in the area.

Tom added more detail and Tai discovered Tom was also a marine biologist and they'd met on the job.

When the dishes were cleared, Ashlin brought the mousse to the table and Tai dished it up.

Silence fell as they ate it, with the occasional comment on how good it was.

Tai warmed. He loved providing food people relished: it made his heart sing and gave meaning to his work. Not only was he providing sustenance, but also something they enjoyed.

"I'm going to get so fat if I keep dating you," Piper said when she was finished. She kissed his cheek. "Thank you. That was fantastic."

"It was," Ashlin said as she scraped the bowl to get every last bit. She glanced around the table and then said, "What the hell, we're all family," and lifted the bowl to her mouth and licked it clean.

The others laughed, but Tai froze, his heart pounding.

Family.

Was it so easy to be accepted into Piper's world, into her life?

Tai had had to prove himself time and time again wherever he went. There were always chefs at restaurants who had thought less of him until he proved he cooked better than any of them. The restaurant business was highly competitive and he'd risen through the ranks very quickly.

He'd forgotten what it was like not to have to prove himself.

His tribe wouldn't accept Piper that easily.

"Maybe you should give that recipe to me," Michael said. "Then I'll have her completely under my control."

Ashlin snorted. "As if." She stood and cleared the bowls. "Anyone for coffee?"

Chapter 14

It was late by the time they left. Conversation had shifted to what Tom and Piper had been like as children and Ashlin had got out the photo albums. They had spent seven years in Western Australia and Piper pointed out Libby in some of the photos. Libby was in so many, she must almost have been part of the family. When he commented on it, Tom said, "She was. She and Piper used to drive me crazy mothering me. It was great when she moved to Houston."

"We have Libby, Adrian and Kate around for dinner every couple of months," Ashlin said.

Here was a strong family, a strong community really, if he took into account Piper's other friends – George and Elle, Imogen and Chris, Libby and Adrian. They were there for each other.

He wasn't sure if there were still any of his family photos left from before his father had died. There certainly hadn't been many taken afterward. His mother had drifted away and he had been too angry to chase her.

But seeing Piper with her mother, he had to wonder what it would be like to be that close, to actually laugh with his mother or tease her. He couldn't remember what his mother's laugh sounded like.

"So what's your verdict?" Piper asked as she started the car.

He pushed aside his sadness. "You were a cute kid."

"Thanks. I was talking about my parents."

"They're lovely. I can't wait to cook your mom's shrimp bake recipe."

Piper huffed. "I can't believe she gave that to you."

He had the recipe tucked into his pocket. He'd have to make it for Piper sometime soon. "Tom and Casey were nice too."

"He was, wasn't he? I have a suspicion Casey is going to be the one. They looked so in love, didn't they?"

He nodded. There had been something special between them.

They pulled up at her apartment and Tai followed her inside. It was becoming a habit for him to stay the night there. He liked spending time with Piper and the shorter commute to work, but it wasn't a relaxing space. Piper was messy and the traffic noise was constant. Plus she didn't have a garden, and he liked to connect with nature regularly.

He'd have to convince her his place was better – though at least they could be alone here.

If he wanted to he could take her clothes off in the kitchen and have her over the kitchen table without anyone walking in.

Grinning at the idea, he proceeded to make it a reality.

***

Piper woke on Monday morning and stretched, groaning as her muscles responded. Last night had been amazing. Tai had fit in so well with her parents and when they'd got home, he'd shown her other possible uses for a kitchen table.

She grinned.

"You look like you're up to no good." Tai's voice was low and sexy.

Piper turned her head to find him watching her. Her skin heated. "I was thinking about last night." It was amazing that a single look from him could turn her on. The intensity of his gaze struck deep at her core.

Tai smiled. "Your parents were nice. I see where you get your urge to help. Your whole family does good things."

Piper paused and adjusted her focus to her family.

She hadn't ever thought of it that way, but now she did she realized both her father and brother worked tirelessly to help the environment, and her mother was involved in a number of women's charities and mentoring programs. And though she'd always *wanted* to help people, she hadn't actually done anything like the rest of her family. She needed to find something to do. She wanted to feel fulfilled in her career, to feel as if she were improving someone's life.

She wanted to be able to look in the mirror and know she'd done something good.

Which meant she had a lot more thinking to do.

***

Piper's phone rang as they arrived at the Wooden Spoon.

"I've got about twenty thousand dollars in items for the auction," Imogen told her.

Piper's mouth dropped open. They'd been talking about the auction last week and their list of ideas had been impressive, but Imogen had actually come through with the goods. Piper hadn't dreamed so big. "That's fantastic."

"Libby and some of her friends are donating signed books and the chance to appear in their stories, Adrian is going to give a small, private concert to a bidder, and George has arranged a few memorabilia things to auction off. Is Tai going to give cooking classes?"

They'd talked about it but he hadn't made a decision. "I'll check and call you back."

She hung up and went into Tai's office. "Imogen is a miracle worker," she said. She listed all the things they had to auction. By the time she was finished, Tai's jaw had dropped. She smiled. "Have you decided about those classes?"

He blinked and closed his mouth. "Yeah, I'll do them." He shook his head in disbelief. "I never expected this."

Neither had Piper, but she wasn't going to knock it back. "It's amazing what can happen when you work at it."

"And when you know people," Tai said.

He was right. It would have been a lot harder without the contacts they had.

"A couple of chefs have agreed to cook meals for people in their own homes as well." Tai flicked through the notes on his desk and handed her a list of names with the details. "And I've got some artwork to sell from the rez."

"This is great." They'd definitely raise enough for a school bus if people bid fiercely for the items. "I'll give George a call and ask how he's going with the concert. If we lock in a date we can start advertising."

"Where will we advertise?" he asked.

"I'll ask Patti from the *Age* to do a piece. She'll be able to tell me the other places to advertise and of course George will have contacts too." Excited at the prospect this was all coming together, Piper left the room again.

A youth center would mean so much to people like Bradley. The thought of him made her pause. It had broken her heart to hold him while he'd cried the day before. He needed more than a youth center. He needed someone who loved him – he needed a whole family who cared, not just a few people who couldn't always be there for him.

Checking the time she saw he'd be at school already. She'd call him this evening.

She sighed. It was a difficult situation without an easy solution. She had no idea how many more children on the reservation needed a little bit more encouragement or a place to hang out while their parents were working. It was tough. She couldn't imagine what it would be like to be working so hard to provide everything you could for your children, and not being able to be there when they needed you.

Tai ducked his head in. "Want to go to the movies tonight?"

Piper sat back, surprised. "Sure. What's on?"

"Don't know. You decide. I'll be finished here by five." He left.

It was a nice idea. They hadn't done anything remotely date-like in their few weeks together. It would be great to do something normal.

She brought up the local theater website. She had no idea what kind of movies Tai liked. Was he an action adventure guy, did he like comedy, thriller or romance? She didn't know much normal stuff about him at all. What was his favorite color? Did he like dogs or cats? Was he a rock, jazz, pop, heavy metal or traditional music fan? She would have to ask him.

Reviewing the list of movies, Piper wrote down a few she

would be happy with. They all began about the same time so Tai could make the final decision later. Then she rang one of her favorite restaurants and booked a table for two. If they were going on a date, she wasn't going to let Tai cook. He deserved a break. With that organized she focused on the cookbook.

Piper spoke to Eyota for half an hour, discussing the best way to approach members of the tribe for their stories.

"Some of our older members don't trust white people," Eyota explained. "It won't matter that you're there for Tai. They remember clearly their treatment, the way the white man tried to suffocate our culture, and this will feel the same way to them." She paused. "I'll come with you when I can, but I hope you have a good memory as some won't like you recording them or taking notes."

Piper hadn't considered that aspect of the project. As a reporter she occasionally had people who didn't want to talk to her, but most wanted their five seconds of fame.

The research she'd done so far had uncovered a history of oppression, forced migration and poor treatment by American settlers. She would have to earn the Queches' trust.

They arranged to meet the next day and Eyota would organize the interviews. "It might take a couple of days. You can stay with me if you like."

"Do you have enough room?" Bradley was already staying with her.

"Of course."

"That would be lovely." She hung up and wrote down her interview questions.

***

At six o'clock Piper picked Tai up from his house. She'd been home to pack a bag for her trip to the reservation and to get ready for their date night. Her next-door neighbor had agreed to look after Moggy while she was away.

Tai was still in the shower when she arrived so Piper sat in the kitchen and chatted to Adahy.

"When's your single coming out?"

"Next week," he said, grinning. "I can't wait. It's going to be amazing to hear it on the radio."

Piper remembered getting her first byline in a paper. She imagined it was a similar feeling.

Tai came out, dressed in jean shorts and a black shirt. The top button was undone, showing a hint of his chest, but it was enough for Piper to imagine pressing her lips against that spot. She cleared her throat and said, "Ready to go?"

"Yeah."

Piper drove them to an Italian restaurant she'd always loved.

"Good choice," Tai said when he saw it. "This is one of my favorite places."

"Do you eat out much?"

"Hardly ever," he said. "I'm either at the restaurant or at home cooking for Adahy and Rayen."

"You must really love cooking," she said.

"I do." He smiled at her as the waiter showed them to their table. "Ka' sa' taught me when I was eight. It was something for me to do, something else to think about … Anyhow I loved it. It was all a big mystery, working out what flavors went with what and figuring out how long I had to cook things. There was never any doubt I would become a chef."

"How did it happen?" she asked.

"I was cooking at one of the food vendors at a powwow in Houston. A chef came, tried one of my dishes and insisted on being introduced to the person who had made it." He grinned. "He took me on as an apprentice straight away."

"How old were you?"

"Sixteen."

"Do you still keep in contact with that chef?"

He shook his head. "The man was a tyrant. He taught me some fantastic techniques but he also taught me how not to treat my staff. I was pleased to finish with him."

They ordered their meals and drinks. Piper took a breadstick out of its packet. "So where did you go next?"

He named the restaurant. "The head chef there so much nicer but I didn't learn a lot about food there. He was the first person to provide dinner for his staff."

"That must have been great."

"Yeah. I didn't have a lot of money then."

"Did you go home much?"

He shook his head.

It must have been hard. After growing up in the reservation community and then to be thrown into Houston with no family or friends. "You must have been determined."

He gave her a wry smile. "Ka' sa' says stubborn. It was difficult at first. As an apprentice I lived above the restaurant where I worked and Chef took the rent out of my pay. I knew no one, so when I wasn't working, I was studying to finish high school. After that I studied business because I wanted my own restaurant one day."

"It didn't take you long to achieve it."

"Stubborn," he said again. "When I finished my apprenticeship I moved to a one-bedroom apartment and shared with whichever apprentice needed a place to stay. I gave them the bedroom and slept on the couch, but they paid half the rent. We ate at the restaurant and I was frugal."

Piper couldn't imagine living like that. She'd moved out of home when she'd gone to college, but her parents had paid for it all. She'd waitressed for extra spending money. It made his successes all the more extraordinary.

Dinner was served and she asked, "What did your parents think about you moving out of home so young?"

He'd mentioned Eyota but had never mentioned his parents. Would he tell her about them?

Tai was silent for a long time. "Mom was thrilled it got me out of the rez and into a steady job. She wanted me to succeed."

It was the first time he'd mentioned his mother. "She must be proud of you."

"Maybe." He took a mouthful of his carbonara and avoided her eyes.

The closed Tai had appeared again. Piper acknowledged the sting of rejection. He didn't want to share his family with her, when she'd been so open with him.

Tai swallowed and sighed. "We're not very close. After Dad died she had to work a lot. Ka' sa' raised us."

Wanting more, Piper asked, "Where does she work?"

"She's just been made a senior manager at Walmart."

"Do you see her much?"

He shook his head. "Between my work and hers we rarely

find time. She lives on the other side of Houston."

He didn't seem to mind, which was odd, considering how close he was with his grandmother, Adahy and Rayen. She didn't push it. Instead she asked, "When did your dad die?"

"I was eight." He pulled on his braid. "I don't want to talk about it."

He was shutting her out and it hurt more than it should. She reminded herself they'd only been dating for a few weeks. Perhaps it was too early to go into past hurts. She didn't need to know everything about him.

But she *wanted* to know. She wanted to learn everything about him.

Forcing a smile on her face, she asked, "Which movie do you want to see?"

***

It turned out Tai was a comedy and action adventure fan. They decided on an action film and grabbed some chocolate from the candy bar before they went in.

As the lights went down Piper couldn't concentrate on the movie. She needed to review things. She'd known Tai a month. During that time she'd reassessed her career, introduced him to her family and he'd met her friends. They'd discussed what she liked to do and he'd even heard myriad stories about her childhood.

She'd also been there for him when Jerry died.

And in return she'd met none of his friends, he'd told her the minimum about his parents, and while she knew his culture was important to him, she knew little else.

She sighed. Perhaps she was being unfair. She had met most of his family, and been to the reservation, which he clearly didn't share with just anyone. Plus she'd known from the beginning he was a private person.

But still it hurt.

Maybe he wasn't as invested in this relationship as she was.

Until she figured it out she needed to rein in her emotions and treat the whole thing more casually, because right now her feelings were galloping ahead toward an ill-defined goal shining in the distance. Just because they'd been spending every night together didn't mean Tai was serious about her. She needed to remember that. She wriggled in her chair to get comfortable and concentrated on the movie.

**

"It was a good movie," Tai said as Piper drove them home. He'd really enjoyed the evening. It was nice to go out for a meal he didn't have to cook for a change, and to do something normal with Piper.

"Yeah," she said without her usual enthusiasm.

He frowned. There was something wrong. "Didn't you like it?"

She shrugged. "It didn't really grab me." There was indifference in her tone, which he'd never heard before. In fact Piper had been very quiet since they left the restaurant.

"You can choose next time," he said. He'd not actually asked what types of movies she liked. He glanced at her.

"Thanks." She smiled, but it didn't reach her eyes.

Alarmed at her lack of response, he asked, "What's wrong?"

"I'm a little tired."

He'd never been in the car with Piper when she hadn't filled the drive with conversation, except for that first time on the reservation when they didn't know each other. Even tonight at the restaurant she'd been asking him questions about his family. Questions he didn't want to answer because it was so hard to explain how he felt about his parents even now.

And when he hadn't answered, she'd stopped asking. Stopped talking at all. And he'd been too relieved to realize.

They pulled into his driveway. Piper tapped her hand on the steering wheel. "I won't stay tonight," she said. "It's late and I need to get an early start tomorrow to get to the reservation."

"Staying here saves half an hour off your trip," he said. But if she stayed he might have to tell her about his parents. Did he want to go into his past now?

No. He never wanted to go there.

He sighed. She'd been so open with him about her family, it was only fair that he tell her about his. He took a deep breath and covered her hand on the steering wheel. "I don't talk about my parents to anyone."

Hurt flashed across her face before she masked it. "Why not?"

He couldn't have this conversation in the car. It was too small, too crowded. He needed fresh air and space. "Will you come out the back with me?"

She hesitated and then turned off the engine.

He led her through the house and out onto the lawn, moving to the trees. He sat down and pulled her down next to him.

Silence descended. Where did he start? He hated talking about his parents, but he wanted Piper to understand why. He wanted her to understand him, because she'd come to mean so much to him.

Which meant he had to tell her the whole story.

Taking a deep breath he steeled himself. "My father suffered from depression like Jerry. Some days he was fine and he'd play with Adahy and me, and have a good time, and other days it was so bad we couldn't get any response from him. On those days we'd go over to Ka' sa's place." He paused. "Dad couldn't work because of the depression, so Mom did. She worked long hours and we only saw her in the evenings and on the weekends." He used to love her warm hugs and the way she'd read them stories before they went to bed.

"As I got older I recognized when Dad was going into his depressive phases so I'd tell Ka' sa', and do my best to be good and take care of Adahy so we wouldn't bother him. We used to play him songs to cheer him up." At three, Adahy had picked up their father's guitar and started playing. It was much too big for him but it hadn't mattered. It was the one thing that halted the depression for a while. His father would show Adahy how to strum the strings and where to put his fingers so he got different notes.

"One day he was worse than usual. I wanted to stay home from school but he made me go. I made him a card during class, and ran home during the lunch break to give it to him."

Images flashed across his mind, bright and colorful.

Pushing open the door, calling for his dad.

Seeing the foot sticking out from behind the sofa.

Moving around and seeing blood, so much blood.

Recognizing his father's shirt because he couldn't recognize his face.

Tai squeezed his eyes shut.

Piper's arm came around him and he leaned in to her, drawing strength from her comfort.

He swallowed the lump in his throat.

"I found him," he said finally, his voice dull. "He'd shot himself."

Chapter 15

Piper gasped.

Tai remembered so clearly the confusion, the panic and then the revulsion. At first he'd tried to wake his father but he hadn't responded and Tai had got the sticky blood on him. He rubbed his hands against his shorts now as if it were still there.

"I eventually ran to Ka' sa's. I didn't want to leave him but I couldn't remember her phone number." His mind had gone completely blank, but the one thing he'd known was he couldn't let Adahy see their father like that.

"Ka' sa' took over. It must have been just as horrific for her."

Piper brushed away tears on his cheeks he hadn't realized were there.

"I'm so sorry. I shouldn't have made you relive that." Her voice was full of sorrow.

He drew in a shaky breath. "I want you to know about me." He kissed her hand. "It's just my childhood wasn't as happy as yours. It's hard for me to talk about."

"I understand now."

If he was baring his soul he should keep going. He didn't want to go through this twice. "Mom was absolutely devastated. They loved each other so much and he'd left her. She went to pieces and hadn't the strength to comfort us, so we moved in with Ka' sa'. I thought she was sending me away because she blamed me. I should have stayed home and been with Dad. He wouldn't have done it if I'd been there."

"You know that's not true," Piper said.

"I do now. It took me a long time to realize it." He spent years blaming himself, no matter what his grandmother said. Years of feeling like he'd killed his father. "After her initial grieving, Mom started working weekends and I thought it was because she didn't want to be with us. Later Ka' sa' told me it had been her way of coping. If she kept busy, she didn't have to remember her husband had killed himself." He sighed. "We haven't been close since I was eight. When I was old enough to understand the suicide wasn't my fault, I blamed her for deserting us." He played with one of Piper's earrings. "We've been strangers for so long and it wasn't until I saw your family photos the other night that I realized how much I was missing out on. But it's probably too late to fix it."

"Do you want to repair your relationship?" Piper asked.

He shrugged. He'd resented her for so long. He wasn't sure there was enough icing to fill those holes. "When I saw your photos I remembered the time before Dad died when we were a happy family. I miss that."

Adahy had always climbed into their mother's lap as soon as she finally got home. Tai hadn't been able to do that. He hadn't been able to forget it was his grandmother he'd run to and his grandmother who had dried his tears, comforted him and pushed aside her own grief for his.

He would always be indebted to her.

"Maybe you could invite her to dinner one day when Adahy and Rayen are free. See how it goes."

"Maybe." It seemed like an insurmountable chasm to cross and he was scared of taking the first step.

Piper got up and pulled him to his feet, wrapping her arms around him. "You are an incredible person," she said. "You have achieved so much after such a horrific experience. You're so strong, Tai." She kissed him slowly and he drew comfort from her lips. "If you want to fix things with your mom, I'll be by your side the whole way."

He held her tightly. Somehow she knew the right things to say. And the thought of her by his side did give him courage.

"I'll check everyone's schedule."

They walked back to the house hand in hand.

He felt a little bit lighter having told her his story. She'd not judged him for blocking out his mother and she hadn't pitied him for finding his father: she'd just been there for him, a silent support.

He appreciated it.

He hadn't realized how much he'd kept to himself until Piper came along. Hadn't realized how much he needed to show the tribe he was strong and he could help them.

"What time are you leaving in the morning?" he asked as they entered his bedroom.

"Around seven."

"Who are you meeting with?"

She told him the names. Some of them were likely to give her a little bit of trouble. "A couple of guys had really bad childhoods. They don't like or trust white people," he said.

Piper nodded. "Eyota explained. I'll do my best to convince them that the point of the interviews is to preserve their culture, not destroy or appropriate it. But I'll play it by ear."

He hadn't considered Piper's skin color when he asked her to help him with his cookbook. He'd known she would do a great job, but the elders had had bad experiences with white men. It was too late now. He would see how Piper went over the next couple of days and, if she didn't have any luck, he'd talk with the elders when he went down on Sunday.

Climbing into bed he pulled Piper close. He needed to hold her.

"Sweet dreams," she said, kissing him softly.

"Good night."

He fell asleep almost instantly with her in his arms.

***

Piper had a fair quota of nerves bubbling around in her stomach when she arrived on the reservation the next day. Eyota had explained that some of the oldest members on the reservation had not only been taken away to boarding school and punished for practicing their culture, but had also been cheated by oil companies who said they had their best interest at heart. They didn't trust easily.

Eyota came out to greet her when she arrived. "We've got time for an iced tea before the first meeting," she said. "I want to ask you what you said to Bradley on Sunday. He was much happier yesterday."

"I didn't really say much," Piper said, surprised. She placed her bag next to the sofa and went through to the kitchen. "We talked about feeling guilty and he explained to me it wasn't my fault for what happened to Rayen. It might have triggered that it wasn't his fault with Jerry."

"Well, I thank you for it. I was really worried about him. He's talking more now, and while he's still got a way to go, it's a step in the right direction." Eyota poured the tea. "Now tell me, why are you helping Tai with his cookbook?"

Piper blinked. It wasn't a question she'd expected. "He asked me to, and I've got the time."

Eyota tilted her head down and frowned. "So if you had been working, you wouldn't have helped him?"

"No, it's not that. I wouldn't have been able to dedicate the time to it that I can now, but I would have helped anyway."

"Why?"

What answer was Eyota expecting from her? "Because it's Tai's goal and I want to help him however I can. I'm genuinely interested in his cultural heritage. I don't know much at all about the tribes."

Tai's grandmother nodded as if satisfied. "There may be stories the elders aren't willing to tell."

"That's fine. I can't make them say anything they don't want to say. What we do include in the cookbook is going to need to be relevant anyway. Stories about hunting and gathering or about cultural celebrations are likely to lead to dishes made as a result of those things."

"Will you only record the relevant things?" Eyota asked.

Piper had been considering that. She had no idea what information she would gather from the interviews, but she wanted to record everything. She could also write some articles about what she'd learned if the tribe agreed to it. "I'll take down everything," she said. "If there's enough, I could even collate all the stories and put copies in the general store for everyone to access."

"I have bigger plans than that," Eyota told her. "I want my tribe's history and stories recorded and published so the whole world can read them. I'd like you to consider turning what you learn into a book for us. If you agree, I'll get Tai to draw up a similar ghost-writing contract for you with me."

Piper blinked. The idea thrilled her. "I'd love to," she said. "What kind of structure were you thinking of?"

Eyota handed her a piece of paper with a chapter outline on it. She was prepared.

Piper scanned it. "This looks great. I might need to add a few more questions to my list." She scribbled down some notes.

"I'm pleased you agreed. I want someone who would come with an open mind, but not be blind to our failings – a fresh pair of eyes. You'll be great. Now, we'd better get going if we're going to be on time."

As Piper followed Eyota out to the car she thought she might have passed a test.

***

They wrapped up the interviews before school ended for the day so they were at home when Bradley arrived. The first two had gone well, with those elders more than happy to chat about their culture and everything they knew. The last one was a little trickier. Piper suspected Eyota had chosen the most open-minded people first so as to ease Piper into it gently. The last man, Stan, was the tribe's chief. He was grumpy and doing the interview because Eyota had sweet-talked him. "If this wasn't for Tai, I wouldn't invite you into my home," he told Piper with a glare.

"I appreciate your time," she said.

He harrumphed and proceeded to grumble about the white man for a bit before Eyota brought him back on topic. He refused to let Piper record his voice or take notes, so she sat back and gave him her undivided attention.

The man had a memory like a steel trap. He remembered dates, names and specific details from more than fifty years ago. Piper itched to write it down. Her recall wasn't so good. Instead she listened, asked questions and tried to commit as much as she could to memory.

When they left his house, she got out her laptop and furiously typed as much as she could remember while Eyota drove home.

Eyota laughed. "Give him a few more sessions with you and you'll win him over. Then he'll let you record him. You asked some good questions and, though he won't acknowledge it to you, he will keep it in mind."

It was good to know, but still she captured what she could.

They pulled up to the house as Bradley arrived home.

"Hi, Piper." He stood back, a little unsure.

Piper opened her arms. "Hi. Don't I get a hug?"

He smiled and hugged her, squeezing tightly. "You're staying tonight, aren't you?"

"Sure am."

"You want to go swimming in the lake?"

Piper paused. She had the rest of her notes to write down, but there was so much hope in his eyes. "Do you have any homework?"

"Some math."

Piper glanced at Eyota.

"You two can go to the lake as long as you're home by five. Then Bradley can do his homework."

"All right!" Bradley said and ran inside to change.

"He does seem happier today," Piper said.

"You're kind to go with him. I know how much you want to write your notes. I'll record what I remember while you're at the lake," she said.

"Thank you." Piper went inside to change, and then she and Bradley walked down to the lake.

There were already a few kids swimming. She waved to those she recognized.

"One day I'm going to swim across the whole lake," Bradley said.

It was a very big lake. "That's a great goal. How far can you swim now?"

"Not very. I get tired and have to come back." He hunched his shoulders.

"Do you ever have a rest and float?"

"I don't know how to float," he said.

It was the first thing her mother had taught her when she was learning to swim. If she turned over and floated on her back, she'd be able to rest until she had the energy to swim back.

"Want me to teach you?" she asked.

"Yes, please."

They waded out a little deeper and Piper put her hand under Bradley's back to support him. "You need to use your hands a little, to keep you up," she said and she showed him what she meant.

Bradley practiced and it wasn't long before he floated by himself. "I reckon I could make it across the lake like this," he said.

Alarmed, Piper said, "You mustn't try it by yourself. It's too dangerous. But if you tell Eyota about it, she'll help you." There had to be another option. "Maybe you can find out how wide the lake is and measure the same distance along the shore. Then you can practice swimming the distance, but if you get tired, it will still be shallow enough for you to put your feet down. You can make a start mark on the shore and then mark where you get to and aim to do a little further each day."

He thought about it. "That's a good idea."

Piper smiled in relief. "We should head back now." The sun had dipped lower behind the trees.

"Aw, do we have to?"

Piper grinned. "Yes. We promised Eyota we would be back by five and we both have homework to do."

"What homework do you have?" he asked as they waded out of the lake.

"I'm recording tribal stories for Tai to use in his cookbook. I interviewed some people today and I need to write up my notes to make sure they make sense."

"Grandpa used to tell me lots of stories," Bradley said quietly.

Perhaps that was another way she could help the boy. "I'd love to hear them."

He widened his eyes. "Really?"

"Absolutely. After you've done your homework, I can

interview you."

He stood visibly taller. "Can you write down that they were Grandpa's stories?" he asked.

"Sure, if you want me to."

He nodded. "That way no one will forget him."

Piper didn't know what to say to that.

When they arrived back at the house, Eyota said, "You've got time for a shower before dinner."

Bradley hurried to get the first shower and Piper turned to Tai's grandmother.

"Is there anything I can do to help?"

"No, I've got it all under control. How was the swim?"

"Lovely, though I may have given Bradley an idea." She explained how he wanted to swim across the lake and how she'd taught him to float. "I suggested he swim the same distance along the shore before he tried across the lake."

"I'll keep an eye on him," Eyota promised. "It will be good if he has a goal to keep him occupied."

***

After dinner Piper helped Bradley with his homework and then interviewed him. The boy had an incredible memory and enjoyed repeating the stories his grandfather had told him. When they were finished, Piper tucked him in, read him a story and kissed him good night.

Eyota was making tea in the kitchen when Piper came out. "Those stories he was telling you are spot on," she said. "Told the way my parents told Jerry's father and me."

Piper had forgotten Jerry was Eyota's nephew. "How are you?" She wondered whether anyone had stopped to ask the old woman the question, because she was always so sure of herself.

Eyota sighed. "I am sad, but I need to be strong for Bradley. Jerry will be in a better place now with the ancestors and his wife."

"It must be hard to lose your nephew and your son to the same thing."

"Tai told you?" Eyota raised an eyebrow.

"We spoke about it last night." She still felt badly about the way she'd behaved. Sure, she'd been hurt by his reluctance to share his past with her, but now knowing what he'd been through, she understood.

She would have been reluctant to share too.

"It's good he has someone to talk to. My Tai feels he has to do everything himself – feels he has to be strong for the tribe."

"I imagine he's had a good role model," Piper said.

Eyota nodded. "There have been times when I've had to be the strong one for my family."

"Do other families have as sad a history as yours?"

"There are few who haven't been affected by something. Of course there are different levels."

"Do you know a solution?"

"Nothing this complicated is easy to fix."

***

Piper spent the whole week on the reservation. With the extra work Eyota wanted her to do, it made sense. She helped in the afternoons when children would drop by for a chat or a meal or a lift home. To Piper it seemed Eyota's house was an unofficial youth center. She lived close enough to the school for the kids to walk over and many liked to sit and listen to the stories the old woman told.

Eyota had an amazing knowledge of the tribe's history and its cultural traditions. Piper suspected Eyota could have written the book herself, with little input from the other members of the reservation. Piper wasn't sure why she'd asked her to do it.

A couple of times, children stayed overnight, sleeping on one of the bunk beds or on the couch. When Piper asked Eyota about it, she said one family didn't like staying on their own while their mother was working night shift, and some brothers had heard their father had lost badly on the races that day and their mother had said to stay with Eyota.

It wasn't all bad news though – just the occasional kid needing help. Plenty of the reservation families were doing well, despite their disadvantages.

Piper made a few phone calls to George and Imogen to discuss the fundraising efforts. George had set a date for the concert in late September and had a massive line-up of stars performing, including a few flying in from other parts of the country.

On Friday Eyota invited some members of the tribe over to discuss what facilities the youth center would need. She was adamant about the need for a kitchen and bathroom and small bedrooms where families could stay together. "We have a lot of foster parents on the reservation, but most of them are full. Some kids need a safe, warm place to sleep occasionally and others for an extended period of time."

"We'd need a caretaker then," Piper said. "Someone who will sleep overnight to chaperone the kids."

"It would be nice if we got a permanent caretaker rather than just a roster of different volunteers," Eyota said. "The children need consistency in their lives."

Piper made a note. "It would have to be a paid position. There wouldn't be many who could afford to do it full time for free." Though it would be incredibly rewarding to be the person these kids turned to for help.

Eyota didn't comment.

Piper realized it was what Eyota was effectively doing anyway. Perhaps she needed to rethink her assumptions.

"A couple of communal rooms would be good – maybe a pool table, or table tennis table, something to keep the kids occupied," Bill said.

"We could get others in to teach additional classes like basket weaving, pottery, language classes or traditional weapons," Peta added.

Piper wrote down the ideas. "Rayen wants to hold self-defense classes too, but perhaps the school would be a better place."

"Yes, that should be done sooner rather than later," Eyota said.

"Do we need to go to the tribal council for input?" Piper asked. She wasn't entirely sure how planning worked on the reservation, but she suspected such a project would need to be approved by someone.

"Once we have a plan," Eyota said. "As with any group of people it's better to give them an option to consider and modify than to start from scratch. Everyone will have their own opinion on what is best."

Piper understood politics.

Eyota wrapped up the meeting and the other attendees left.

Bradley came into the kitchen and dumped his school bag on the floor. "What are you doing?" he asked, looking at the paper spread over the table.

Piper wasn't sure how much Eyota and Tai wanted to say about the youth center until they had raised the money and it had been given the go ahead.

"Working on a project," Eyota said. "Tell me, what do kids like to do after school?"

Bradley shrugged. "Some play sport, some take extra classes and others go swimming in the lake."

"Do they complain about being bored?" Piper asked.

"Some of the older kids do."

"We'll have a chat to them too. Do you have any homework?" Eyota asked.

He nodded. "Some reading."

"Why don't you do that while we finish here?"

Piper waited until he left the room. "Do we have any other interviews tomorrow?" she asked. It was the weekend and Tai was coming.

"Just one."

Piper wanted to get a draft done on the first section of the cookbook before he arrived so she had something to show him.

"Do you need help with dinner?"

"No, honey. You do the work you need to do. I know you want to show Tai what you've done."

Piper nodded her thanks. She took her laptop into the small living room, where Bradley was on the sofa reading his book. Piper sat on the chair next to him and began collating her notes. She had two main files, one with the skeleton for the cookbook and the other with the skeleton for the history book. Going through her interview notes, she copied the relevant stories to the equivalent sections in both documents. When it was done, it was time for dinner.

She chatted to Bradley about his day at school and then read him a story before he went to bed. Afterward she settled in the living room with Eyota and worked on refining the stories into a format that would suit the cookbook.

***

Tai had missed Piper more than he'd expected to. After close to two weeks of spending every night together it had been lonely going to bed by himself. He called her every evening when he was taking his dinner break and she'd sounded enthusiastic about the information she'd gathered so far. He was glad she was enjoying it, and pleased his tribe interested her.

On Saturday morning he left early to get to the reservation. Adahy was going for the weekend so Tai hitched a ride with him. After the funeral Adahy had received a lot of requests for music lessons and the first group session was today.

They stopped at the general store to buy a couple of items Eyota had asked for.

"Tai, Adahy. Good to see you boys." Gary had been running the store since Tai was a kid.

"How're things?" Tai asked.

"That white girl of yours is what everyone's talking about. Some aren't happy Eyota didn't choose a tribe member to write our history."

It was a job going to an outsider. "She's a good researcher."

"Good at interviewing too. She's impressed some, even those who didn't want to be impressed."

Tai smiled. "Piper has a way about her."

"That she does. She's been in and bought every book on the tribe we have. Said she wanted to check what had already been done so she could add to it and not repeat it."

Adahy put the bread and milk on the counter and Gary rang it up.

"You sending your boy to my lessons?" Adahy asked.

"Yeah, he'll be there. He cooked the fish from Tai's last lesson yesterday and damn it was good."

Tai was pleased. He hoped the people coming to his lessons would continue to practice when they got home. Gary's son was fourteen and as sharp as a tack.

"He can't decide whether he wants to be a rock star or a chef," Gary continued.

"He'll be great at whatever he chooses," Tai said.

Gary nodded in agreement.

They left the store and drove the rest of the way to their grandmother's place.

The first person he saw when he arrived was Piper. She was out the front of the house, watering the plants. She waved and smiled when the car pulled up. Tai jumped out of the car and swept her up into his arms.

She squealed, managing to hold the hose so they didn't get soaked.

He kissed her, closing his eyes and enjoying her taste. "I missed you."

"I missed you too."

"Do I get a greeting like that?" Adahy asked, grinning.

Tai turned and glared at him.

"Just kidding." He grabbed his guitar and bag from the trunk.

"What plans do you have today?" Tai asked.

"I've got one more interview and Eyota is going to Jerry's place to sort out some of the stuff there. Bradley's going with her," Piper told him.

It was likely to be hard for both of them and Tai wanted to be there. "Who's the interview with?"

"Stan. I spoke to him on Tuesday, but he's agreed to let me come back and record what he has to say."

Tai was impressed. Stan was not one to trust easily. "Gary said the whole rez has been talking about you."

Piper looked alarmed. "I haven't upset anyone, have I?"

He shook his head. "Not really. There are a few grumbles, but most are impressed with your sensitivity."

She breathed out a sigh of relief and turned off the hose.

Together they went inside.

"Stan rang to say he'll meet us at Jerry's place," Eyota said as they walked in. Tai gave her a hug.

Bradley came out of his room with a backpack on. "Hi, Tai; hi, Adahy."

"Hey, Bradley, how're things?"

The boy shrugged. "Not bad. Piper's been helping me with my homework and I aced my math test yesterday."

Tai pictured Piper sitting down with Bradley, helping him. He smiled. "That's great."

"Have you got everything you need?" Eyota asked Bradley.

He nodded.

"Then let's go."

Piper gathered her satchel and followed them to the pickup. During the drive out to Jerry's place she told Tai about the work she'd done on the cookbook. He was surprised with how much she'd completed in less than a week, but he shouldn't have been. He remembered how committed she'd been to the profile articles she'd written and how exhausted she'd been at the end.

She didn't seem exhausted now. In fact she was the most relaxed he'd seen her. Perhaps reservation life was good for her.

He paused. It wasn't something he'd considered before. For some people reservation life was like a prison sentence and others thrived on being part of their culture. He hadn't considered whether Piper could be accepted there, and hadn't asked her what she thought of the stories she'd been told. His traditions were ingrained in him, which was why he spent the week before Jerry's funeral on the reservation, doing what needed to be done.

He would have to ask her.

His stomach dropped. If he was thinking of asking her about his culture, if he was imagining her here regularly, it meant their relationship had slipped into the serious lane.

And that couldn't happen.

Not with the membership laws as they were.

He had to do something, but the idea of splitting up with Piper made his heart ache.

"Where do we start?" Bradley's voice pierced his thoughts.

Tai blinked and was relieved by the distraction. Jerry had left everything to Bradley. He'd once told Tai that Teresa wouldn't want it and Carl wouldn't appreciate it.

"How about the living room?" Tai led Bradley through. "All of this is yours, Bradley," he said. "You can keep everything if you want to."

Bradley bit his lip. "It's weird to go through Grandpa's things."

Eyota walked over. "I know, honey. There are some things that are clearly trash though, and it's OK to throw them out." She picked up a collection of bottle tops in a jar and offered it to him, eyebrows up in a question.

The boy nodded.

"And his clothes can go to someone who needs them, because they won't fit you," Tai said.

"Can I keep his traditional jacket?" Bradley asked in a small voice.

"You can keep whatever you like," Piper said going over to him and giving him a hug. "You tell us if you want to stop, or if you want to keep something, and we'll do it. You're in charge today."

He smiled a small smile.

Tai hadn't been involved in sorting out his father's things after he had died. He wasn't sure who had done it, but Eyota had given him a couple of keepsakes, and Adahy had been given his father's guitar.

"Why don't you come with me now, and we'll fetch the jacket and anything else you want from the bedroom?" his grandmother said.

Bradley kept hold of Piper's hand and the three of them walked into the bedroom. Piper exchanged a look with Tai as she went.

She did something to his heart. It always swelled and tightened when she was around.

"The kid's got a thing for Piper," Adahy observed.

"I'm glad he's got her," Tai said. He'd had his grandmother, as Bradley did, but he'd still felt so alone. Shaking off the melancholy, he said, "Shall we start in the kitchen?" There was bound to be a lot of food that needed to be thrown out.

They hadn't been working for too long, pulling items out of the fridge and throwing them in the trash, before Eyota called, "Adahy, come and see what we've found."

Tai followed Adahy into the living room, where Bradley was sitting with a banjo on his lap.

"It was my father's banjolin," Eyota said. "I never knew where it had gone. My brother must have inherited it and given it to Jerry."

Tai frowned. "Banjolin?"

"My father made it. It's got the body of a banjo and the neck of a mandolin – banjolin," Eyota explained.

"Cool." Adahy crouched down next to Bradley. "Can I give it a go?"

Bradley gave the instrument to Adahy.

Adahy strummed the strings and made adjustments to the notes. "The strings are old, probably need replacing," he said, before he proceeded to play a little ditty.

Bradley watched Adahy with envy.

"I'd keep hold of this if I were you," Adahy said, handing it back.

"I can't play," he said.

"I'll teach you. You can come to my class this afternoon."

"Really?" The boy's eyes lit up.

"Really."

Bradley placed the banjolin back in the cotton bag it had been in. "Thanks!"

That's what Bradley needed. Something to keep him occupied. It gave him less time to dwell on what he'd seen, what he'd experienced.

Tai returned to the kitchen and continued sorting the food. When he was done, he went through the cupboards. There was a lot of cutlery and crockery but it was all in decent condition. He didn't want to discard anything that might help Bradley when he was older.

As he finished in the kitchen, Stan arrived. Tai showed him in and Stan dropped onto a chair at the kitchen table.

"I'm only agreeing to do this because Eyota asked me," he said as Piper walked in.

"I know we both appreciate it, Mr. Bullock," Piper said.

"Well, let's get on with it then."

Tai flashed Piper a smile. She didn't seem the least bit perturbed by Stan's behavior. "I'll go help in the other room," he said. "Yell if you need me."

He made himself scarce.

Chapter 16

"Are you going to start that thing?" Hearing Stan's voice, Piper realized she was staring after Tai, smiling.

She cleared her throat and found him waiting impatiently. "Yes, I'm sorry." She turned on the recorder. "I'm here with Stan Bullock, Chief of the Queche tribe." She gave the day and date. "He has agreed to speak about the history of his tribe." She turned to him. "Where would you like to begin?"

He smiled as if pleased she'd let him be in charge of what he said. "We shall start with honoring the ancestors," he said.

Piper settled in for an education.

***

It was close to midday when Eyota and Bradley walked in. Stan was telling Piper about tribal membership. "To be a member of our tribe your mother must be a Queche. We don't follow blood quantum laws like other tribes do."

Piper paused while making a note. "You mean if your father is Queche and your mother isn't, you're not considered part of the tribe?"

"No." Stan pressed his lips firmly together.

"I've been trying to get the council to change that law for years," Eyota said. "It's time for lunch. We've cleaned out the garbage and packed up clothes that can go to a thrift shop."

Did Tai know about the law? Surely with his dedication to

his culture he would. But that would mean he had no intention of their relationship going further than it had. She couldn't imagine him wanting children who weren't part of his tribe.

Perhaps he wasn't serious about their relationship.

Unease swirled around her stomach and she did her best to ignore it. She'd talk to Tai when they were alone.

Pushing her feelings aside, she asked Bradley, "How did it go?"

He shrugged. "It was all right. Grandpa has a lot of stuff."

"He was a hoarder, like his father," Eyota said.

"His father was a hoarder because everything was taken away from him," Stan said. "We went to the same boarding school."

"What was that like?" Bradley asked, pulling out a chair.

"Like losing your soul," Stan said.

Eyota clicked her tongue. "You can discuss that later," she said. "Why don't you come back to my place for lunch, and you and Piper can continue your interview there?"

"All right," Stan agreed.

Tai came into the kitchen as Piper turned off the recorder and packed up her notes. Outside the pickup tray was full of items from Jerry's house but there was room for Adahy, Bradley and Stan, who had walked over.

When they arrived back at Eyota's, she and Tai went into the kitchen to prepare lunch while Adahy and Bradley sat on the sofa, and Adahy showed the boy how to find the notes on the banjolin.

"What do you think of our culture?" Stan spoke, directing the question at Piper.

Piper sat in one of the armchairs. "It has a long memory and lovely traditions. I don't know a lot about my great-grandparents and even less about their parents. We don't tend to honor our past like you do. Perhaps that's why we keep making the same mistakes."

"And our way of living?"

She wasn't sure if he was referring to the past or the present. "Being mindful of the environment and making sure you care for it so it sustains you in the future is something we can all learn from," she said. "By the time the people in charge do something about it, it may be too late." She'd spent evenings talking with her father and brother about global warming and the effects of industry. Her father had chosen to fight the battle from inside one of the companies, hoping to drive change, while her brother was trying from the side of science. Each knew there was a long way to go.

Stan seemed satisfied.

Tai called them in to the kitchen for lunch and they sat around the table catching up with news of the reservation. There was a lot happening and Piper had realized from her few days there that everyone supported each other. Many of them were related but all wanted to ensure the survival of their culture.

They spoke about school with Bradley and the youth center with Stan.

"We have something to discuss with the council," Eyota told Stan. "We have a fundraising event planned to raise money for a youth center."

Stan frowned at her. "We can't raise that kind of money on the reservation."

"That's why we're going off rez," Tai told him. "It was Piper's idea."

"Actually one of my friends had the idea," Piper said quickly. "We're all organizing it."

Stan was unimpressed. "What idea?"

Piper looked to Tai. It was probably better coming from him.

"We're running an online auction and people have donated thousands of dollars in items," Tai said. "Then we've organized a rock concert. The headlining act is Kent Downer."

"The concert is going to be amazing," Adahy said. "I can't wait to do it."

"How much do you expect to raise?" Stan asked.

Tai gave him a ballpark figure and the chief's eyebrows went up. "Impressive. Have you got a contract with these people?"

Tai and Piper exchanged a glance. "No," Piper said. She refused to believe George or Imogen wouldn't hold up their end of the bargain.

"Then I won't believe it until the money is in the council's account."

Piper made no comment. She understood his sentiments, considering how his people had been treated over the centuries.

"You're right," Eyota said. "We'll need to draw up an agreement with George and Imogen and one with the tribal council to ensure the money is spent on what it was intended for."

Stan stared at her, outrage on his face. "You think we would squander the money?"

Eyota shook her head. "No, but the council may have different priorities. There are housing shortages and other issues which the council might want to address first."

He looked at her for a minute more before he conceded. "You may have a point."

Piper let out a quiet breath.

"I need to get going," Adahy said, getting to his feet. "I've got to set up for class. You coming, Bradley?"

Bradley stuffed the remaining food in his mouth and ran to get his banjolin.

Tai stood and collected the plates, while Piper asked, "Would you like to continue the interview?" She wasn't going to make the mistake of assuming Stan would still want to talk.

"Might as well get it written down," he said. "My people had no written language. We were nomads and there was no point carrying around things that could be stored in your head. Besides, so much is lost when it is on paper."

"There's no reason why we can't film the stories," Piper said. "It could be a great way of preserving the traditions. Many people prefer watching things to reading. We could do both."

Eyota pursed her lips. "It would need to be professional, and that costs money."

Piper thought quickly. "Is there anyone in the tribe who's interested in film making?" she asked.

"What about Neil?" Eyota said.

Tai nodded. "He's studying at college at the moment."

"Perhaps he would be willing to do it. He might be able to borrow the college's equipment or even do it as one of his assignments." Piper knew there was a real art to working out the best visual angle and then to editing interviews together. She had a couple of friends who worked in television news.

"I'll investigate it," Stan said. "Let's continue as we were."

Piper checked her notes and asked him a question.

***

It was getting dark when the interview finally wound down. Adahy had returned from his lesson and Bradley sat outside under a tree practicing what he had learned.

Eyota had thrown together some finger food so they could eat while still talking and Adahy had joined the table to listen.

Piper's head was filled with names, dates, relationships and traditions. She needed some downtime.

First, though: "Thank you for your time," she said to Stan, shaking his hand.

"I do this for my tribe," he said.

She nodded. His attitude was nothing to do with her, and she was grateful for his knowledge.

When Stan had left, Tai turned to her and put an arm around her waist. "Do you want to go for a walk?"

She did. A full moon was rising so there was plenty of light, and she needed to clear her head. "Yes, please." She followed him out of the house and along the path that led to the lake. When it opened out so it was wide enough for both of them, he took her hand.

She'd missed having him around over the past few days. She enjoyed being with him, even if they didn't speak or were doing different things. It was one of the reasons she'd spent her days last week at the restaurant. It didn't matter if Tai was cooking and she was planning the cookbook, what mattered were the times when she would surface, or he would pop his head into the break room and they would have a quick chat before going back to what they were doing.

She loved being around him. She loved his strength, his humor, his sensitivity and his compassion. She loved him.

The idea gave her little start, but then she smiled. Everything about it felt right. She was walking next to the man she wanted to spend the rest of her life with. The only question was how did he feel about her?

The question of tribal membership popped back into her

head, but before she could ask, Tai said, "Mom's coming to the cooking class tomorrow." His voice was loud in the silence, though he spoke quietly.

They hadn't talked any further about his mother during the week. "How do you feel about it?"

"Nervous," he admitted and stopped walking. He turned to Piper and took her other hand. "Adahy invited her when he decided he was going to stay overnight."

"Does Adahy understand why your relationship is strained?" she asked.

"We've never spoken about it, but I'm sure he suspects."

"So what are you going to do?"

He shrugged and sighed. "I don't know. How am I supposed to start the conversation?" He was genuinely at a loss.

"How about starting with, Can we talk? And then tell her you wish your relationship was better."

"There's so much that hasn't been said. I could make things worse."

He was right. "Is it better to try and fail, or to not try at all?"

"I need to try." He pulled her into his arms and Piper hugged him. This was where she wanted to be.

In his arms, filled with her love for him, supporting him however she could. Dare she tell him how she felt? Or was it too soon?

Tai bent his head and kissed her and the words were lost.

***

For the first time, Tai wasn't looking forward to the cooking class. Today it meant talking with his mother, and he wasn't sure how to handle it.

Part of him hoped she wouldn't turn up. But Piper was right. It was better he spoke to his mother, cleared the air and tried to salvage something out of their relationship. He'd loved her when he was younger, had missed her like crazy after their father had died, before the guilt had turned to resentment in his teenage years.

He wanted to reclaim the future.

Piper walked into the kitchen, her hair neatly combed, and dressed for the day in a pair of blue shorts and a red tank top. It didn't matter what she wore: she was beautiful. "Morning," she said, kissing him.

He poured her a coffee. "Morning. Did you sleep all right?"

They had spent the night in different rooms. He, Adahy and Bradley had shared the room with the two bunk beds in it and Piper had slept in Rayen's bedroom.

"Yeah. I've become used to the wildlife that makes noise in the night," she said. "Have you figured out what to say when your mom arrives?"

He had words running around his head, but what came out of his mouth might be a whole different thing. "Yes."

Before she could say anything else, Bradley padded into the kitchen wearing his pajamas. He gave Piper a hug.

"Do you want some cereal?" she asked him.

He nodded, yawning.

Piper got the bowl and gave it to the boy, who thanked her.

Tai smiled. The two of them had fallen into a routine over the past couple of days. He liked watching Piper and Bradley together. She was good with children. She'd make a good mother one day. He could imagine a little Piper running around with Piper's honey blond hair and his brown eyes.

No.

His hand stopped halfway between the table and his mouth, and coffee splashed out onto his lap. The burning liquid got him moving again – he jumped up and found a dish cloth to mop up the spill.

"Are you all right?" Piper asked, coming over.

He couldn't look at her, couldn't reconcile what he knew with how he felt. "Yeah. I'll just get changed." He fled the kitchen, his skin cold, his heart tight.

He loved Piper.

He could imagine spending the rest of his life with her.

And the thought didn't scare him at all.

But he couldn't possibly marry her. She wasn't Queche. Any children they had wouldn't be accepted into the tribe. He couldn't bring any child into the world if it would rob them of that belonging. If they had no heritage to claim. It was hard enough being Native American as it was. He'd let their relationship go on too long, not wanting to end it, and now he had to. Before she felt the same way about him.

It was so difficult. Piper understood some of the struggles of his people. She'd been gathering stories for days and, last night before they went to bed, she'd shown him what she'd done. It was written with sensitivity and compassion.

But it didn't matter. She wasn't a member of any tribe. She couldn't ever truly know.

And he could never be with her.

He barged into the room he was sharing and Adahy woke up with a start.

"What's happened? What's wrong?" He rubbed his eyes and sat up.

"Spilled coffee on my crotch," Tai said.

Adahy swore. "Geez, next time be more quiet about it." He stretched. "I thought the house was on fire."

Tai ignored him, focusing on finding another pair of shorts and getting changed.

Then he sat down on the bottom bunk across from Adahy and put his head in his hands. He couldn't deal with the thought of losing Piper now. Not when his mother was due at any minute. There was way too much to cope with.

"Hey, Tai, what's up?" Adahy climbed down from the top bunk and sat next to him.

"Nothing." Tai wasn't going to dump his worries on his brother. Adahy didn't need them. Tai had always kept things to himself and he wasn't going to start sharing now.

"Don't lie to me." Adahy's voice was angry.

Surprised, Tai looked up.

"I'm an adult, Tai. You don't need to keep anything from me any more. I can handle it."

Tai opened his mouth but no words came out. He'd never realized Adahy had noticed what he'd done.

"I know you were trying to protect me, but I'm a big boy. What's got you so freaked?"

Tai was at a loss. The only person he had confided in was Piper.

Should he tell the truth?

"It's Mom," he said finally, choosing the lesser of the two issues.

"What about her?"

"It's the first time she's come to a cooking lesson."

"And what? You think she'll hate the food?"

Tai shook his head. "We've never been close."

"You should stop blaming her for Dad's death," Adahy said. "It wasn't her fault."

Tai's jaw dropped open. "I don't. Who told you that?"

Adahy shrugged. "Mom. I asked her once why you never hugged her."

He shook his head. "You've got it the wrong way around. I always thought she blamed me."

There was a knock on the door and Eyota's voice called, "Boys, your mother's here."

"Be right there," Adahy called back. He turned to Tai. "Why would she blame an eight-year-old kid?"

"I blamed myself, so it made sense to me."

Adahy stared at him. "I never realized."

Tai got to his feet. He wanted to end the conversation more than he wanted to put off seeing his mother.

His brother put a hand on his arm. "You didn't kill Dad. He killed himself."

The image came unbidden to his mind. He stamped it away. "I know."

But it didn't make the visions go away.

He left the room and walked into the kitchen, where his mother was sitting at the table with his grandmother, Bradley and Piper.

Piper laughed at something Jackie said.

Tai's heart squeezed. He didn't know what to do about either of these women.

"Hi Mom," Adahy said, coming into the room behind Tai and kissing his mother on the cheek.

"Hi, Ada. Tai." She greeted him with a nod and a small smile.

He nodded back to her. He couldn't do it now. "I'd better go and set up everything." He needed to get out of there.

"Do you want a hand?" Piper asked.

"No. I'll see you later." He was abrupt and the hurt on Piper's face didn't make it any easier, but he needed space and air.

He left the house and strode toward the school. He was far earlier than he needed to be, but it didn't matter. Adahy or Eyota would drive the pickup over to the school with the kids later.

Right now he needed to think.

Chapter 17

Piper forced a smile onto her face after Tai left. She knew he was nervous about talking with his mother, but he'd barely looked at her either.

"Have you known Tai long?" Jackie asked her.

Piper liked her first impression of Tai's mom. She was friendly, though she was uncertain around her oldest son.

"About a month," she answered. "I met him at one of Adahy's concerts and then I had to interview him for the *Houston Age*."

"You wrote that ridiculous profile in today's paper?" Jackie was indignant.

Piper's stomach clenched. "I wrote *an* article. I haven't seen what they printed. Do you have the paper, Eyota?"

"Yes. It's on the coffee table. I haven't unwrapped it yet." She turned to Jackie. "We went through Jerry's house yesterday."

Piper fetched the paper and unwrapped it, flicking through until a lift-out slipped onto the table. *The People of Houston.*

They'd done it as a magazine rather than weekly feature articles. She found Tai's profile and began to read, walking back into the kitchen as she did so. She felt sick. "This isn't what I wrote." She sat down. "This is garbage." They'd taken bits of both articles she'd written and mashed them together, adding statistics that made the reservation appear as if it were getting millions of dollars in handouts from the government.

But how had they got the other article?

Her work laptop – they must have gone through the files after she'd left. She paged through the rest of the articles, which were largely unchanged.

Why would Geraldine do that?

She got to her feet, her skin prickling. Tai was going to be furious. "Excuse me for a minute. I need to make a phone call." She stalked outside without waiting for a response and dialed Geraldine's number, but nothing happened. No reception.

She walked back in. "There's no reception."

"You can use my phone," Eyota said, looking up from the article.

"Thanks." She stalked over and dialed the number. "Geraldine, it's Piper."

"Piper. Have you seen the profiles?" Her tone was pleased.

Anger stirred. "Yes, I've got them in front of me. What the hell did you do to my story on Tai?"

"We made a few necessary editorial changes. Don't you like them?"

"No, it's shit," she said. "You completely massacred the story and implied things that aren't true."

"What I did was make the story consumable for our readers. It's my job as editor to ensure everything that we publish is suitable for the *Age*."

Piper's mouth dropped open. "I don't care if you're the editor. You made wholesale changes to the article that weren't warranted."

"I say they were. Do you think Mr. Woods will be unhappy?"

That was an understatement. "Yes, I think Tai will want you to print a retraction."

"It's good exposure for his little restaurant. Great publicity."

"No it's *not*." Piper couldn't believe how little Geraldine seemed to care about the fact that she'd completely misrepresented Tai.

"We seem to be in disagreement. It's lucky you no longer work at the *Age*."

"That's for sure. I'm so incredibly disappointed in you, Geraldine. I thought you were better than this." Piper hung up the phone and growled in frustration. Eyota, Adahy and Jackie were looking at her. She ran a hand through her hair and tried to calm down. "She didn't care. She completely misrepresented Tai and your culture, and she doesn't give a hoot." Piper paced up and down the kitchen, waving her hands around. She stopped and addressed Eyota. "I'm so sorry. I never expected this."

"I take it they changed what you wrote," Jackie said.

"Yes. I can show you the original if you like." She didn't want Tai's mother thinking the worst of her.

"Yes, please."

Piper turned on her laptop and passed it over to the woman. "I did two versions because I wasn't sure which one Tai would want." She walked away, taking deep breaths, trying to calm herself. She'd promised Tai she would write an accurate article, she'd promised not to be like that travel reporter – and she hadn't been able to keep that promise.

Jackie shifted the screen so Eyota could read as well. The women read in silence and Adahy stood up to read over their shoulder. Bradley left the table and began to practice the song Adahy had taught him yesterday in the living room.

Jackie had tears in her eyes when she finished reading. "I didn't know any of that," she said. "He's worked so hard. I'm so proud of him."

Eyota patted her hand. "You should tell him some time."

Jackie bit her lip.

Her reaction made Piper forget her concerns for the moment. Tai was going to try to bridge the distance with his mother today. It seemed both mother and son were unsure how to approach each other.

"It's a good article, Piper," Adahy said. "I can't understand why they laid you off."

"You're not working?" Jackie asked.

"Not for the paper. I'm doing some work for Tai on a cookbook and some things for Eyota."

"Piper's recording the stories of the tribe," Eyota told her daughter-in-law. "Though she had a good idea yesterday – that we should film the elders telling them instead."

"I know someone who could do that," Jackie said.

"Who?" Adahy asked.

She blushed. "A friend."

Piper bet the friend was male.

"Do you have a boyfriend, Mom?" Adahy asked, picking up the same signs Piper had.

Jackie reddened further. "No, ah, well I guess, yes?"

"Cool, what's his name?" There wasn't much that fazed Adahy, and it had been twenty years since his father died.

"Hugh," she said, waiting for Eyota's reaction.

Eyota smiled. "You'll have to bring Hugh out to the reservation next time you come," she said. "I'd like to meet him."

How would Tai react to the news? He'd loved his father: that had been clear when he'd spoken of him. Would he see his mother's boyfriend as a betrayal?

She wasn't sure.

"What does he do?" Adahy asked.

"He's a cameraman for the local news," she said, naming the station.

Piper sat up. "Is that Hugh Jordan?"

"Yes."

Piper had worked with Hugh when she'd interviewed Emily, Kate's nanny who had accused Adrian of cheating on her. He was a really nice man. "He's lovely."

Jackie beamed at her.

The sounds of kids calling to each other entered the kitchen.

"That's our sign it's time to get to class," Eyota said.

Piper wasn't sure whether she should go. She wanted to give Tai a chance to talk to his mother alone, but she didn't want anyone to show him that article before she had a chance to prepare him. She sighed. His relationship with his mother was more important. She'd sort out the article after lunch. "I'll stay here and work on my notes."

"You've been working all week," Eyota said.

Piper smiled. "Compared to the hours I was doing at the paper, I've been positively slack."

"I don't want you working too hard," Eyota said, frowning.

Piper stood up to walk her to the door. "Trust me, I'm fine. I'll use the quiet to check what I may have missed."

She gave Bradley a hug and waved to the kids waiting outside.

"I'll make sure Tai brings you a plate," Adahy said.

"I'll walk down when you're due to finish," she responded. She'd met enough people on the reservation now to talk to others while Tai spoke with his mother.

When they were gone, Piper sat down at the kitchen table, pleased to be alone. She had enjoyed staying with Eyota over the week, but it was the first time in a long time she hadn't had time to herself and it was something she really needed. How was Tai going to react when he saw that article? She felt sick just thinking about it. She shook her head. There was no point worrying about it. They'd deal with the article together.

In the meantime she would make the changes she'd discussed with Tai the night before and work on the next section, before walking over to the school for lunch.

She'd give Tai plenty of space if he needed it, and would encourage him to speak with his mother.

And then they could talk.

***

Tai's head was not in the lesson. He spoke automatically, taking his students through the correct way to cook shrimp.

Piper hadn't come to the lesson and he was glad – she clouded his thoughts.

Now however, he was all too aware of his mother in the room. She stood at one of the tables not far from him and listened intently.

He felt like a child who had to give a presentation in front of the whole school. Not that he could remember a time when his mother had actually made it to any of his school events. He brushed off the resentment. It was in the past and it was time to move forward. He walked around the classroom, checking how people were doing, offering tips and advice where needed. His final stop was in front of his mother and Adahy.

"How's it going?" he asked.

Her smile was cautious. "I think I'm doing it right."

Tai checked her pan. "Have a taste and see if it needs any more spice."

She did as he asked her and said, "It tastes good to me."

"Then you're doing it right," he said.

His mother positively beamed at him. He'd never seen her that happy around him. Maybe she would be willing to talk.

When the class finished and everything had been cleaned up, they took the food outside to share with others who had arrived for lunch. Piper was there, but she dished up her food and went to talk to one of the elders of the tribe who she must have interviewed during the week. He was relieved. He couldn't deal with her and his mother at the same time.

He dished up his own portion and sat down on one of the benches, a little apart from the others. If anyone wanted to talk to him, they'd come over.

Jackie glanced at him and took a deep breath as if preparing herself. Then she walked over. Tai's skin tightened in an automatic response.

"Mind if I sit down?"

He gestured to the spot next to himself. "Go ahead."

She was silent for a moment before saying, "Piper showed me the articles she did on you – not the one the paper published, but the others."

Surprised, he glanced at her. He hadn't realized his profile had been published.

"They're very good. You've done so much work." She hesitated. "I'm proud of you."

Someone could have knocked him down with a feather. He had no idea what to say, no idea how to react.

She sighed and then got to her feet. "I wanted you to know."

Tai put a hand on her arm. "Wait. Sit down, please." He sighed as well. "I don't know what to say. You've never told me that before."

"You never seemed to need it."

His armor had worked well. Tai got to his feet. "Do you want to go for a walk?" He couldn't sit here and discuss this with so many people around.

"Sure."

They left their bowls on the seat and walked out of the school grounds toward the lake.

The day was muggy but the shade of the trees offered some relief.

"You should come to the Wooden Spoon some time," he said, choosing the safest topic. "Bring some friends and you can have a meal on the house." He had no idea if his mother had any friends, and wasn't that a sad indication of how well he knew her?

"I'd like that. People are always impressed when I tell them my son owns it. I've never read a bad review."

"We aim to please." It was weird to hear his mother bragged about his achievements. He expected her to mention Adahy but not him.

At the lake edge they stopped walking and stood side by side. There were a couple of canoes in the distance and some kids splashing and playing down the shore, but where they were it was still.

Tai didn't know how to start the conversation. Should he apologize, say he would like to know her better?

"I went to Piper's parents' for dinner last week," he said. "Her mother showed me their family albums from when Piper was a kid. Some of them reminded me of photos we took before Dad died."

His mother took a sharp intake of breath.

It wasn't often that any of them mentioned his father.

"We don't have many from after." He wasn't blaming her: he was trying to explain.

"Tai, I'm sorry. I didn't deal well with your father's death," his mother said, turning to him. "I knew he was depressed, but I also knew how much he loved all of us and I thought it would be enough." Her eyes filled with pain. "I was wrong and I blame myself for being so in love that I didn't pay more attention to the signs."

Tai took a step back. "I thought you blamed me."

Jackie's eyes widened. "Of course not." She reached out to him, holding his hand. "You were only a boy. You couldn't possibly have stopped it."

Tai held on to her hand, the first connection he'd had to her in a long time. "I blamed myself. I knew something wasn't right that morning before I went to school. I should have stayed with him. It's why I went home at lunchtime. I wanted to cheer him up."

"I didn't know what to say to you. How do you comfort a child who has found his father dead? I fell apart and I will forever be indebted to Eyota for taking charge and caring for you boys." Her eyes were filled with grief. "When I finally came to my senses I didn't know how to bridge the distance between us. You'd withdrawn, grown up – you didn't want me around and I didn't blame you. I hadn't been there when you needed me the most."

It appeared they had misunderstood each other all along.

It was time to fix things. He stepped forward, bridging the gap between them and wrapped his arms around her. "I'm sorry."

She hugged him fiercely, and sobbed against his neck. "I'm so, so sorry."

Tai's heart lifted as he held his mother. It would take them a while to get used to each other, for the awkwardness to completely fade, but they'd made a start.

***

Piper saw Tai and his mother walking back to the school. They weren't talking but their body language was more relaxed than it had been when they'd walked off together. She hoped it meant they'd spoken and patched things up a little.

A shadow above her made her look up. It was Stan and his face was as dark as a thundercloud.

"Is this what you call a decent article?" He slammed the profile magazine down on the table in front of her.

Holy hell. He was going to cause a scene and Tai hadn't seen it yet. "I didn't write that," she said as Tai walked over.

"Isn't that your name on the byline?" He pointed to it.

"Yes."

"What's going on?" Tai put a hand on Piper's shoulder.

"You said your girlfriend was sympathetic to our cause, that she would write a fair and balanced book on our history. I say this proves otherwise." He thrust the paper at Tai.

"Tai, they changed my article," Piper said, turning to him as he took the paper and read. She held her breath.

Finally he looked up. His eyes were hard. He reminded her of the Tai he was when she first met him – aloof and uninterested. "I thought you only sent one article."

"I did," she insisted, getting to her feet. "They must have taken the other one from my laptop."

He was silent for a long moment. "I trusted you. You promised me a fair representation." His voice was so cold.

Worry skittered through her. "I called Geraldine and told her you'd want a retraction. I'll put the original up on my blog."

"It's too late. The damage is done."

She was aware that all eyes were on them, watching. She didn't want to fight in public. "Can we go and talk about this?"

Tai looked around and noticed the attention. He stalked away, down the path that led to Eyota's house.

Piper hurried to catch up with him. "I'm so sorry, Tai. I never believed Geraldine would do this, otherwise I wouldn't have convinced you to do the interview."

"How do I know it *was* Geraldine? How do I know it wasn't you?"

Her worry slid into anger. "If you could even think that then you don't know me very well at all."

"Maybe I don't." He turned around. "We should go our separate ways."

All the air left Piper's lungs. She gasped for breath. "You're kidding me."

"No. You'll never truly understand me and my culture."

She couldn't form any words as she watched him walk away. Hadn't she spent the last week immersing herself in his culture, learning about it, writing about it and loving it? Hadn't he said what she'd written so far for the cookbook was good, insightful, just what he was looking for?

What the hell was going on with him? He couldn't break up with her over the article. She knew it was a big deal to him, but what they had was more than that.

Wasn't it?

She didn't know what to do. Should she go after him, tell him she loved him, ask him to listen to her? Maybe it would be better to wait until he'd calmed down. Give him time to think things through. He didn't like to be rushed into anything. There had to be some way she could convince him she respected his culture and his beliefs.

Slowly she walked to Eyota's house. Everyone was still at the school having lunch. She couldn't stay here. Not if he was serious. It would be too awkward.

She gathered her things, left Eyota and Bradley a note to say she'd been called back to Houston and that she'd call them during the week.

Then she drove home.

She was just outside the reservation when her numbness thawed. She pulled over to the side of the road and cried.

Chapter 18

Tai strode down the path, not caring which direction he was going, just needing to get away.

It was done.

He'd broken up with Piper.

He'd been agonizing over the decision for the past few hours, but he couldn't come up with another solution. It was Piper or his tribe.

He couldn't turn his back on his people, his culture, his world. He'd put too much into it; it meant too much to him. He couldn't possibly have children knowing they would not be allowed to be part of that world.

She'd handed him the perfect excuse to break up with her and he'd grabbed it desperately.

It was better this way.

Better to break up before she fell in love.

But never in his wildest dreams had he imagined it would hurt like this. It was hard to breathe, his heart clenched so tightly.

He crashed through the forest, allowing branches to whip him, providing resistance to where he wanted to go.

Which was as far away from Piper as he could get.

Eventually he stopped, and looked around, breathing heavily. She wasn't coming after him. The thought stabbed his heart but he ignored it.

What was he going to do now? Did he go back to the school and hope Piper had left? He couldn't just hide out here in the forest, as much as he wanted to. He'd just reconciled with his mother and he had to go back to say goodbye to her.

Hoping like hell Piper was gone, he turned around and headed slowly back to the school.

***

"There you are!" Adahy lifted a hand in greeting. "Where's Piper?"

Just hearing her name caused his heart to beat faster. "I don't know." He glared, hoping his brother would take the hint.

"You two have a fight?" He fell into step with his brother.

"It's none of your business."

Adahy held up his hands. "I'm trying to help. You look agitated."

Tai stopped, huffed out a breath. It wasn't fair for him to take his anger out on Adahy. He wasn't doing anything wrong. "We broke up."

"This isn't about the article, is it?"

"No. I realized it will never work. She's not Queche."

Adahy's mouth dropped open. "You split up with your gorgeous sweetheart of a girlfriend because she's white?" He shook his head. "I thought you were smarter than that."

"You're supposed to be on my side," Tai reminded him.

"Not when you do something so dumb."

Annoyed, Tai turned to him. "I'm sure you've read the article. She doesn't understand us. She doesn't fit in."

"She was fitting in fine this weekend," Adahy said and squinted at him. "What's the real problem? Is she shit in bed?"

Tai blinked and then blinked again. He couldn't keep up with his brother. "No."

"Has she become clingy and nagging?"

"No." Piper had always given him the space he needed.

"Then what?"

"It won't work." He didn't want to stand here justifying his decision to his brother. Adahy didn't understand what the tribe meant to him. He didn't realize how hard Tai fought to save it, to support it, to make it self-sufficient. How he needed to make sure others didn't suffer like he had. He couldn't jeopardize all of that for his own needs.

He needed to continue to work with the council to help preserve their culture, their peace of mind, their identity.

And he needed to make sure his children were part of that.

Pushing past Adahy he continued to the school.

And immediately wished he hadn't, when Stan cornered him. "What did she have to say for herself?" he demanded.

Tai sighed. He might have used the article as an excuse to break up with Piper but he couldn't let the others believe it was her fault. "She didn't write the article, Stan."

"What a load of trash. Of course she did. It says so right on the top."

"Her editor changed it."

"That's convenient."

He ran a hand through his hair. "Can we just drop it? It's too late now."

It was another negative portrayal of a Native American.

One day he might even stop being surprised by it.

***

Piper called Eyota on Monday morning to apologize for leaving without saying goodbye.

"I hope everything is all right," Eyota said.

Piper had no idea what Tai had told them. "It's fine. I'll send through the first chapter by the end of the week."

"Take your time. There's no rush."

"Is Bradley there?" She didn't want him to think she'd deserted him.

"I'll put him on."

"Hey, Piper." He sounded a little sad.

"Hi, Bradley. I'm sorry I had to rush off yesterday. I didn't get a chance to wish you good luck on your spelling bee today."

"I think I'll ace it after your help." His voice perked up.

"I'm sure you will. I'll give you a call later in the week to see how it went."

"OK. Bye, Piper."

She hung up. No matter what happened between her and Tai, she wasn't going to desert Bradley.

The thought of Tai made her sad. He hadn't called like she'd hoped he would, but she had a plan. She was going to work on the recipe book this morning and then head to the restaurant mid afternoon when it was quiet, and talk with him.

She would tell him what Geraldine had said, she would tell him she loved him, and she would support him and his tribe in whatever way she could.

Surely he would forgive her.

***

At three o'clock Piper drove to the Wooden Spoon. The back door was locked, which was unusual. She knocked and Kath answered. "Is he here?" Piper asked.

Kath shuffled her feet. "He is," she said. "But I'm not allowed to let you in."

Piper gaped at her. "What?"

"I asked how the recipe book was coming and he said you weren't welcome in the kitchen any more."

Piper was suddenly short of breath. "Could you check again for me?" She hated to put Kath in a difficult position but she may have misunderstood. "I can meet him in the restaurant."

Kath nodded.

A few minutes later she was back. "No. He's busy." She fidgeted with her hands.

"Thanks, Kath," Piper managed to say, and walked away. He wouldn't even talk to her. After all they had been through together and he wouldn't give her a chance to explain.

How could he believe she'd written that article?

Unless he'd just used it as an excuse to break up. Maybe she'd unknowingly put out some kind of "I love you" vibes and it had freaked him out. But the least he could do was be honest with her. She would make him tell her the truth.

Fueled by anger, she entered the restaurant through the front door, waving to the waiter and moving purposefully toward the kitchen as if she had a right to be there. No one tried to stop her.

She would have loved to see them try.

Pushing open the doors separating the kitchen from the restaurant, she ignored the few staff in there prepping for dinner. Kath saw her but didn't move.

Tai was in his office, working on his computer. He was still wearing his chef's uniform, his hair was tied back in his usual braid and his eyes were focused on whatever it was he was reading.

He looked so good, her heart hurt.

Striding into his office she was rewarded with a satisfying look of shock before his face pulled on the mask of disinterest.

"Did you really believe you could break up with me and not let me defend myself?" she asked. She didn't wait for an answer. "You know I didn't write that article. I showed you the two I did write, so don't you dare use that as an excuse." She took a breath. "As for understanding your culture, I find it absolutely fascinating. I loved spending time on the reservation and getting to know everyone. No, I didn't grow up with your traditions so they don't have the same meaning to me as they do to you, but that doesn't mean I don't respect your right to believe them."

Tai stared at her, his expression unchanging as if he was uninterested in what she had to say. Doubt slid insidiously inside her. How could he look at her like that? Not a flicker of emotion. They had shared so much.

She went on the attack to get some sort of response from him. "But maybe you used my race as an excuse to break up with me." She remembered what Stan had told her and everything clicked into place. "That's it, isn't it? It's because I'm not Queche. You never intended this to be anything more than a fling. You would never marry anyone who wasn't part of your tribe."

He said nothing, but his eye twitched.

He had known about the tribal laws. He had never considered what they had serious. Being hit by a truck would have been less painful.

"Well, let me give you some advice. Next time you decide to date a white woman, tell her at the start that it's just casual, that your tribal laws won't allow it to be more serious. Tell her before she falls in love with you." Her voice broke. "Save her the heartbreak you're putting me through."

He flinched.

At least something got through to him.

"You don't need to worry about me coming around again. We're both clear on where we stand."

With as much dignity as she could muster, Piper turned and walked out of the office, out of the kitchen and out of Tai's life.

Only when she reached her car did she let the tears fall.

***

Tai waited until the kitchen door had closed behind Piper before he lowered his head into his hands.

What a mess.

He had never wanted it to come to this. He'd been selfish, trying to fool himself that what they had was just casual because he loved spending time with her.

It wasn't going to work. It couldn't …

And then she'd said she loved him.

It was like being hit by lightning. A spark of electricity, excitement, joy, before he remembered it couldn't be. He'd wanted to end the relationship before she loved him. He hadn't wanted to hurt her. He was hurting enough for the both of them.

"You all right, Chef?" Kath hovered at the doorway. She'd probably heard the whole thing.

"Fine. I've got work to do." He turned away from her, dismissing her, and waited until she left.

Whose stupid idea had it been to put a glass window in his office? All he wanted to do was shut himself in and hide from the world but that wouldn't work.

No, he had to keep busy.

His phone rang and he grabbed it, desperate for the distraction.

"Tai, I want to talk to you about the concert," George said.

Would there be a concert now? Would Piper get so upset that she'd ask George to cancel it?

"What do you need?"

"Numbers of people attending from the reservation," he said. "Tickets go on sale tomorrow and I need to hold back the right amount for the kids who are coming."

Tai frowned. "What kids?"

"Piper asked for the kids from the reservation to get free

tickets, because they can't afford it and the money is going to help them."

Tai leaned back in his chair as emotion swamped him. She hadn't told him. The kids would love it. "I'm not sure. Let me make some calls and I'll get back to you."

"Great. I'm so excited about this. I reckon we should make it an annual event."

Tai was used to George's enthusiasm. "Let's see how this one goes first."

After a bit more discussion they hung up and Tai called his grandmother. He explained about the tickets.

"I know. Piper was talking with the school. They can organize transport for a hundred children."

Would George be willing to give away so many tickets? "I'll check the numbers with George."

"Wonderful. Can you tell Piper that Bradley will be one of the children going so she won't need to take him?"

Tai hesitated. "You'd better tell her yourself."

"Why?" His grandmother's voice was concerned.

"We broke up. I'll talk to you later, Ka' sa'." He hung up before she asked him any more questions.

He had to stop thinking about Piper, stop talking to people who knew her. It was better they had a clean break, but with the concert, that was likely to be difficult. He had to survive the next couple of weeks and then the event would be over and no one should ever mention Piper to him again. He could cope with that.

He would have to.

He called George back and gave him the number.

"Fantastic. We've been promoting the hell out of the concert and tickets go on sale tomorrow. I'll know by the end of the day how successful the promo has been."

Tai was suddenly nervous. What if no one was interested in attending such a diverse concert? Kent Downer might be enough of a draw card but there were no guarantees. "Will you let me know?"

"Sure."

Tai hung up. He had work he needed to go on with.

And a woman he needed to forget.

***

Piper allowed herself an hour for crying and self-pity and then threw herself into work. The quicker she finished the cookbook the sooner she could put Tai behind her.

She worked late into the night, only stopping when she couldn't keep her eyes open. Then she fell into bed and slept.

The next day she did the same, working from the moment she got up until she fell asleep at her table.

By Wednesday evening the cookbook was ready for its final read-through. She pushed back from the table and breathed a sigh of relief. By the end of tomorrow she could send the manuscript to Tai and she wouldn't have to see him again.

The thought caused her more pain than relief.

Needing a distraction she cleaned her house, picking up the snack wrappers and rewashing the clothes that Moggy had been using as a bed for weeks. She was becoming a hermit.

She had to get out of her apartment and back into civilization.

But not tonight. She was so tired she needed to sleep, but in the morning she would head to Eat, Drink, Read and go through the manuscript there.

***

Piper got up early on Thursday and fussed with her appearance to make herself feel more confident, and then she drove to Elle's café.

It was busy with the morning coffee rush so she took a seat and waited for Nora to take her order.

While the girls were making her coffee, she fired up her laptop and began to read through the recipe book.

She was pleased with what she had done. The Queche stories flowed nicely into the recipe sections and were easy to read.

"Hi! I haven't seen you in a while." Elle delivered her order and sat down across from her. "Where have you been hiding?"

"On the reservation." Piper told her about the two ghost-writing projects.

"Wow, that must be interesting. Tai's keen to share his

culture with you."

At the mention of Tai's name Piper swallowed the lump in her throat.

"What's wrong? You don't look so good."

"Nothing." She didn't want to tell her friend yet. It hurt too much to talk about it and she didn't want to start crying here. "Just tired."

"You've been working hard." Elle smiled. "Oh, hey, George was going to call you and Tai today. He wanted to go over the concert plans."

Piper was supposed to be taking Bradley. "He'd better call Tai. But I'll call George later and see if there's anything I can do to help."

"It's mostly sorted. Imogen is checking the details of the auction website today and it should go live tomorrow."

Piper had been so out of touch with what was going on. Her friends had done amazing things to get the fundraiser off the ground and she'd barely done anything. "I'll give her a call too." Imogen's wedding was in a couple of weeks and Piper knew nothing about it except that she was a bridesmaid.

She'd promised herself when she was laid off that she would be a better friend, not work all the time, but somehow she'd replaced work with Tai and the ghost-writing projects, and *still* neglected her friends.

Had she always been so self-absorbed?

"I've got to run. I'll talk to you later." Elle stood up and went to serve a customer.

Piper sighed.

She was a mess. She'd been so excited learning about Tai's culture that she'd neglected not only her friends, but also her search for permanent employment. She still had a couple more weeks of work on the manuscript for Eyota, assuming she still wanted to go ahead with it, and the money from both projects would last her a couple of months. But she had to find a job.

She'd start looking as soon as she'd finished the cookbook.

***

Piper returned to her apartment after lunch, and at the end of the day, she was satisfied with the cookbook. All it required was the recipes, which Tai could easily add in himself. She sent him the file, agonizing over the email until she was sure it sounded as professional as she could make it.

Then she got up to find something for dinner. She switched on the radio and found a station playing cheerful tunes. As part of her new resolution, she was determined not to work past six o'clock. Her evenings would be spent reading books, watching television or catching up with family and friends.

As she checked her cupboard for food, a song came on the radio that she recognized immediately – Adahy's single. She grinned and turned up the volume, tapping her feet in time with the music. She should call him and tell him it was playing.

She froze with her hand outstretched to the phone. Maybe he wouldn't want to hear from her now she and Tai had broken up. Had she not only lost Tai, but Rayen and Adahy too? Tears sprang to her eyes and she blinked them back.

As she was debating whether she should call, the phone rang. Piper turned down the music and answered.

"Have you had dinner yet?" It was Imogen.

"No."

"Great. I'll bring pizza." She hung up before Piper could ask what was going on. She wasn't in the mood to socialize but it would be good to talk to her friend. She needed to tell someone about Tai.

She went to the fridge to check if she had anything she could offer Imogen to drink.

Her laptop pinged with an incoming message. It was from Tai.

Manuscript fine. Payment in account. Contract is complete.

That was it. Nothing that would suggest he felt anything for her. She squeezed her eyes shut to stop the tears. She wasn't going to cry. Imogen would be here soon.

When the knock at the door came, Piper had two glasses out and a bottle of white wine.

She opened the door and stepped back in surprise. Imogen stood holding two pizza boxes and with her were Libby and Elle.

"Girls' night," Imogen announced, walking in and putting the pizza on the coffee table in front of the sofa.

Piper hugged Elle and Libby and closed the door before she turned. "We didn't have anything planned, did we?" Her brain may have been distracted this week but she was almost certain they hadn't had a date.

"You looked like you needed cheering up at the café today," Elle said. "So I called the others."

"We've barely seen you since you got cozy with Tai," Libby said. "Not that we blame you."

At Tai's name Piper turned away, and busied herself getting extra glasses out, blinking back the tears. Damn it, she didn't want to cry any more.

"Honey, what happened?" Imogen asked, coming over and putting her arm around Piper's waist.

All the restraint she'd built up around herself during the day crumbled at her friend's gentle question. Tears sprung to her eyes. She tried blinking them away but they were coming too fast. "He broke up with me," she said. She wiped her eyes and turned to pour the wine.

"Why? What's wrong with him?" Libby asked.

Piper smiled a little. She swallowed down the lump in her throat and handed the wine to Libby and Elle. "First he said it was because of the article I wrote. Did you see it? Geraldine changed the whole damned thing and it was garbage. Then when I went to explain and he didn't listen, I realized it was actually because I'm not part of the tribe. Membership passes down through the mother's side so if we had children they wouldn't be Queche. To him it was just a fling all along."

"Oh, honey, that's awful," Libby said.

"He never mentioned it earlier?" Imogen asked.

Piper shook her head.

Elle frowned. "Is there any way they can change it?"

Piper stopped with her wine glass halfway to her mouth. "Eyota did say she's been trying to change the law for years." But she hadn't said what the problem was.

Did Tai know? Did he even care?

Piper thought about the way Tai had greeted her after they'd been apart for a few days. She'd been sure he cared for her. But the Tai who had sat across from her at the restaurant was not the same person.

She shook her head. "I told him I loved him and he just sat there. If he loved me, he would have thought of changing the laws rather than just giving me up." She took a big gulp of her wine to numb the pain.

"Maybe he doesn't know he *can* change it," Imogen suggested. "He might come to his senses."

Or he might move on.

She didn't have a lot of choice. She'd told him she loved him and he hadn't seemed to care. She'd seem pathetic and desperate if she kept trying. She wasn't going to throw herself at someone who didn't love her.

"It's hard," Libby said. "I was a wreck when Adrian broke up with me. I was sure I'd never see him again. But the interview you did with Emily showed him I cared and he'd been wrong."

She didn't think anything she did would overcome Tai's commitment to his tribe and, if she was rational about it, she could understand his point of view. If the roles were reversed, she'd want her children to inherit her culture.

But perhaps he would reconsider if she helped with the finishing touches of the concert and auction, if she wrote the best damn history of his tribe and if she took Bradley to the concert like she promised. If none of that changed his mind, then she would have to move on.

However hard it would be.

Right now though, she wanted a distraction. She grabbed a piece of pizza. "Tell me how the wedding plans are going," she said to Imogen.

Imogen hesitated. "We don't need to talk about it, Piper. You're hurting and I don't want to be insensitive."

Piper shook her head. "I insist. I want proof happily ever after does exist," she said. "Tell me everything."

After a little bit of cajoling, Imogen smiled. "All right. It's like this."

***

Tai felt like a bear with a sore tooth – cranky and aching all the time. He snapped at his staff, fought with Adahy and even yelled at Rayen.

All the while Piper haunted him.

People would mention her name or something would happen that would remind him of her. In the restaurant he'd occasionally forget and look for her in the break room because he had something to share.

Her spirit had infused itself in every part of his life. His three favorite places – the restaurant, his home and the reservation – now all reminded him of her.

But that didn't mean they could be together.

He shook away the thought. Today he needed to be focused. His mother was out in the restaurant with her friend, Hugh, and Adahy. Though he hated going out into the seating area, he had to.

He'd arranged for them to sit at one of the most secluded tables. It was the same one Piper and Rayen had sat at when they'd gone out together.

Damn it. There she was again. Would she ever leave his thoughts?

At the table he kissed his mother's cheek and shook Hugh's hand. The man was in his mid fifties, with short dark hair and a slim build.

"Nice to finally meet you," Hugh said. "Your mother talks about you so often, I feel as if I know you."

That surprised him. "Likewise," he lied.

He didn't know a lot about Hugh, but his mother liked him. He would have to invite them both around to the house for a meal soon.

"Have you read the work Piper has done on the book for Eyota?" Jackie asked. "She emailed me a copy yesterday. It's wonderful."

He hadn't told his mother they'd broken up. "No."

"Oh. You'll have to ask her to see it. She's even done a marketing plan. She has a friend who's in the publishing industry, I think."

"I'd better get back to the kitchen," he said, desperate to escape. "I'll leave you to enjoy your meal."

His mother looked a little worried about his abrupt manner so he bent down and kissed her cheek, forcing a smile to his face. "Duty calls. Let the waiter know if you need anything." He left.

Why was it he couldn't escape Piper as easily?

Chapter 19

The Friday before the concert, Tai drove to the reservation. He'd agreed to chaperone the excursion and that included the bus trip into Houston. They were leaving early on Saturday morning in order to arrive in time to watch the sound check and do a little bit of sight-seeing.

When he arrived at his grandmother's house he found Bradley packing an overnight bag. "Where are you off to?" Tai asked, giving him a hug.

Bradley's eyes were wide with excitement. "After the concert, I'm staying at Piper's place and she's taking me to the Space Center on Sunday and then bringing me home."

Tai flinched at the mention of Piper's name. "When did you organize that?" he asked.

"Yesterday. We were talking about my science class and the planets, and she said I had to go to the space center."

Why was Bradley talking to Piper? "Did she come to the rez to go over the book?"

"No. She calls me a couple times a week." Bradley zipped up his bag and carried it to the front door.

Tai frowned. Why would she?

His grandmother came out of the kitchen and greeted him. "I'm glad you're here. I want you to read over Piper's manuscript. I'm pretty happy with it, but I'd like another opinion."

It was the last thing he wanted to do. He didn't want to read her work, but he couldn't escape. Better to get it over with. "Where is it?"

"In the kitchen."

Tai sat down and began.

The writing was easy to read. It was a casual, conversational style — like someone was talking to him rather than like he was reading. The introduction described where the tribe was at currently. Then the following chapters were broken down into sections of white man's history and when the land had been theirs, as well as including the myths and legends of the tribe.

It was written with sensitivity and compassion. He flicked through, only reading passages. In sections he felt her anger at the treatment of his people and her respect for how they had overcome it.

Overwhelmed, he pushed it aside. "It looks fine," he said to his grandmother who had been sitting at the table weaving a basket.

Eyota raised her eyebrows. "I thought it was better than fine," she said. "I thought it was excellent."

"She has a way of writing what you want to see." That's all it was. That's all he could let it be.

"What did you see?" his grandmother asked.

He looked up at her then. She watched him steadily, with those eyes that could gaze into his soul. He couldn't lie to her, much as he wanted to. "She respects our tribe," he said. It made it so much more difficult.

Eyota nodded. "I also felt her anger at our experiences and her joy at our stories."

Tai didn't want to listen. "She's good at what she does."

Eyota put down her basket with a sound of disgust. "I didn't believe Adahy when he told me you were behaving like a child, but I see now he was right. Since the two of you broke up I've heard nothing but tales of your anger. If you miss her so much, you should win her back."

Tai pushed to his feet. "I don't want her back." He'd never told a bigger lie in his life.

"Nonsense. You've been moping around for weeks."

"*I* broke up with *her*," he said, the anger building. "I

wouldn't have done it if I wanted her."

Eyota's mouth dropped open, then she scrutinized him. "Why did you?"

It was none of her business. It was none of anyone's business.

But he always felt he had to explain himself to his grandmother. She deserved it.

He just had to come up with an excuse she would believe.

"We have nothing in common. My focus is on helping my tribe and my people and she wrote an article that betrayed all that."

The disbelief on his grandmother's face had him dropping his gaze. "I know you don't believe she wrote that. She showed me her articles. Besides, you just read that manuscript, didn't you?" she asked. "She is interested and not because she was paid to be. That girl is fascinated by our culture."

"But she doesn't fit in," he said desperately.

"Of course she does. I've had numerous people ask when she's coming back and when the book will be finished."

Eyota was right. He closed his eyes, his heart sore. He had to tell the truth.

He said, "If we had children, they wouldn't be part of the tribe. Tribal membership is passed down through the mother."

Her eyes widened. "If you're considering children, she must mean a great deal to you." She was silent for a long moment, before she said, "An official recognition by the tribe doesn't make any children you have more or less Queche in my eyes or in your own. You will bring them up to respect our history, to learn our language, to honor our traditions. They will be our family and they will be our tribe."

She made it sound simple.

Did it really matter whether it was official? Would it matter to his children?

Before he could speak, she asked, "Does a marriage certificate mean you are more committed to your partner than you were the day before?" she asked. She shook her head. "Of course not. If you love her, you can't let her go. Love is much too important."

"But the tribe …"

Eyota waved her hand. "You have done your share for the tribe. Besides, I've been trying to get the tribal council to change those rules for years. There aren't enough of us now to keep going with old ways that limit our growth. They'll make us extinct. It's just Stan dragging his heels."

Tai stared at her. Could there really be an opportunity to change it?

He didn't know what to do. He'd been so dedicated to his people for so long. He'd done everything by the book, but Eyota was suggesting the book could be rewritten.

"Are you scared of love?" The question came out of nowhere.

He blinked but didn't answer.

"I know your father's death affected you greatly, and your mother fell apart, but it wasn't because she loved too much – it was because she didn't know how to cope."

Tai had never consciously considered that. He'd always sworn to himself he would never abandon his children if something like that happened to him, but he'd never thought he was scared of loving.

When he said nothing she said, "Why don't you go for a walk? Clear your head. But don't forget, our history is full of intermarriage between tribes and between races. That should not be your deciding factor."

Eager to escape, Tai almost ran out the door.

He avoided the lake. It was early evening and there'd still be some swimmers down there. He didn't want to speak to anyone, see anyone. Everyone was so sure he should be with Piper, but they didn't know his heart. Only he did. Was she right for him? They were so different.

He loved to cook; she preferred to buy her food.

She was messy; he was neat.

He was of the Queche people; she was white.

She had a very happy family with parents who loved each other, and his was recovering from dysfunction and his father had committed suicide.

He didn't drink alcohol, but she always had a bottle of wine in her fridge.

He rode a motorcycle; she drove a car.

Tai arrived at the stream and sat down. He sighed and closed his eyes.

Focusing on his breathing, he listened to the noises of the forest around him. He needed a few minutes to center himself, loosen the tightness in his chest and ease the pain in his heart. Somewhere to the right of him a crow squawked.

Piper's image came unbidden to his mind's eye. She was beautiful, but it was her smile that really got him. It was as if she was having the time of her life.

He grinned at the image.

What did he know about her? She worked hard. When he'd asked for her help with the recipe book he never imagined she would do it so quickly, but she'd embraced the challenge and run with it. She liked to be challenged.

She liked to bring issues to the public's attention. She wanted to help people. She was determined. He remembered her persistence in getting that first interview. Thank goodness for it.

Her writing was beautiful and she had a way of presenting the information that made him want to read on. And she had sensitivity and a knack of knowing when there was more underneath.

Piper loved her family and her friends. She'd fit in easily with his own. She liked people no matter their race, their background, their circumstances. She felt responsible for those around her. She had been devastated when Rayen had been assaulted, had blamed herself. She'd been there for Bradley when he needed someone to talk to. Hell, she'd been there for him as well when he'd despaired over Jerry's death.

He loved that she'd known something was wrong and had come to help.

He loved her.

Tai opened his eyes as the thought reverberated in his consciousness.

That was the key.

He *did* love Piper.

But there was still the issue of tribal membership. Eyota *said* she was trying to get the council to change it – could she?

He ran a hand over the rock he was sitting on, allowing the

233

surface to rub his skin. He had to talk to Stan, had to ask him if there was a possibility.

If the law could be changed he would choose Piper in an instant.

And that was his answer.

He got to his feet and headed to Stan's house.

***

Stan answered the door almost immediately. "Quit your pounding. What's the emergency?"

Tai blinked and un-fisted his hand. He hadn't realized he'd knocked so loudly. "Sorry."

Stan grunted. "What do you want?"

Tai swallowed heavily and took a breath. "I wanted to ask you about a matter of law," he said. "Tribal membership."

"What about it?"

"It's passed down the maternal line. Are there any plans to change this?"

Stan squinted at him. "Is this about your girl?"

He couldn't call Piper his girl any more. "Yes."

"You'd better come in." Stan held the door open and Tai followed him into the living room. "You planning on marrying her?"

His heart clenched. "I want to, but the law …"

Stan sighed. "Tai, I'm an old man. I've experienced more abuse by the white man than anyone should ever have to. I was sure Piper would be another to take advantage of us. That article seemed to prove it."

Tai didn't say a word. He didn't want to interrupt Stan.

"If you'd asked me a month ago if the laws should change I would have said no. I didn't want anyone diluting our tribe." He grasped his braid. "But that girl is different. Eyota showed me her manuscript – she has recorded our history beautifully." He shook his head as if he couldn't believe it. "She and her friends arranged that concert and the auction. Eyota told me the preliminary figures yesterday. It will help our tribe tremendously."

Tai held his breath.

"And then there's you to consider." Stan nodded at Tai.

"Don't think the council doesn't recognize everything you do for our tribe. I saw your passion for her when you defended her to me. We would hate to lose you."

Tai didn't tell him he'd chosen the tribe over the love of his life.

"Plus Eyota's been nagging me about that law extra hard since you first brought Piper to the rez. That woman is like a dog with a bone when she wants something." Stan slapped both hands on his lap. "I will propose changing the law at the next meeting. I was the one vetoing it all these years, so I think it will get approved."

His heart stopped. "Really?"

"Yes, really." Stan scowled at him and got to his feet. "Now go and do what you need to before I change my mind."

Tai walked out of Stan's house in a daze, hope swelling in his chest. There was a chance any children he and Piper had would be accepted into the tribe. And if it didn't happen this time it was tabled at council, he was optimistic it would get approved some time in the future.

But after all the things he'd said, would Piper be willing to take him back? He'd been cruel, dismissive, had pushed her away. But he'd make it up to her. He'd explain, she'd listen and she'd forgive.

Piper always listened to the facts before she made a decision; she was logical, balanced and willing to listen.

He had to believe it.

Because he couldn't bear to consider the alternative.

***

The moment Tai stepped on the bus to head to Houston, his stomach started to churn. In a few short hours he would see Piper. He would speak with her, apologize and find out if she would forgive him.

Eyota had told him Piper was meeting the bus at the stadium where the kids were going backstage to watch the sound checks before heading to the bayou for lunch.

Ignoring the churn, he focused on his task, which was checking off the names of the kids who were on the bus. When he was satisfied, the bus drove off.

Inside it was noisy. The kids ranged from as young as eight right up to eighteen, and they were excited. Tai sat at the front and kept an eye on things, but there were no problems. The kids were thrilled to be on an excursion to the city, and on their best, if loudest, behavior.

He ran through what he wanted to say to Piper, but they arrived before he came up with a decent sentence, let alone a whole explanation.

They pulled into the parking lot and Bradley ran to the front of the bus.

Tai put a hand out to stop him. "Whoa! Wait until the bus has stopped," he said.

"But there's Piper!"

Tai glanced out the window and his heart stopped.

It was indeed Piper.

His heart kicked into gear again, this time at double speed, and the nausea whipped up his stomach like a hurricane.

She looked amazing.

She was dressed in a patterned, knee-length skirt and a fitted red top. She was smiling and waving at the bus, and he wished the smile were for him.

The bus stopped and the doors opened.

"Slowly," Tai advised, and let go of Bradley, who raced down the steps and into Piper's arms.

She laughed and hugged him back.

If only it could be that easy for him.

He waited until all the children had disembarked before he got off. Piper hadn't noticed him and while he was tempted to go straight up to her and drag her away, now wasn't the time. They had children to look after.

Piper directed them all to the backstage door where George was waiting. He gave each child a backstage pass.

"All right. You need to stick together. No wandering off, otherwise you'll get me into trouble," George said.

There were a few murmurs of agreement before George let them inside.

Tai stayed at the back to make sure no one got left behind, or indeed tried to wander off.

His eyes kept finding Piper wherever she stood, which was

generally at the front, with Bradley, her faithful shadow, at her side.

George showed them the dressing rooms, where the kids got to meet Kent Downer. Kent spoke with them for a few minutes, and signed autographs, before George hustled them to the next spot.

Tai hadn't seen Adrian in costume before. It was strange. He hung back to shake his hand.

"The kids are having a great time," he said.

"Sure are. It's a blast to meet them all," Adrian replied.

Just then Tai noticed a couple of kids hanging back, glancing around as if they were going to sneak off. "I'll catch up with you later. Good luck tonight." Tai called out to the kids, who jumped guiltily, groaned and continued following the group.

George led them into the seating area, where they sat to watch the sound check. He explained what was going on.

Tai couldn't concentrate on the words. His eyes were firmly fixed on the back of Piper's head, willing her to turn around.

She didn't.

What could he possibly say to make up for how he had treated her?

How could he show her he was sorry, that he didn't mean what he'd said?

In front of him children stood up and he brought his attention back to what was going on. The sound check was finished and it was time to go. Tai stood up to wait for the kids to file out of their seats and found himself face to face with Piper.

He froze, drinking in every aspect of her. She had darkness under her eyes that told him she wasn't sleeping much.

"Tai," she said.

It had to be a good sign she was willing to acknowledge him. "Piper." He longed to reach out and touch her, but one of the other chaperones called out for them to hurry up. There was a busload of children waiting for them.

As Piper turned to go, he blurted, "Could I have a word with you later?"

She nodded, not letting any emotion show. "Sure." She

walked off at George's call. The relief was immense. After how cruel he had been to her, he'd been expecting anger or complete dismissal, not agreement.

Maybe he had a chance.

"Are you and Piper still fighting?" Bradley asked.

"We're not fighting," he said. They had to be talking to do that.

Bradley squinted up at him and then shrugged, and joined the others.

**

There was no chance to talk to Piper before they got on the bus to head for the bayou and a picnic lunch.

At the park, both he and Piper were surrounded by the children wanting to talk to them about their week, or something at school. Normally he loved listening to the kids and encouraging them, but today he wanted Piper alone.

She wasn't making it any easier for him. She laughed and played with the children, always just out of his reach.

After lunch they went to the Museum of Natural Science and he again had to bring up the rear with Piper at the front.

It was agonizing to have her so close and not be able to speak to her.

But he needed to be alone with her to say what he wanted to say.

**

Dinner was a fast-food extravaganza because it was the cheapest to do on a budget. Then they all returned to the stadium and found their seats.

Tai was getting desperate. If he didn't talk to Piper now, he wouldn't get another chance tonight. Bradley was going home with her after the concert and he was taking the bus back to the reservation.

Unfortunately she was also at the other end of the seating row to him. He leaned over to one of the other chaperones in front of him. "I need to talk to Piper for a moment. Are you fine with the kids?"

"Sure."

Relieved, he jumped up and walked down one of the empty rows until he got to Piper. Then the nerves kicked in again.

"Can I talk to you a minute?" he asked, when she glanced up at him.

She indicated the empty chair next to her. "Have a seat."

He squirmed. "Privately."

A frown crossed briefly over Piper's face, but she spoke with the other chaperone on her side and then followed Tai out into the foyer. There were people milling around, but it was about as private as he was going to get.

But now he had her to himself, he wasn't sure where to start.

"What did you want?" Piper asked, her tone polite.

It was too polite. There was no emotion there. Perhaps she didn't love him any more. He swore to himself. There was only one way he was going to find out. "To apologize," he said. "And to explain."

She was silent, waiting for him to continue.

"You were right about the article. I knew you hadn't written it, that it wasn't your fault. I told Stan after you left. I used it as an excuse to break up with you."

She showed no surprise, no change of expression at all. "Why?"

"I did know about the tribal laws from the beginning. I wanted to tell you, to explain it couldn't be serious, but I didn't know how to bring it up. I enjoyed being with you and I didn't want that to end. I was so *very* selfish." He ran a hand through his hair. This was the hardest bit. "And then I realized we'd become *more*. I panicked. It happened so fast. I didn't want to love you because it couldn't work out." He was making a mess of it.

"So you're telling me this to ease your conscience? To give me a nicer goodbye?"

The words terrified him. "No."

She crossed her arms. "Tai, I know how important your tribe is to you. I understand you want your children to be part of that. But I won't keep dating you until you find a nice Queche girl. I deserve more than that." Her eyes flashed.

She didn't understand what he was trying to say.

He took hold of her hands. "That was the reason I pushed you away, but I've been so miserable. Everything I did, everywhere I went, reminded me of you. So many people would mention your name and I would ache right here." He touched his chest. "Eyota finally had enough of my temper and spoke to me. She made me realize that tribal membership is in the heart, not on a piece of paper. As long as we raised our children right. And anyway Stan is going to propose to change the law." He smiled. "You won him over with your manuscript."

Piper's lips curved upward in a hopeful smile. "So what are you saying?"

What was he saying? Couldn't she tell?

But, no, he hadn't told her. His heart full with hope he said, "I love you. You brought the sun into my life, a shelter from the storm, and the hope instead of despair."

Piper's smile was as bright as that sun. She flung her arms around his neck. "I'm so glad you realized." She kissed him and her taste was so familiar, so right. "I love you too."

Tai wrapped his arms around her, not willing to let go. "I'm so sorry," he murmured. "So very sorry for those horrible things I said to you. I was hurting so badly, but I had to push you away. I'd hoped you hadn't fallen in love with me yet, like I had with you."

"How could I not love you?" Piper asked. "You're the most giving, generous and kind man."

She still loved him. His chest wasn't big enough for the emotion swirling inside of him. He leaned his forehead against hers. "You make me feel like I can be that kind of person," he said. He'd had meaning to his life before she came along, but now he also had true happiness.

They would make a life together.

They would build a family

They would love.

Epilogue

"I can't believe in the year since I got married, the three of you have fallen in love and now Piper is getting married," Libby said as she slid into her royal purple bridesmaid dress, which had been specially designed to fit over her sizeable baby bump.

Piper barely believed it herself.

It was her wedding day.

She never would have imagined when she'd met the surly but gorgeous Taima Woods that she would be walking down the aisle to marry him in eight short months.

But sure enough, here she was on the reservation, in the house that had been Jerry's and was now where she, Tai and Bradley stayed when they came, getting ready for her wedding.

Imogen dabbed a tissue at her eyes. "Quiet, you'll start me crying." She poured glasses of champagne and handed them around to Rayen, Piper, Elle and Ashlin.

Elle shook her head. "I'll have iced tea too."

Piper whirled around to face her friend. "Is there something you're not telling us?" she asked.

Elle glanced away. "No."

Libby and Imogen put down their glasses and looked at Elle.

"Spill," Piper demanded.

"This is your day," Elle protested.

"And I want to know, so tell me."

Elle sighed. "I was going to wait until after. I didn't consider the alcohol."

Piper clenched her hands together, waiting.

"I'm pregnant. George and I are having a baby." Her smile was radiant.

Piper's squeals were added to Libby's and Imogen's, and they surrounded Elle, giving her a group hug.

Kate hopped up and down. "Another baby! It'll be best friends with ours." She was thrilled Libby was having a baby and couldn't wait to meet her new cousin.

"When are you due?" Libby asked.

"Not until September. I'm just glad the dress still fits. I was panicking I might put on weight." She smoothed down the front of her bridesmaid dress.

"You're not showing at all," Imogen assured her.

"May your child have wisdom and strength," Rayen said, with a smile.

"Congratulations, Elle," Piper's mother said, giving her a hug. "How does Toby feel about it?"

Elle glanced to the living room, where her son was waiting with Piper's father. "We haven't told him yet. He wouldn't be able to keep it a secret. He's been hoping for a brother for a while now, so I think he'll be happy."

Piper was so happy for her friend. Elle and George had got married in December because, after Imogen's garden wedding, George had declared he couldn't wait any longer. They had married a couple of weeks before Christmas in a beautiful venue overlooking lush gardens, just north of Houston.

And now they had a baby on the way.

Piper hugged her friend again.

"Girls, if we're not going to be late, we need to finish up here," Ashlin said.

Piper checked the time. Her mother was right. They were due at the lake in twenty minutes.

"Tai won't mind waiting a little," Rayen said.

Piper grinned at her soon to be cousin. "But I do!" She couldn't wait to marry him, to make their promises and to start on the next stage of their life together.

Imogen carefully lifted the wedding dress off the bed and

Piper slipped out of her kimono wrap. She stepped into the dress and held it in place while Imogen and Ashlin did it up.

It fit perfectly. Imogen had done an amazing job designing exactly the type of dress Piper wanted. It was strapless, tightly fitting around her waist before flaring out to a slightly full skirt. Just enough bounce for fun, but not enough to be difficult to walk in.

"You're beautiful, darling," her mother said, tears welling in her eyes.

Piper's own eyes watered in response.

"Don't!" Imogen commanded. "No crying until after the ceremony."

They all laughed at the mock severity.

"Come on, ladies," Michael called from the living room. "We need to get moving."

Piper slipped on the beaded sandals Rayen had made her – a tradition of the tribe – and stood up. "How do I look?"

"Like my baby grown up," her mother said.

"Like a woman in love," Libby said.

"Like my new cousin." Rayen smiled at her.

"Like the happiest woman in the world," Imogen said.

"Like a bride," Elle told her.

Piper choked back tears. She *was* the luckiest woman in the world to have such wonderful friends and to be marrying her best friend of all.

"Let's go then," she said and walked out to greet her father.

***

The ceremony was being held at the edge of the lake. The whole tribe had been invited, and Tai's staff, as well as Piper's family and friends. From the car she saw Tai and the groomsmen – Adahy, George, Tom and Bradley – standing at the lake's edge. She and Tai had agreed on a ceremony that mixed traditions from both of their cultures.

Tai was absolutely stunning in his tribal garb. Adahy and Bradley wore similar clothing, and George and Tom were wearing black suits.

Bradley fussed with his sleeves. Piper smiled. She'd fallen in love with the boy too, and she and Tai had been fostering him for months. He had moved to Houston with them, but they returned to the reservation each weekend, and during the school vacations Bradley and Piper spent more time there, staying in Jerry's house. They were investigating how they could adopt him.

Being a freelance journalist meant she had the flexibility to choose her jobs and work where she wanted to work. She was also project managing the construction of the youth center, which required her presence on the reservation regularly.

"Are you ready?" her father asked, reaching a hand in through the door.

Piper blinked. All the others were waiting for her outside the car. Taking her father's hand, she stood up and let Imogen fuss with her dress.

Then with a nod to Adrian to say she was ready, she rested her hand in the crook of her father's arm and followed Toby, Kate and her bridesmaids down the aisle, while Adrian played an acoustic version of her favorite love song.

Her eyes met Tai's and her heart lifted. She smiled so widely she suspected she resembled the Cheshire Cat, but she didn't care. The man she was going to spend the rest of her life with was right in front of her and his gaze told her he was as happy about it as she was.

Finally she reached his side. With a few words from the clergyman, her father had given her away, and she held Tai's hand.

"I love you," she mouthed at him, not really listening to the ceremony.

He grinned at her and, quick as a flash, kissed her on the mouth.

"Wait a minute. There'll be plenty of time for that later," the clergyman grumbled.

The assembled crowd chuckled.

Piper didn't care because he was right. Today was just the beginning.

They had their whole lives ahead of them.

A lifetime of love and family.

Thank you for reading!

I hope you enjoyed the book. It would be super awesome if you could leave a review wherever you bought it, because I love to hear what you thought of the story (yes, even if you didn't like it!)

If you've only just discovered the Texan Quartet, make sure you check out Libby, Imogen and George's stories too. The first book is What Goes on Tour.

Acknowledgements

A book is never completed in isolation. For Into the Fire I had many people who provided me with in-formation and whom I need to thank: Teena, for her information about journalism and newspapers; the Rayne's Writers Research group, who provided me with information about Native Americans, in particular JoAnn, Shane and PB; Michael, for his information about banjolins – I told you I could work it into the story!; and a huge thank you to my beta reader, James, who read the entire book over a weekend and gave me some invaluable advice about my representation of Native Americans.

In this story, Taima is of the Queche tribe. After much deliberation I chose to make up a tribe rather than use an existing tribe for a number of reasons: the reservation needed to be within easy driving distance of Houston so that Tai could return on the weekend; I wasn't able to get in touch with the relevant tribe to ensure my reservation information was correct, and I didn't want to get it wrong; and many tribes from that area of Texas, which are considered by some sources to be extinct (such as the Karankawa), have people claiming to be descendants, so I didn't want to offend anyone by appropriating their culture. I sincerely hope that I cause no offence for making up a tribe and a reservation.

Finally I must thank the team at Momentum: Joel, Ashley, Patrick, Michelle, Kate and Jon. As always you've helped me publish the best work I can, and I appreciate your hard work and endless patience in answering my never-ending emails.

What Goes on Tour

The Texan Quartet # 1

What goes on tour, stays on tour ... or does it?

Few people know that socially awkward Adrian Hart is actually rock God, Kent Downer, and that's the way Adrian likes it. His privacy is essential, especially now that he has guardianship of his orphaned, ten-year-old niece, Kate. But when the nanny quits in the middle of his Australian tour Adrian finds himself in a bind.

Until Libby Myles walks into his life.

Libby has only ever wanted to become a full-time author and prove to her parents that she can make it on her own. On the surface, the temporary job as the nanny for Kent Downer's niece looks perfect—the pay is fabulous, the hours are short and Kate is a big fan—it's the rock star that's the issue.

Arrogant and way too attractive for anyone's good, Kent Downer has enough swagger to power a small city. But when he's out of costume he's different—shy and uncertain. For Libby it's a far harder combination to resist. She needs to find a balance between work, writing and ignoring her attraction to the rock star, because if she falls for him, it could mean the end of her dream.

But when a horrible scandal is unleashed—putting young Kate in danger—there's more heat between Libby and Adrian than just sexual attraction. Libby must figure out if Adrian ever cared for her, or if it was all just part of the show ...

http://www.claireboston.com/books/the-texan-quartet/

All that Sparkles

The Texan Quartet # 2

Imogen Fontaine is living every girl's dream.

She is a fashion designer for her family's haute couture label, lives in a mansion, has a great circle of friends and is the apple of her father's eye. Everything is perfect.

Until the day that Christian, the boy at the center of her childhood heartbreak, walks back into her life.

From there her life starts to unravel, as long-kept secrets are revealed. Imogen learns that her past was built on lies and betrayal, shattering the illusion of her perfect existence. She must seek out the truth if she has any hope of forging a new path for herself and discovering true freedom.

But can she convince Christian that there is a place for him in her new life?

http://www.claireboston.com/books/the-texan-quartet/all-that-sparkles/

Under the Covers

The Texan Quartet # 3

What if the one time you didn't want love was when you truly needed it?

Forced to flee her abusive ex, alone with no support, Elle is determined to rebuild her life and protect her five-year-old son. Not one to take the easy road, she opens a bookshop café, but opening day al-most ends in disaster. In the midst of this chaos, the last thing she needs is a man as charming as George Jones getting in her way.

George has always been a sucker for a damsel in distress, and Elle ticks all the boxes. But Elle's not interested in being rescued by anyone, especially not him. She knows her taste in men can't be trusted, but fighting George's charisma is harder than she expected. And George, who is not one to ignore an itch, has found there's something about Elle that's got under his skin.

When Elle's ex turns up to cause trouble, George must overcome his boyish flirtatiousness if he's to convince Elle to trust herself and let him into her life. But can Elle put her past behind her before it overwhelms her present?

http://www.claireboston.com/books/the-texan-quartet/

Lightning Source UK Ltd.
Milton Keynes UK
UKOW01f0936241017
311553UK00001B/39/P